All the F*cks I Cannot Give

Michael Carlon

Also by Michael Carlon

The Last Homily
Winning Streak
Uncorking a Murder
Return to Casa Grande

ISBN: 978-0-9979839-5-1
ISBN-0-9979839-5-7

To everyone who has been burned by corporate America
— you are more than just a lever someone had to pull

CHAPTER ONE

Confrontation Isn't My Strong Suit

One might think the worst day in a man's life might be when he finds his wife in bed with another person, but I knew my wife Laura was a lesbian very early into our marriage. No, she didn't have the telltale ring of keys clamped to one of her belt loops by a carabiner, nor did she ever come out and admit, "Kelly, I'm really not into dudes." Come to think of it, the fact that my parents gave me a woman's name may have been what attracted her to me in the first place (apologies for the digression). No, I knew my wife was a lesbian because my twin sister, Josephine—who everybody calls Jo—spotted her in a gay bar shortly after we returned home from our honeymoon ten years ago. FYI, Jo is a lesbian and my father considers her the son he never had. She's also my best friend.

At first, I didn't believe her because the initial photographic evidence of Laura chatting with another woman at a bar appeared innocent. Sure, it was clear she was at our town's lesbian bar—The Meow Mix—because the name is plastered all over the wall and was captured in every still image Jo sent me. Oddly, all the women were dressed as Schneider from *One Day at a Time* for an event called Pat Harrington Night. So what? I thought to myself. I've heard that oftentimes women feel more comfortable at those places than straight bars because they don't get hit on as much.

When Jo showed me the picture of my wife tongue kissing a woman who resembled Nancy McKeon from *The Facts of Life*, I chalked it up to Laura being a bit curious. I didn't confront her about it because, by nature, I hate confrontation. Nothing scares me more than causing conflict—so I tried to forget about it and buried it. Denial is my absolute favorite defense mechanism.

When I caught Laura in the act with my eyes, that was different. It was on a day I came home from a business trip early. Instead of taking the early morning flight from San Diego to NY, I decided to take a red-eye so I could get to our suburban Connecticut home early as a surprise to my wife. She was surprised alright, especially when I walked in on her and our handywoman Ella doing more than just playing doctor in our bed; the back of my wife's head resembled a bear fishing for salmon swimming upstream.

A more aggressive man would have offered to join them, but part of being non-confrontational means I'm also not the least bit aggressive—I simply coughed loudly to make my presence known. Ella opened her eyes and stared at me with a look of shock on her face. Laura unburied her face from between her girlfriend's thighs thus ending the gynecological exam, turned around and simply said, "Oh fuck." She then rolled over, pulled our sheets over the two of them, and reached for the pack of cigarettes on our cherry wood nightstand.

At the time I wanted to say something other than, "Since when do you smoke?" but that was the only phrase I could muster.

"I didn't expect you until later," Laura said while maintaining eye contact and exhaling a plume of smoke through her nose.

"I wanted to surprise you, so I took the red-eye."

"I told you never to take the red-eye since you're always grumpy when you don't get enough sleep."

"Apparently that's not the only reason," I muttered under my breath.

I remember turning around so Ella could get dressed with some degree of privacy. After she left the room, Laura confirmed what my sister had been telling me all along—she is, in fact, drumroll please, a lesbian and only married me to appease her conservative parents who loved that their wild child of a daughter was settling down with a white-collar guy who had a good job; it certainly explained why we were on the quarterly plan when it came to sex! Incidentally, that was supposed to be a night of matrimonial congress, but congress decided to take a ten-year hiatus—that's right, I have not had sex with another human being in ten years.

I remember being more shocked than angry and, since we've already established that I have a hard time dealing with conflict, I agreed to Laura's proposition that we live in an open marriage, which we've done for the past decade. She argued that it would give us the best of both worlds: the freedom to explore other people and the appearance of living a normal life, which would appease both of our families. Ever since then, I've buried myself in work and focused on my career and not chasing some serious tail. I can't say the same for Laura, who chose to bury herself in beaver like a fat man at a Las Vegas buffet.

So while that was a pretty shitty day for Kelly Carson, that's me if you haven't guessed, it wasn't the worst day of my life. No, that would be today, the day my spineless boss fired me…over the telephone.

CHAPTER TWO

My Spineless Boss

I work in the field of marketing research, and before I educate you more on what that means, let me just make something perfectly clear—no one in this field says to themselves, "I want to study consumer opinion for the rest of my life." No one goes to school for a degree in market research; people who wind up in this field have dreams of becoming psychologists, sociologists, anthropologists, or any of the other ologists one can become after almost a decade of higher education. For one reason or another, though, they wind up selling out and applying their research skills to marketing problems—my story isn't unique in that regard.

I was all set to earn a Ph.D. in clinical psychology from a prestigious university but decided to take my father's advice and work for a year before returning to school. I took a job at a well-known New York-based advertising agency and that's where I saw my first focus group.

The topic was what people would want in a website from their bank, and the guy leading the discussion looked like he was having a blast engaging people in conversation and asking probing follow-up questions.

At the time, I thought it looked like a cross between group therapy and improvisational theatre, and I knew right then and there that I wanted to do that for the rest of my life, so I turned down the opportunity to earn my doctorate and pursued running focus groups full time.

Seventeen years ago, I left the agency world to work for a research company called Stahl and Partners run by an inspiring woman named Michele Stahl who had a penchant for French wine, younger men, and a cocaine habit that would shock Charlie Sheen. She was looking for the next generation of moderators to run her business so she could retire early and spend her days in Hawaii with her collection of antique coke spoons and boy toys of the week. While she was, and this is putting it mildly, bat shit crazy, she had moments of lucidity when she taught me the ins and outs of leading group discussions and keeping clients happy. According to her, the key to the latter was offering sexual services after each night of research and submitting to their every demand. That's one of two bits of advice I didn't take from her, the other being never to believe a drug dealer when he says he'll be over in twenty minutes. I didn't take that advice because, well, I've never required the services of a drug dealer—I'm as square as they come.

A little over two years ago, I walked into the office, and Michele informed me and the rest of the staff that she had sold her firm to Omnivore, a large holding company, and that we would be integrated into their research division. She also informed us that she made twenty million dollars on the sale; even though she had a three-year earn out, I never saw her again and often wonder if she lived to see her mid-fifties. The following day I met my new boss, Pete Jackson.

You know Pete Jackson—even if you've never met him, you know him. Why do I say this? Because he exists in every American high school. He was likely the captain of the lacrosse team, maybe the student council president. Always had a positive, go get 'em attitude even though you knew he was full of shit and said whatever he needed to in order to get ahead. Ring any bells?

My first meeting with Pete was one I'll never forget. He sauntered into a conference room 15 minutes late for an "all-hands" meeting he called. He was wearing a plaid sport coat and trendy green Coke-bottle glasses and was clearly trying to look younger than his fifty-seven years by dressing down with a pair of designer jeans and black sneakers, which, for all intents and purposes, looked orthopedic. As he walked into the room, he tucked the Nalgene water bottle he was never seen without under his arm and started clapping as if to suggest we should all clap when he entered.

"Team!" he exclaimed. "Thanks for coming. I've heard so many good things about all of you and I can only imagine what you've heard about me. I can assure you only half of what you heard is true."

Actually, what I had heard was that Pete was about one percent businessman and ninety-nine percent bullshit, but that for some reason the board liked that ratio well enough to believe he could double the revenue in our department.

"I like to be scrappy, so don't expect anything too formal from me, and the only thing I expect from you is that you kill it and crush it every day."

Right then and there, I knew this asshole had no idea what we did as moderators. We don't kill, we don't crush —we talk to strangers and turn their stories into insights our clients can use to make better decisions. No killing required.

"Who here wants to take Pork Chop Hill with me?"

After he said "Pork Chop Hill," I made a mental note to revise my résumé that afternoon.

Much to my surprise, the other people in the room all stood up and cheered; one even let out a hoo-rah with a little vibrato as if he were Al Pacino's understudy in Scent of a Woman: The Musical.

I remained sitting, unable to comprehend the shitstorm that just walked into the room.

"What's your name?" Pete said to me.

"Kelly," I replied.

"Kelly? That's a girl's name."

I could tell the minute he heard my name that this was what his response would be. Call it a would-be woman's intuition.

"It's the name my parents gave me."

I told you before that my parents named me Kelly, but I didn't mention why. Now's as good a time as any. Three months into her pregnancy, my mother was told she was having twin girls—now in the 70s, ultrasounds were not a perfect science, and the equipment my mother's doctor used couldn't pick up the dangling thing between my legs that's the telltale differentiator between boys and girls. As such, my mother and father told their friends they were having twin girls and planned accordingly.

My parents decided on the names Kelly and Josephine in honor of their mothers. When we were born, they were as shocked as anyone that I was, in fact, a boy. Because they already had clothes embroidered with the names Kelly and Josephine, and because my parents are cheap bastards, they went with Kelly not thinking about the hell it would put me through. No one can fuck you like family.

"Your parents have a sick sense of humor," Pete said. "I have a question for you, Kelly. Are you a hunter or are you a farmer?"

"I'm a moderator," I replied.

"Yeah, all of you are moderators, but what I want to know is, what kind of moderator are you. Do you hunt or do you farm? Do you chase after business looking to kill it, or do you sit on the sidelines waiting for it to sprout, because I got news for you, I want hunters, not farmers."

"I billed 1.5 million last year, Pete. I'm not sure if I did that hunting or farming, but I ate pretty well." It would have been great if I actually said this, but true to my nature, I just thought it.

Pete turned around and left the room, but not before looking back and saying "Hunters." He then pounded his chest like Tarzan and walked down the hall.

Over the next year, he treated me like a red-headed stepchild; I knew he wanted to fire me because, well, he would often pass me in the hall and say, "I really want to fire your ass, Kelly." The problem was, I was his most profitable resource and firing me would have been like shooting himself in the foot. While I mean that metaphorically, the hyper-testosteroned goon actually did wind up shooting himself in the foot.

He invited himself hunting with some actual hunters and smartly, the people he was with only gave him a .22, which was barely enough to take down a squirrel, let alone a deer, but they smelled an idiot when they saw him and were nervous about giving him too much firepower. As dumb as they figured him for, they didn't expect him to play with the trigger when the barrel was resting on his shoe. For this reason, he was working from home in the beginning of December.

My job requires a lot of travel and I see my fair share of airports every week. Just five minutes ago, my phone rang while I was in the Delta Sky Club at Los Angeles International Airport. With three weeks to go before Christmas, I was eager to my way back to New York after finishing a project to understand how recently divorced women in their forties approach dating. It was commissioned by a skin care client looking to market a new miracle in a bottle face care product. The caller ID on my phone read FuckFace. Because I am non-confrontational by nature, I get some revenge by giving people I don't like derogatory nicknames in my phone's address book. Petty? Yes, but definitely satisfying. I picked up the phone and here Pete's voice on the other end.

"Kelly, I'm glad I caught you."

He never calls me, so I immediately knew something was up.

"Why the hell didn't you pick up the first time I called?"

"Because I fucking hate you." Okay, I thought it, I didn't say it. The truth is, I was in a trance making some edits to the novel I've been writing for three years and, at first, didn't even feel the phone vibrate in my pocket. You see, in addition to being a moderator, I'm also an aspiring novelist.

"How did Project Beaver go?"

Since I was talking to recently divorced women, and

since he's a complete sexist, he referred to the study I just wrapped as Project Beaver.

"Client is very pleased."

"Did you get any?"

"No, Pete, I didn't get any. What do you need?"

"Figures. Fucking farmers never get any."

My conversation with Pete was interrupted by an attractive woman who motions for my attention. She clearly saw I'm on the phone but didn't seem to give a shit.

"Pete, can you hold on a second?"

"What the fuck, do not put me on hold. No one puts Pete Jackson on hold!"

As if you needed any more proof of his assholery, Pete Jackson talks about Pete Jackson in the third person.

I turned my attention to the woman; she's familiar looking but I can't place her.

"What?" I ask.

"Can you watch my bag while I go to the ladies' room?"

"We are in the Delta lounge, your bag will be fine."

"What's the big deal, just watch it okay?"

"Fine," I replied and watched her walk away. I noticed that other people couldn't take their eyes off her and some began to whisper. Then I hear Pete Jackson's voice again.

"Farmer Kelly, where are you?"

"Here, sorry. Why are you calling me?"

"Well I'll get right to it. There's no easy way to say this but…"

I immediately envisioned him sitting at home with his injured foot wrapped in maxi pads because he was too cheap to buy the bandages his doctor recommended.

"…the business has been soft lately and you are a lever I have to pull."

I couldn't believe what I was hearing. Was this idiot firing me over the telephone three weeks before Christmas?

"What does that mean, a lever?"

"Let me put it in farming terms for you. Let's say you're a farmer, right, which of course you are. Let's say that for seventeen years, your farming feeds you very well. Crops come up year after year, but then all of a sudden, there's a drought. No crops."

"But there hasn't been a drought. I've grown my business 20 percent over last year. I'm on the road more than anybody else."

By this time, the familiar-looking mystery woman returned to her bags and took the seat across from mine.

Pete continued, "Right. The drought hasn't hit you yet, but it hit Heather, Laurie, and Brian."

He named three of my colleagues who haven't had a project since October.

"So why aren't you talking to them?"

"Because they are hunters."

I have seen porn with better plotlines than the story he tried to sell me.

"Apparently not very good ones." In true Carson form, I thought it but didn't say it.

"Listen, the fact is they're cheaper than you. I can actually hire three more hunters for what we pay you, and I need more hunters. It's not personal, it's just business."

The Godfather is one of my favorite films and while normally I'd appreciate the reference, given the circumstances under which it was said, I didn't.

"Look, we will honor your bonus and pay you a severance of two months. After that, kemosabe, I suggest

you learn to hunt."
He terminated the call before I could reply.

CHAPTER THREE

Meeting Terri Flynn

I look up from my phone and find the woman sitting across from me staring into my eyes. She's also chewing gum and snapping it loudly. Normally gum chewing, or any type of chewing for that matter, is a pet peeve, but I let it slide because she's a redhead, and in my experience, they're an 11 on the 10-point crazy scale, and the last thing I want to do is start an argument with a ginger in an airport lounge.

"Did you just get fired?" she asks bluntly.

"Excuse me?"

"You have a look on your face like you just got fired. I've seen that look before. Up-and-coming actors always have that same look after they bomb auditions."

So she's a redhead and an actor—that's twice the crazy, and I'm not in the mood for crazy.

"Why didn't you stand up for yourself?" She has no intention of letting this conversation die.

"I'd rather not talk about it."

"That's your problem. You're the type of guy who

would rather not deal with conflict. It's no wonder your former boss doesn't respect you."

Who the fuck does this woman think she is pretending to have insight into my life?

"Is that so?"

"Yeah. I mean look at you. You're a good-looking guy who is obviously successful based on the way you dress and that thousand-dollar laptop bag, but you don't have an ounce of fight in you."

I mentioned before that I ate well last year so yes, it's true that I've done well for myself, but what I don't need now is some ginger actress psychoanalyzing me in the middle of the LAX Delta Sky Club.

"Do you know why I asked you to watch my bags?"

"Enlighten me."

"Because you look safe. I knew you wouldn't rifle through them like some of these other people."

She motioned around to the other lounge guests, who all stared at her, and then me, with mouths agape.

"You think I need Julie fucking Andrews over there to find the pocket rocket I keep in my purse? Hell no."

The woman she was referring to did resemble Julie Andrews, but *Mary Poppins* Julie Andrews, not *Sound of Music* Julie Andrews.

"I think I'd rather be left alone right now."

"Of course you'd rather be left alone, but I'm not going to leave you alone because you need me."

"All I want to do is go back to New York in peace."

"How funny, I'm going to New York too. Where are you seated?"

The nice thing about flying so much is that I often get upgraded to first class and today, being fired over the telephone notwithstanding, I got the nod from the Delta powers that be that I was worthy of a loyalty upgrade.

"3A," I reply.

She then shows me her boarding pass and points to her seat assignment: 3B. I also notice her name at the bottom of the pass—Terri Flynn.

"Seat buddy!" She cheers with her arms in the air. "This calls for a celebration. Do you want some champagne?"

"Champagne? It's 8 a.m."

"Have them put some cassis in mine. I'll watch your bags."

I walk over to the bar, order a glass of champagne with cassis for her and an OJ for me. When I come back, I see her rifling through my bag. By the time I'm at my seat, she's going through my travel wallet.

"Is Kelly your wife? Why do you have her frequent flyer cards?"

My Kelly sense is tingling and I can foresee what is about to happen, so I don't respond. When she opens my passport to evaluate my picture, she puts two and two together.

"Fuck me in the ass and call me Charlie," she exclaims, much to the chagrin of the family sitting nearby. "Your parents named you Kelly?"

Reluctantly, I explain the circumstances of my birth.

"So what you're telling me is you have a small dick?"

For the record, I have an average-sized penis. While it's certainly not going to cause a woman any massive degree of pain upon penetration, it's also not going to feel like a stick in a cave. But the story of how my parents were expecting twin girls due to the inability to spot my dick on an ultrasound has been told so many times by my parents that I can't help but get defensive about it.

"I was a fetus!" I argue.

"Relax there, Kel, I'm just giving you a hard time. But I can't, in good conscience, call you Kelly and I'm not a last name kind of girl because that's too military and my dad was in the military and I've spent the better part of my adult life trying to undo all the rigidity of my upbringing. So I'm gonna give you a nickname."

Her blue eyes shoot up and to the left while she taps her pointer finger on her lips.

"Clark!" she exclaims.

"That's the best you could do?"

"You remind me of Clark Kent—quiet and reserved, but something about you gives me the impression that Superman's hiding inside. And you know what, Clark, call me 'Lois' because I'm going to help you find your inner superhero."

By this point I realize I don't know anything about her aside from her name and my assumption that she's an actress. My thoughts are interrupted by a voice over the loudspeaker.

"For those of you traveling on Delta Flight 3827 to New York's Kennedy Airport, I am sorry to inform you that due to bad weather in New York, your flight has been canceled. Please see us at the full-service counter and we will do our best to accommodate you."

"Fuck," I say, much to the ire of the family matriarch beside us.

I stand and grab my bag, intending to walk to the counter solo, but Terri follows me. Once we get to there, I ask the representative, a woman named Beverly, why the flight was canceled and not simply delayed until the weather improves.

"The northeast is getting slammed," she responds. For whatever reason, Beverly's counter is adorned by pictures of hand-drawn ninjas. While I'm certainly curious about that, I focus on the travel situation.

"How bad is it?" I ask.

"All airports from New Jersey up to Maine are closed. We can book you on the first flight out tomorrow and offer you a free night in a hotel."

Terri pipes up, "Could you send us anywhere else?"

"Oh, hi, Ms. Flynn, my husband and I are such big fans," Beverly says while blushing. "Of course we could send you anywhere in the US you'd like to go, so long as the airport is open."

"Terri… "

She corrects me, "I told you, Clark, call me 'Lois.'"

"Lois," I say through my teeth, "What are you doing? I need to get back to New York."

"For what? It's not like your boss is going to fire you if you don't show up at work tomorrow."

That stings a little, but I can see her logic.

"What, do you have a wife at home who needs you to knock on Heaven's door and fulfill every sexual desire?"

If only she knew the truth.

"No, but…"

"Then no buts. What you need is an adventure and I'm going to give it to you."

I hear Beverly tapping away incessantly at her keyboard.

"I can get you both on a flight to Maui. It leaves in 40 minutes."

"Lodging?" Terri asks, flashing a Hollywood smile if I

ever saw one.

"That's against the rules in this situation, but let me see what I can do."

Beverly taps no fewer than 100 keystrokes then looks up and smiles.

"Ritz Carlton okay? That's where we put our flight attendants and I can get you in there for two nights"

"Deal," Terri says.

Before I can object, Beverly starts tapping again and the dot matrix printer behind her comes to life. A second later she hands us two boarding passes to Hawaii.

"Come on, Clark, it will be fun."

She walks ahead of me and exits the lounge. I shake my head and against my better judgment, follow her out.

CHAPTER FOUR

At the Gate

While Terri only has a small head start, she's already navigated to a Starbucks kiosk two gates away. There are five people ahead of her in line and they all look like the types who order complicated drinks.

"I don't think we have time for this," I say.

"Relax, Clark, the flight leaves in 40 minutes, plenty of time."

I'm pretty anal about getting on planes early for two reasons: one, it helps me relax, and two, it insures my carry-on makes it to an overhead bin near my seat. I get very anxious when my bags are rows behind where I'm sitting, as it means I'll be getting off the plane later or, worse, inconveniencing the passengers behind me. I never want to be that guy.

"But the flight is likely boarding."

She responds to my protest with a roll of her eyes.

Finally, it's her time to order.

The barista is a blond-haired boy of about sixteen whose name tag reads Squeaker; if the lead singer of

Flock of Seagulls had sex with Bea Arthur and they had a baby, I'm pretty sure it would look like Squeaker.

"Oh my god, Terri, how are you?" Squeaker says in a voice pitched so high I thought the lenses of his glasses would shatter.

"Doing okay, Squeaker. How's your mother?"

"One day at a time. Are you done shooting? I thought the production schedule had you at Universal through the spring."

"I don't want to talk about work, but what I would like is an iced caramel macchiato."

Squeaker takes a plastic cup and writes the order down.

"Will that be all?"

Terri motions to me using the classic hitchhiker's thumb.

"And what kind of drink can I get for you, sir?"

"I'll just take a small coffee?"

Squeaker rolls his eyes and shouts "tall blonde roast" in a tone that scolds me for not ordering in proper Starbucks vernacular.

"That will be $7.69."

Terri turns around and bats her eyes and smiles at me. "How would you feel about buying my coffee?"

I reach into my wallet, take out a ten, and hand it to Squeaker who immediately puts my change into the tip jar.

"Can I get a name for the order?"

Without thinking, I give him my first name.

"Kelly is your name? Is that some kind of joke? You think this is funny? Am I fucking here for your amusement?"

I am perplexed by his response and wonder if other

customers give fake names as a way of being rude and dismissive toward the barista class. Then again, if they are, it's probably in reaction to baristas intentionally misspelling customer names; all's fair in love and war—even when buying overpriced, burnt coffee.

"Excellent Joe Pesci impersonation, Squeaker," Terri proclaims. "But tone it down a bit. You went a little overboard on the Jersey accent."

"Thanks, Terri, just wait over there, honey. Your drinks will be up shortly."

Terri and I walk over to the area designated for pickups.

"Squeaker wants to be an actor."

"You don't say."

"Why are you so grumpy, Clark? We're going to Hawaii, savor the moment!"

A thousand other men in my circumstance would be excited as hell to be taking a free trip to Hawaii with an attractive redheaded actress whom they just met, but all I feel is anxiety. I've just lost my job and need to make a plan for my future; I need to talk this through with my sister, but she's five thousand miles away.

"I just want to get on the plane."

"Kelsy, your order is up," comes a deep voice from behind the counter.

I don't move because my name isn't Kelsy.

"Kelsy," the deep voice says again. "Iced Caramel Macchiato and a tall blonde roast."

I begrudgingly retrieve our order. When I look on the red cup containing my drink, I see that Squeaker added some artwork.

"What's that on your cup?" Terri asks.

"Nothing," I reply curtly.

"It's not nothing, it looks like something. Come on, show it to me."

And that's the first time I show Terri my penis. Well, not MY penis, but the one drawn on my cup. She responds by laughing so hard I think she's going to lose her breakfast.

"I'm glad you find this funny, but what the fuck am I supposed to do with this monstrous cock on my cup?"

"At least you didn't order a venti. It would have been even bigger!"

I take a sip and she loses it again.

"Oh my god, when you drink, the tip looks like it's going into your mouth."

We pass by ten gates and finally get to ours, where I find they're already boarding Zone 2; my anxiety rises ten notches and here's why—this means they've boarded the elderly, families traveling with small children, first class, business class, active military, passengers with premium status, passengers with missing limbs, left-handed people, clergy, atheists, airline union members, people with service animals, and Zone 1. And worst of all, it means our carry-on bags will be checked at the gate.

"Fuck," I say.

"What's the matter, Clark, they didn't leave without us."

"They are going to make us check our bags. I hate checking my bags."

"So what, we check our bags, big fucking deal."

"My bags never make it when I check them."

"Clark, listen to me, they're going to check them right here. The plane is right there. They are going to personally put them on, and because they're getting on so late, they'll be LIFO."

I look at her with a raised eyebrow.

"Last in, first out."

"Isn't that accounting speak?"

"When I moved to LA to pursue acting full time, I took some classes at a community college to appease my parents. I loved accounting."

There's a tall, skinny blonde woman who has joined us at the gate. She's talking on the phone and I overhear the strangest conversation I've ever been privy to.

"Gentle domination is $400 an hour. If you want water sports, that's an extra hundred."

"Did you just hear that?" I whisper to Terri.

"Sure did," she whispers back.

"I wonder what her father did to her?"

"That's the difference between you and me, Clark. You're thinking about her dad, and I'm wondering if the guy she's talking to is going to spring an extra Benjamin so she springs a leak on him. It's only a hundred bucks, fella, get peed on, why don't ya?"

I try to put that out of my mind and approach the gate agent. Just as I suspect, after the three of us hand over our boarding passes, we're told we have to check our carry-on. I'd rather be peed on. I watch as she prints out labels and straps them to our bags.

"Just leave these at the end of the jet bridge and enjoy your flight to Hawaii."

We do as we were told and then board the plane. Thankfully, Beverly transferred our first-class seats to the new flight, so we settle into seats 3A and 3B. As we sit down, the flight attendant, another tall blonde—this one would look at home on a fashion show runway—asks if we want a cocktail before takeoff. My traveling companion orders a vodka-tonic and I opt for a cranberry juice.

"Are you in recovery or something?"

"What? No, I just have a rule about not drinking before 6 p.m."

"Why would you have such a rule?"

"I don't know, I guess I have control issues."

The flight attendant comes back with our drinks and offers to take our Starbucks cups. When I hand her mine, she gives me a dirty look, having assumed I drew the colossal cock on my cup. As such, irreparable damage is done to the passenger/flight attendant relationship.

As a piece of advice, you never want to upset a flight attendant. They can make your flying experience a pleasure or a living hell. For example, say you're on a plane with your own TV screen—if you were rude to a flight attendant when you boarded, don't be surprised if it doesn't work. Conversely, an ounce of kindness will get you an extra snack or maybe even a free drink.

"I didn't draw that," I protest in an attempt to defend myself. She just huffs and walks away.

My phone starts to vibrate, and I awkwardly shift around until I can extricate it from my pocket. I don't recognize the 212 number, but because it's a New York area code, I pick up.

"This is Kelly," I say.

"Please hold for Pam Hart," an effeminate voice says.

I wait a few seconds and the voice that comes on the line sounds like it belongs to Mel Blanc if Mel Blanc smoked no fewer than two thousand cigarettes a day.

"Kelly, this is Pam Hart from the Hart Literary Agency. Is now a good time to tawlk?"

Six months ago, I sent out a number of query letters for a manuscript I was shopping around. Writing has always been a passion of mine and I know how important getting an agent is—the big publishers won't take you seriously if you don't have one. The problem is, it's harder to find an agent who will take a chance on a first-time author than it is to find a virgin in a sorority. I had sent queries to a few hundred agencies and received a few hundred rejection letters—the only one I hadn't heard back from was Hart Literary and now the founder was on the phone.

"I just boarded a flight, but I have a few minutes before they close the door."

My statement is interrupted by the flight attendant coming across the PA system.

"Ladies and gentlemen, we have just closed the airplane door, please turn off and stow all electronic devices and make sure your phones are in airplane mode."

I know from my extensive travels that nothing upsets flight attendants more than people who don't follow this instruction, as if a cellphone will take down an airliner. Nevertheless, I always comply with it for fear of rocking the boat, which I've already done here with that cock-art. However, now was different—I finally have an agent interested in my book, so I don't hang up.

"This will only take a New Yawk minute," Pam says.

I feel a tap on my shoulder and it's the tall blonde stewardess motioning for me to turn off my phone; to say she looks agitated is putting it mildly.

"I'm sorry, it's my agent. Just one minute," I whisper and hold up my index finger to underscore one minute.

I fully realize I sound like every Hollywood asshole she sees on the LA to Hawaii flight and this wins me no points.

"We are interested in representing you, Mr. Carson.

Could you make it to Manhattan for a meeting next Monday morning, say 11?"

I do some quick math; today is Friday and I'm on the way to Hawaii. I would have to leave Hawaii first thing Sunday morning to make a Monday morning meeting. It seems reasonable and since I've just been shitcanned by Pete Jackson, I have nothing else to do Monday. "Absolutely," I reply.

At this point, Eva Braun—the obvious nickname for the Germanic-looking stewardess—is standing to my right with her arms folded and her face red with anger.

"Wonderful. I'll email you a confirmation. See ya then, g'bye."

I hang up and make a grand display of turning off my phone for Eva, who mimes the directions coming over the PA system. While she's showing us how to put on our oxygen masks in the event of a loss of cabin pressure, Terri starts playing twenty questions about my call.

"Agent?"

I tell her about my writing, in the sparest detail, and that Hart is the first agent to call back.

"That's incredible, Clark, but I got bad news for you."

I had a feeling she would attempt to take the wind out of my sails.

"What's that?"

"You failed the first test."

"What do you mean?"

"She asked you to come to a meeting, right?"

"Yes, Monday morning."

"And you didn't propose an alternate time?"

"I didn't want to risk her changing her mind."

"Clark, Clark, Clark," she says, exhaling. "She's already

interested in you. You're her ticket to money and you need to be in control of the conversation. By not pushing back, you just hurt your negotiating position."

This is all new territory for me, the conflict-averse.

"It's not in my nature to push back," I argue.

"You aren't going to last long in the entertainment business if you let people walk all over you."

She says it in a way that indicates there's more story there, but I don't want to probe too deeply; we've only just met, after all.

"I'll put it on the long list of things I have to work on."

"What's it about anyway?"

"What's what about?"

She looks at me as if I have three heads and raises her hands in the air. "Your book."

"It's about a guy who gets fired three weeks before Christmas and goes on an adventure with a Hollywood starlet." I say it deadpan; it's my first attempt at humor since meeting Terri, and I don't know if it's the vodka or if my comment was actually funny, but she begins to laugh.

"If you want to read it, I have a copy on my tablet."

"Good. I'll read it on the flight because I hate watching movies on the plane."

I pull my tablet from my thousand-dollar laptop bag and hand it to her as the pilot's voice comes over the PA.

"We are number one for departure. Flight attendants, please prepare the cabin for takeoff."

Terri immediately grabs my hand and squeezes it hard as we begin our roll down the runway.

"I'm scared to death of flying, Clark, just wanted you to know."

The truth is, I don't mind her choking my hand—it's

been a long time.

CHAPTER FIVE

Baggage Claim

The flight from Los Angeles to Maui is a little over six hours and Terri buries her nose in my book as soon as we level off and her nerves calm down. The book is a comedy and I'm pleased to hear her laughing, seemingly at least once per page. While she's busy reading, I decide to do a little research on my traveling companion as, truth be told, I don't know a thing about her or her work.

I dive back into my fancy bag for my laptop and connect to the plane's Wi-Fi. The first hit I get after searching for Terri Flynn is a story from an online gossip rag talking about how she stormed off the set of *Temporary Layoffs*, the movie she's currently working on. There's no clear reason for her actions, but an unnamed source close to the project suggests it might have to do with a dispute with the director. The researcher in me wants to do some more digging into this, but I realize if she caught me reading tabloid stories about her, it would be an uncomfortable situation, and reading a couple sentences on her wrath is enough to send me fleeing to the Internet

Movie Database.

I enter her name and pull up her filmography. Scrolling to the beginning, I see her career started with a sitcom called *Our Boy Roy*; I vaguely remember it as a take on the rich-white-family-adopts-poor-black-child genre so popular when I was growing up in the 80s. She played Nikki Bates, the tomboy next door neighbor of a gay black couple who adopts a poor white child. The show was cancelled after two seasons and she moved onto a nighttime drama called *LaMaze Academy* about a group of high school students who make a vow to get pregnant; the show was a hit and makes Terri a household name.

As I continue through her filmography, it's clear why I've never heard of her; most of her work is in teenybopper shows and movies and it's not a genre that I was ever into. About midway through her career, after she hit the age of twenty, she pulls an Elizabeth Berkley and stars in a provocative film called *Girls Night In* as an attempt to shed her goody-goody image. It's a complete flop and she doesn't work again for another five years.

The last entry in her filmography is a movie called *Temporary Layoffs*—it's marked "in production" and is a major studio comedy billed as Jimmy Walker's comeback. From the corner of my eye, I see her putting the tablet down, so I quickly close my laptop.

"Your book is really good. How did the name Blaze Hazelwood come into your head?"

Blaze is the lead character. He's a washed-up primetime soap opera star from the 80s looking to become relevant in present day Hollywood. The book centers on his pursuit of fame and the soap operaesque twists and turns that come with it.

"I was on a road trip with a friend of mine and to pass the time we started coming up with alternate versions of popular movies. He offered up *Black to the Future* starring Tyler Perry and I countered with *The Codfather* starring Blaze Hazelwood, which makes no sense because he isn't a real actor, but we both started laughing at how pretentious of a name it was. When I needed a character name for a down-on-his-luck actor from the 80s, Blaze was at the top of my list."

"The story's not just funny, it's smart funny. I read a lot of scripts and you'd be surprised at how much crap is out there. This is better than 90% of what I see."

"Wow, thanks for the compliment."

"I only have one criticism."

Here it comes—the part where my world is crushed.

"Why are you so afraid of conflict?"

"Huh?"

"The writing is great, the story is well paced, and the character development is really strong, but it lacks conflict."

Apparently, I can't even tolerate conflict in my make-believe fictional world.

"I guess I have a hard time with feeling uncomfortable."

"Clark, you have to learn to deal with that. Conflict isn't just a part of life, it's what drives a story forward. You need to carefully create tension and release it throughout the story. Otherwise, people won't keep reading. They won't become invested in the characters or the outcome."

I remain quiet, carefully considering what she said, trying to determine whether I'm upset, and then she hits me with the following.

"Think of it this way—what's the difference between

really good sex and sex that's just mediocre?"

Now would be a bad time to admit that, at 42, I've only had sex with two people—my high school girlfriend and my wife, the latter being the lesbian who hasn't touched me in ten years. As such, I'm no expert on the differences between good sex and bad sex; to me, any sex with a human is pretty unbelievable.

"The best sex I have is with guys who take their time and get into it. They don't just throw down, stick it in and fuck—they are sensual. They kiss me, breathe with me in rhythm, caress my body. They don't just sprint to the finish. They build something beautiful. They change speeds, get me close, then pull back. When the release is delayed until we both can't stand it, the force is overwhelming. That's what you have to do with words, Clark, seduce the reader and give them the best orgasm of their life."

As she speaks, I realize she and I couldn't be any more different. She's so free and I'm so rigid—she makes me realize that while I'm much older than she is, she has lived much more than I have. Plus, her telling me about the overwhelming force of a good orgasm has me at attention, so to speak.

"I'll keep that in mind."

"Good. I'm going to take a nap. Wake me when we land."

She lays her head on my shoulder and sleeps for the rest of the flight. I like the feeling so much I remain as still as possible so I don't wake her. I'm almost motionless for the remaining two hours. I say almost because my penis is constantly reminding me that we're in the midst of a pretty serious dry spell.

#

The plane lands just after 2:30 and fifteen minutes later, we're parked at the gate. Terri sleeps through all of it. I finally move, jostling her just enough to wake her, unbuckle my seatbelt, and grab my bag from under the seat in front of me. Eva, still holding on to her cock and phone-use anger, gives us a halfhearted "Thanks for flying Delta" as we exit the aircraft.

We make our way to baggage claim where bags from our flight have already started going around the carousel. Terri giddily screams, "That's my bag," as hers comes down the chute. I expect mine to follow shortly thereafter, as they were put on the plane at the same time, but no such luck.

"LIFO for me, Clark. I wonder where yours is," my fiery-haired travel companion says.

As I look around baggage claim, I see a digital advertisement for the Stahl Center for Peace and Balance, which is billing itself as Hawaii's premier center for addiction treatment. I wonder if my old boss has anything to do with it and my question's answered when she appears on the screen and says, "If you are speaking peace and balance in your life and want to put your addictions in the rearview mirror, come to the Stahl Center. We are here for you. Namaste."

While three years have passed since I've seen her, she actually looks younger than I remember. I'm momentarily perplexed but then realize it's probably movie magic.

Terri's voice pulls my concentration from the ad. "Clark, I'm proud of you for not freaking out, but your bag appears to be a no-show."

Just my luck. Terri and I walk to the baggage office and

are greeted with an "Aloha" by an overweight Polynesian woman named Mary. I explain my predicament and hand her my boarding pass and checked bag receipt.

"I am so sorry, Mr. Carson, but apparently your bag never made it onto the flight."

"How is that possible?" I ask. "I left it right next to hers at the end of the jet bridge."

"The note here says the baggage compartment was too full and they placed it on the next flight to Maui. Tell me where you're staying and I'll make sure it gets delivered to your room."

The blood drains from my face and I can barely put a sentence together. Terri steps in.

"Mary, thank you for your help. We are staying at the Ritz Carlton in Kapalua."

By now it's four, but due to the time change, it feels much later; we're both hungry and tired and want to get to the hotel.

"If you like, Delta can provide you free transportation to your hotel," Mary says.

Delta is trying so hard to right its wrongs, it's almost endearing and I feel a greater sense of loyalty to them even though they just fucked me. It makes me wonder what my general level of happiness would be if my wife or idiot boss ever took responsibility for screwing me over. We take Mary up on her offer and follow her directions to the shuttle bus.

CHAPTER SIX

One Room Only

The airline's transportation van is a far cry from the limos I'm sure my traveling companion is used to, but it will get us from the airport to the Ritz Carlton in one piece. While I should take in the scenery on the ride to the hotel, I decide to call my twin; she always tracks my flights, and I'm sure she's wondering what the fuck's going on. She picks up the phone with all her characteristic charm.

"What the fuck? Why haven't I heard from you?"

She was born a minute before me and uses this as justification for playing the role of vulgar big sister.

"I'm not going to make it to dinner tomorrow," I reply. We always have dinner on Saturday nights, and she does not like scheduling alterations.

"The snow will be gone by then," she says. "You'll land by three if you take the first flight out of LAX and we'll be at the Bird by six with margaritas in hand by 6:05, so long as Jason's behind the bar."

The Bird is short for our favorite restaurant, Tequila Mockingbird, located one town over from where I live.

Jason is the restaurant's infamous bartender; his drinks are potent and we love him for it. I consider him more than a bartender—he's my therapist and personal pharmacist rolled into one.

"I'm kind of in Hawaii right now."

"Wait, what?" She's never at a loss for words, so I must have really stumped her with this news.

"I'm in Hawaii," I repeat and then relay the entire story, from firing, to Flynn, to fucking Maui.

"First of all, your boss is a spineless bag of fuck nuts."

My sister's way with words is only bested by my father's; seriously, that man could throw together a string of obscenities that would make Quentin Tarantino blush.

"Have you told Fuck Face yet?"

Fuck Face is one of the nicknames Jo has bestowed upon Laura, my lesbian wife. Jo has been out of the closet since puberty and can't stand the fact that my wife uses me as a cover to her family; half her ire is directed at Laura for hurting me and the remainder is a result of Jo not respecting her requiring the assistance of a man in any way.

"No. She doesn't even know I'm not coming home tonight."

"What does she care? As long as you keep paying the bills."

Jo always knows how to hit me where it hurts the most. Yes, it's dawned on me that my wife doesn't want a divorce because that would mean cutting off a nice life for herself —she hasn't worked since the day we got married. Even if she got half my assets, she'd still need someone to take care of her; she has absolutely no financial management skills, or any skills at all, for that matter, aside, perhaps, from muff diving.

"I really don't want to have this discussion now. Can we table it as a potential New Year's resolution?"

"Your New Year's resolution should be to get laid by someone who cares for you."

"I'll take that into consideration."

"Good, but at some point you've got to cut the cord. So is Terri Flynn as hot in person as she is on screen?"

"Hotter," I admit.

"Maybe you should make her your New Year's resolution."

"I had that same fantasy for the last two hours of my flight."

"Well, don't sell yourself short. You've got a lot to offer. Hey, when you get a chance, call Mom. She'd love to hear from you."

At best, my mother and I have a love-hate relationship where I love her and she hates me. Maybe that's too harsh a statement; I like her and she hates me.

"Is she considering apologizing for referring to me as Frank Luntz?"

My mother and father cannot grasp what I do—or make that did—for a living. My sister is a medical doctor, a general practitioner to be more specific, in our hometown of Stamford, Connecticut, and my parents can tell their friends that their daughter is a physician. While I have explained no fewer than one hundred times that I run focus groups for a living, they simply don't comprehend what that means.

One day, during a visit with my parents in Florida, they were watching Fox News in their condo and a republican pollster named Frank Luntz was running a focus group with likely voters after a presidential debate. I pointed at the screen and said, "That's a focus group. My job is to be like that guy."

From then on, they started telling their friends I was like Frank Luntz, which isn't actually a positive thing, depending on what side of the political spectrum you're on.

"Think of it this way," Jo said, "now you can tell them you're unemployed and it's a moot point."

I switch gears from Luntz and general degradation to tell her about the call from Hart Literary.

"Fucking A, that's my kid brother!"

"By one minute!" I remind her. "It's still a long shot, but I'll take it as a win."

Interest from one agent didn't mean I was going to let myself suffer from delusions of grandeur.

"Just remember us little people when you're big and famous."

"I promise, you can be my date to the Oscars when I'm up for best original screenplay."

"Let's not get ahead of ourselves, Grisham. Call me when you get back east."

"Love you, sis."

"Love you too."

By the time my conversation with Jo is over, we're pulling into the Ritz Carlton. Terri and I step from the van and I suck in a big breath of Hawaiian air; for the first time in a long time, I allow myself a moment to take in the natural beauty of my surroundings. This comes to an abrupt end when a well-meaning hotel staffer approaches and says, "Aloha! Can I help you with your bags?"

As the Soul II Soul song goes, "Back to life, back to

reality."

"I don't need any help, but my friend might," I reply.

The bellhop goes around to the back of the van, retrieves Terri's bag, and leads us into the hotel where we're greeted with no fewer than a dozen more Alohas. I retrieve the piece of paper that Beverly gave me back in LAX and hand it to a young woman named Mimi at the front desk who looks over at the two of us and frowns. I'm preparing myself to hear "there's been a mistake" and find out we're really at the Aloha Motor Inn, but I'm spared disappointment.

"Only here for two nights?"

She has the accent of an island girl from the musical *South Pacific*, and I wonder whether it's real or put on to add a fabricated authenticity to the Ritz Carlton experience in Maui.

Terri pipes up, "Unfortunately."

"Boo hoo," Mimi says. "Not really enough time to really see Maui."

At this point I'm a combination of tired, hungry, and cranky and want nothing more than to get into my room and lie down. Therefore I want all small talk cut to a minimum and am coming across less patient than I normally would.

After a few dozen keystrokes, Mimi looks up and says, "I have you in a suite on the top floor, room 3827. Nice view of ocean."

"I think there's been a mistake, don't we each have a room?" I ask, as I have no intention of sharing a room with this actress.

I see a look of concern come over Terri's face and assume she's thinking the same thing—that is, until I hear an all too familiar noise come from her stomach.

"Clark, I need to get upstairs now."

"But what about the room situation?"

"We have no other rooms available," Mimi adds. "Two keys okey dokey for you?"

"That's fine," Terri says loudly, then takes a deep, almost panicked breath.

I take the keys from Mimi and Terri power-walks to the elevator, me trailing with her suitcase and purse.

We ride the elevator to the 38th floor and if I don't know better, the fiery red-haired actress is meditating the entire way up. The doors open and she rushes out.

She beats me to the room and looks back with a near-murderous (maybe fully murderous) rage. I wave the key in front of the door, but it remains locked.

"Sometimes if these things get too close to a cell phone, they deactivate."

"Open the fucking door, Clark."

I try the other key and the light goes from red to green; I hear a click and Terri pushes her way in.

I'd tell you all about the opulence of this suite, but my mind is on my traveling companion, who makes a beeline for the bathroom. A second later, I'm put in the uncomfortable position of hearing an ultra-violent wreckage of the suite's sole bathroom. Terri's colon begins to disgorge in an all-out, rapid-fire manner akin to the scene in *Predator* where Arnold Schwarzenegger, Jesse Ventura, and the rest of the gang shoot up the jungle, desperate to kill whatever animal is picking them off one by one.

I'll admit another thing about me—I'm not a poop guy. I don't enjoy discussing bowel movements and am invariably discreet about my own. After Laura and I married and moved in together, I would take care of my business in the downstairs bathroom while she slept upstairs. I did this for the sake of romance, assuming she would appreciate the gesture. Instead, she accused me of being anal retentive.

After the onslaught, things go quiet in the bathroom and I hear Terri let out a "phew." What happens next is even more shocking.

"Clark, I need something out of my bag."

I look down at my feet and see Terri's pocketbook.

"Ummm do you want me to leave it right outside the door?"

"Well, no, silly, I really can't get up. Just bring it in here to me."

I am stunned. This actress, whom I've known for about eight hours, wants me to enter her bathroom crime scene. My system shuts down until she follows up with, "Clark, are you still there?"

"What is it you need?"

"Go in my purse. There's a ziplock bag with baby wipes. I can't use the sandpaper in the bathroom."

I open her purse and find the wipes. I also come across a battery-operated device about two and a half inches long with "Pocket Rocket" written up the side. She wasn't lying in the Sky Club.

I approach the door and knock.

"No need to knock, Clark. I know you're the only one here."

I walk in and am pleasantly surprised when I find the white marble floor is not defiled in a Jackson Pollock-inspired fecal splattering. My relief, though, is counterbalanced with how repulsive the smell is—it reminds me of the men's room on the lower level of Grand Central Terminal on a hot summer day.

Terri is sitting on the toilet with a towel across her lap and an expression of utter relief across her face.

"You didn't think I was going to give you a free show, did you?"

"Ummm…" is all I can say. Unlike the rumors around Danny Thomas, this is not the kind of show I'm into.

She holds up her hands and I soft-toss her the wipes. She catches them, thank god—an error here could put me in an even worse position.

"Your work is done here, Superman."

I hurry out and step onto the balcony, far from the bathroom horror show, and admire the grand view of the Pacific. It's paradise and it's all mine for the next two nights.

I hear the toilet flush and the sink turn on; a moment later, Terri is by my side.

"You were a real hero in there, Clark. But now my tank is empty, let's go eat."

I worry that maybe she needs a little more time before reloading, but she leads the way from the room, and I follow.

CHAPTER SEVEN

The Hotel Bar

We arrive at the hotel's restaurant and are informed by the hostess that there's a thirty-minute wait for a table. She invites us to have a drink at the bar, and Terri is eager to satiate her thirst for alcohol.

I spend a lot of time on the road, and there is no better place for people watching than the hotel bar. I've seen more poor decisions made in the hotel's watering hole than in boardrooms across the country—and I work in marketing. They are a magnet for call girls looking to provide a little comfort to men who are lonely and thinking about the ones back home. How's that for irony?

Men, though, aren't the only travelers looking for a little road romance; women are sometimes just as bad. One time I saw a client of mine leave a hotel bar in Indianapolis with a doctor she'd known for all of twenty seconds. Apparently she was looking to play doctor while her husband stayed home with the kids.

Terri orders a vodka gimlet and I get a glass of red wine.

"Classy, Clark."

I can't drink hard alcohol. I mean, I can, but you never know which Kelly you're going to get when vodka, tequila, or whiskey is introduced to my system—so I play it safe and stick with wine. I realize most of our conversations have been focused on me, so partly out of politeness and partly out of curiosity, I ask Terri about the film she's working on.

She brushes off the question, "I really don't want to talk about myself."

I detect defensiveness. Since I'm trained to ask questions for a living and know not to automatically accept first answers as gospel, I don't let my question die but instead ask something innocuous with the hope of following it up with something more specific about her current project.

"What's it like working on a movie set?"

"Nice try, but I'm not interested in discussing my life with you at this point."

I'm off put by her reply and she can tell.

"Look, I'm an actress and I have to talk about my projects all the time. Now, I just want to have a little fun and relax."

"Considering what I heard upstairs, I figured talking about a film set would be easy," I say sarcastically.

"Everybody shits, Clark. It's natural."

She says this a bit too loudly and some people look around, but Terri isn't the least bit embarrassed. I, on the other hand, turn bright read, as I assume the other patrons are thinking I've recently experienced some bathroom trauma— mean, I have, but...

"When was the last time you got laid, Clark?"

Her career is off limits, but my sex life is on the table?

How's that for fairness?

"I don't really want to discuss my sex life."

"Would you rather discuss bowel movements?"

I seriously don't know how, but she's clearly read into the fact that I'm uncomfortable with the topic of defecation.

"A long time," I say in response to her first question.

"Why, Clark? You're a handsome guy who clearly has some jingle in his pocket, why has it been so long?"

This is a natural time to tell her that I'm married to a lesbian, but that's not a conversation I really want to have either.

"I guess it's not a priority."

The truth is, although I'm in my early forties, I'm still sexually inexperienced and the thought of taking a new partner after being inactive for over ten years produces enough anxiety for me to stick with self-satisfaction.

"I think you should get laid tonight, Clark. It might help you relax."

"Is that an invitation?" I say with a wink and a smile.

She coughs on a pretzel she's just stuffed in her mouth and washes with a sip from her gimlet.

"Don't get the wrong idea, it's not an offer. But I can read you like a book and you, my friend, need some vagina therapy."

"Can we drop this conversation?"

"You know what your problem is?" Terri says while exhaling slowly, as if she's a therapist who's just uncovered a breakthrough insight into her patient.

"What?" I ask and take a long pull on my wine.

"You give too many fucks."

"Run that by me again," I say using my best Gary

Coleman impersonation.

"Don't Arnold Jackson me when I am preaching the truth."

I'm impressed with her knowledge of 80s sitcoms; if she weren't so crazy, I'd consider asking her out.

"Why do you say I give too many fucks?"

"I've only known you half a day, but I've seen you give a fuck about what time you board a plane, when your luggage will arrive, a harmless cock on your coffee cup, my bathroom habits. You even give a fuck about sharing a free room with me in Maui. I'm sure I've only scratched the surface of all the fucks you give. The only thing you don't give a fuck about, ironically, is fucking!"

And that brings us right back to my nonexistent sex life.

"My advice to you, Clark, in order to become the Superman you were meant to be, is to give fewer fucks."

At this point, we're interrupted by the hostess, who looks like a deer in headlights—then again, who wouldn't after overhearing the psychoanalysis I just went through.

We walk to our table in silence then order another round of drinks. Fortunately, we're seated outside, and the crashing of waves against the shore momentarily distracts me from the fact that in the past twelve hours, I've lost my job, my luggage, and quite possibly my mind as I followed an emotionally challenged starlet on a trip to Hawaii.

And then right on time: "What are you going to do about your job situation, Clark?"

"I guess I'll start networking when I get back to New York…"

She interrupts before I finish my thought.

"Wrong!" She pounds her fist on the table hard enough to shake the silverware. "You failed the second test I've given you, Clark."

Wait, what? I don't even know what the first test was.

"The correct answer is: 'I'm not going to give a FUCK about my job, Lois.'"

"Are really going to do the whole Lois and Clark thing all weekend?"

"What, you give a fuck about what I call you?"

I don't have to think hard about my response.

"No, I guess I don't give a fuck."

"You are learning," she says and laughs.

"What was the first test I failed?"

"What did we do back at LAX after we left the Sky Club?"

"Went to Starbucks, but how could that be a test?"

"Who paid?"

"I did."

"Why?"

"Because you asked me to?"

"But why did you say yes?"

"Because I am a nice guy?"

"Exactly. You are too nice, Clark. When a woman meets a man, she gives him these little tests and puts him in one of three categories based on his responses—potential sex partner, friend, or loser. You went right into the friend zone because you did exactly what I asked you to do."

I'll admit it, I'm more confused than a TSA agent in a self-empowerment seminar.

"So I shouldn't be nice?"

"Not if you want to get laid. Women don't respect nice in a potential bedmate. They like a little bit of attitude. Nice should only come later."

"I'll never understand women."

I'm spared her reflections by our waiter, who greets us with another fucking "Aloha." I order pork tenderloin, and Terri selects the fish of the day.

"Well I've learned another thing you don't give a fuck about besides fucking," she chimes in.

"What's that?"

"Your health."

I raise an eyebrow to express my confusion.

"Pigs are filthy animals. I don't eat filthy animals." Terri surprises me by quoting *Pulp Fiction*.

"I'm impressed."

"I'm just trying to get you to loosen up, and by George, I think I've done it."

I don't know many people who can go from quoting *Pulp Fiction* to paraphrasing *My Fair Lady*. While Terri is crazy and impulsive, she's unlike any woman I've ever met and I think I'm starting to develop feelings of some sort.

While I'm grappling with this realization, she's scanning the restaurant, as if conducting a visual survey of the patrons.

"What are you looking for?"

"Not what, but who."

"Okay, I'll bite. Who are you looking for?"

"Someone for you to fuck." She says it while focused on the bar. I glance around as well and see two single women chatting.

"Limited prospects for you, I'm afraid. Wait, there's Maria."

"Maria who?"

"You'll remember—the woman from the Delta Sky Club at LAX who looked like Julie Andrews."

I look around and find her, then protest. "Oh yeah,

that's her, but she looks more like Mary Poppins than Fraulein Maria."

Terri rolls her eyes. "Do you really give a fuck what Julie Andrews character she looks like?"

I know better than to answer in the affirmative.

"Tell me, Clark, what would your opening line be?"

I haven't approached a woman at a bar in a long time—to say I lack game is an understatement. But I consider my options and have an epiphany.

"Okay, I've got something."

"Great. Lay it on me."

Here goes nothing, I think, then, "Allo, luv. Me name is Bert and I'd like to sweep your lady chimney."

My joke catches Terri by surprise and she bursts out laughing.

"You know, Clark, if you opened with that, she'd most likely tell you to go feed the birds, but it's damn funny. Seriously, what would you say to her?"

"I really don't know… Maybe something like, 'How do you like Maui so far?'"

"Fucking shit, Clark. The easiest openers to ignore give the option of a one-word response. You need to come stronger. Think about it from an author's perspective—what do you have to do on the first page?"

"Capture the reader."

"Right. Ask about Maui, or the weather, or anything mundane and she closes the cover on you and that's that."

I see her point, but I'm well outside of my area of expertise.

"Okay, what would you say if you were me?"

"That's cheating, Clark."

"I'm going to change your nickname from Lois to Yoda

unless you answer my question."

"Fair enough. Okay, I'd go up and ask if she could help settle a debate we're having and then point back to our table."

"Why would she want to do that?"

"Because her curiosity is piqued. It's also a great way to separate her from her friend, which is the primary objective."

"Interesting. So if I use that and bring her back to the table, what then?"

"Leave that to me." She says this using her best James Earl Jones impersonation.

"Okay."

"Okay what?"

"Okay, I'll give it a shot after dinner."

"Why wait that long?"

"Our food will be here any minute."

"Do you really give a fuck about the food at a time like this, Clark? You need pussy more than dinner."

I don't reply.

"Go on and do it."

"I'll try."

"No! Do or do not. There is no 'try.'"

Like Luke on Dagobah, I try to channel The Force as I leave the table and approach the Julie Andrews-looking gal at the bar.

I get to the bar and see she's in a seemingly deep conversation with her companion—I get cold feet and cut a beeline to the men's room. I do my business, wash my hands, stare at myself in the mirror and notice how tired I look. If I was a Julie Andrews lookalike, I wouldn't fuck me. I'd like nothing more than to go back to my table, eat dinner, and call it a night, but by this point, I know Terri well enough to know I'll never hear the end of it if I don't at least approach Julie.

"You can do this, Kelly Carson," I say to my exhausted reflection. "Just fucking do it. Stop giving so many fucking fucks."

I'm dismayed to hear a toilet flush and see a tall blond man resembling actor Ted McGinley coming out of the stall—another fuck given. He looks at me judgmentally and we share an awkward twenty seconds at the sink.

I leave McGinley and the men's room behind and head back to the bar; Julie's now alone and I assume her drinking companion is in the ladies' room, so I swallow my pride and make my approach but not before looking back to see Terri pointing at her wrist, suggesting that time is running out.

I tap Julie's shoulder.

"Excuse me." I say.

"Hi," she says back, giving me a look up and down.

"I'm having a debate with a friend of mine over there and I was wondering if you could help settle an argument between us."

I point to Terri and Julie looks over to make sure I'm telling the truth.

"What's the debate?"

Shit! I have no idea what to say and have to think of something quick.

"It's classified," is the best I can come up with.

"Excuse me?" she says while giggling.

"Sorry," I say nervously but am comforted somewhat that she laughed and think of something to follow it. "It's just that my friend over there made me promise I wouldn't tell you before you come over. She's worried I'll corrupt your point of view."

"Okay," she says mischievously, "I'll bite."

"Carl," she says to the muscular bartender, "tell my friend I'm going to the table over there for a minute, in case she returns before I get back."

"No problem," he says in broken English.

As she gets up from the stool, I see she's wearing a very short black evening dress that hugs her rear end so tightly I can see she's wearing a thong. I'm starting to believe she's not only out of my league, but out of George Clooney's as well.

We get to the table and I sit down. Julie remains standing.

"Clark, why don't you introduce me to your friend?"

"I'm Brenda," she says before I can apologize for not getting her name.

"I'm…"

Before Terri can say "Lois," which she was undoubtedly about to, Brenda interrupts.

"You are Terri Flynn! Oh my God, I was like your biggest fan when I was a kid! *Our Boy Roy* was literally my favorite show. Can I get a selfie?"

Before Terri can reply, Brenda grabs her phone, swoops into the seat next to Terri, and snaps a picture. The expression on Terri's face suggests she's not the least bit happy.

"Please, don't post that on social media. I'm trying to keep a low profile here in Hawaii."

The look on Brenda's face suggests it's too late.

"Okay, so, what are you two debating?"

As if to get back at me for bringing a fan over, Terri

answers, "Whether a woman can truly love a man with a small cock. Clark here says yes, but I disagree."

Of course this makes it look like I'm either Terri's gay friend or that my views are based on small-cock ownership.

"That's a hard one to answer."

Brenda's choice of words is not lost on me.

"On the one hand, I find that guys with smaller dicks try harder in other areas, but on the other, I like a man who can get the job done."

Terri turns to me and says, "You hear that, Clark, looks like I'm right. Thank you, Brenda."

Brenda looks toward the bar and sees her friend is back.

"I gotta go. So nice meeting you. And, Clark," she says with a giggle, "good luck with everything."

After she's gone, I turn to Terri and ask, "Was that the best you could come up with?"

"Nope," she says. "But I spent half of my career distancing myself from that show and it pisses me off when people mention it."

"You realize your dick comment did nothing to hurt her and she's the one who brought up the show."

"Do you seriously give a fuck about that, Clark?"

"Kind of." I know that's not the right answer, but it's the truth.

Our exchange is once again interrupted by the waiter, who's arrived with our dinner. We devour our meals in silence.

CHAPTER EIGHT

Another Failed Test

After eating, Terri wants a nightcap, so we go back to the bar. She gets a vodka gimlet and I get a glass of cab. She's turned the head of the Ted McGinley-looking guy from the restroom and she's apparently noticed the resemblance as well.

"Do you see that guy over there?"

"The blond?" I ask.

"Yeah. Do you think he looks like Ted…"

"McGinley?" I ask before she finishes her thought.

"Yeah. The guy known for killing sitcoms."

"Right. First *Happy Days*, then *Love Boat*, and finally, *Married with Children*."

"I wish to hell he'd show up on the *Kardashians*!" Terri quips.

"That would prove there's a God and that He loves us."

"There's a God, all right," Terri says.

Let's see, we've talked about sex, so next up should be religion followed by politics.

"How do you know?" I ask. I'm a lapsed Catholic and

now only attend Mass on four occasions—Christmas, Easter, funerals, and weddings; in a good year, that's only twice, but in a bad year, the sky's the limit.

"Because, I believe in one God, the Father almighty, creator of Heaven and earth…"

She goes on to recite the entire profession of faith. This chick is throwing curveballs at me like Dwight Gooden before he started sniffing lines of coke the length of a first baseline.

"Why are you looking at me like I have three heads?" she says after she's completed the prayer.

"It's been a long day; I got fired, flew to Hawaii with someone I barely know, have openly discussed my nonexistent sex life with said person, tried to pick up a girl that's way out of my league, and am now discussing religion over cocktails at"—I look at my watch—"eight o'clock, which is well after midnight on the east coast."

"Don't tell me you give a fuck about what time it is," she retorts.

"No I don't give a fuck about what time it is," I say a little too loudly, causing fellow drinkers to turn around. "But it's safe to say I've had a pretty strange day."

"Do you want a Xanax or something?"

I guess we've bypassed politics and gone straight to drugs.

"No I don't want a Xanax. I think I just need a minute alone."

I look over my shoulder and see a gated path leading to the beach.

"I'm just going to walk to the shore for a minute," I say. "I'll be back."

"Okay, Ahnuld," she replies, sounding more like Dana

Carvey than Schwarzenegger. "I'll be here, sitting by myself, pretty little actress that I am."

Whatever mind trick she just tried to play on me doesn't work and I get up from our high-top table, walk through the gate, and follow the path down to the shore.

Once I reach the water's edge, I remove my shoes so I can feel the water on my toes. While I normally hate the feeling of sand sticking to my feet, I decide not to give a fuck. I look to my right and see a full moon rising in the sky and "Bad Moon Rising" starts playing in my head.

I've always loved Creedence Clearwater Revival, but when I was younger, my sister made fun of me for mishearing the lyrics. Instead of singing, "There's a bad moon on the rise," I thought the lyrics were, "There's a bathroom on the right." To this day, if anyone asks where the bathroom is, Jo always tells them it's on the right, much to their chagrin, unless, of course, the bathroom happens to be right there on the right. Alright?

I take a deep breath and just as the water is coming around my toes and I allow myself my own little moment of Zen, my phone starts vibrating. I take it out and check the caller ID, which reads FishFace. I don't really want to talk to my wife, but I pick up because she's probably wondering where the hell I am.

I put the phone to my ear and before I say a word, she asks, "Where the hell are you?"

I know she won't believe me, but I say "Maui" anyway.

"Very funny, but where are you really? It snowed here and no one came to plow the driveway."

Well, at least that mystery is solved—she didn't call to see where I was, she called to complain that our plow guy didn't show.

"Did you call Angelo?" I ask.

"I was hoping you could do it," she replies.

I pay for this woman's cell phone, yet she refuses to use it to help with any household chores.

"When we got married, you agreed to take care of everything outside the house and I agreed to take care of everything inside the house, remember? I had that explicitly written into our wedding vows."

Yeah, we also promised to remain faithful to each other until the day we died, but she conveniently forgot about that.

"I'll call him tomorrow."

"Tomorrow?" she says, loud enough for the crabs under the sand to hear. "That's too late. I have Pilates tomorrow and won't be able to get out of the driveway."

I'd remind her that the Range Rover Sport, which I'm still paying off, can handle the snow on the driveway, but in true Carson fashion, I only think it.

"Fine," I reply. Another fuck I shouldn't give.

"There, that's a nice Kelly," she says. "When are you coming home anyway?"

"Monday." I hang up and call Angelo, who picks up before I even hear the phone ringing.

"Yo, KC, this snow is making it rain!"

Angelo's been one of my best friends since high school, and I know right away that he's stoned out of his gourd by the pitch and tempo of his voice. It's after midnight, but always 4:20 in Angelo's world.

"Hey, I just talked to Laura…"

"How is old Tartar Sauce doing?"

When Laura finally came out to me and I broke the news to Angelo, he immediately went into nickname mode. He tried multiple nicknames, including Beavertown, Fish Lips, and Clambake, but Tartar Sauce is the one that stuck. I didn't say he was evolved, but he plows a mean driveway.

"She's anxious that our driveway hasn't been done yet."

"Wait," he says while inhaling something that likely isn't legal, "where are you? I thought you were coming home tonight."

"Dude, I'm in Maui. Long story."

"Maui wowie? What the fuck are you doing in Maui?" He lets out a little cough.

"Long story," I start, ready to keep this conversation plow-centric, but then I tell him all of it.

"Motherfucking pussy," he says, referring to my former boss. "Dude, they got great weed out there, though."

I'm not a weed guy. Never have been, likely never will be.

"I'll have to take your word for it. Listen, about my driveway…"

"Just tell Filet-O-Fish I'll get to it before the dawn breaks."

Angelo can be poetic when he wants to be.

"But listen, if you run into an actress named Terri Flynn, try and hit that shit."

This comment catches me off guard. I'd left out the part about meeting Terri because I know how much of a dirtbag he is.

"Who's Terri Flynn?" I ask, pretending not to know.

"Dude," he says, sounding like he's inhaling again, "she's one of the hottest pieces of ass in Hollywood. Her scenes from *Girls Night In* are all in my spank bank."

I'm sure Terri would love to know that Angelo from

Connecticut masturbates to the film that nearly killed her career.

"And why would I see her in Maui?"

"Dude, check it out, I've got a Google alert on my phone for any Terri Flynn news—I'm a huge fan. Something came across my phone like a half hour ago because some chick took a selfie with Terri in Maui and hit it with hashtags TerriFlynn and ClarksSmallDick. I'm not sure what the last one's about, but it's trending."

Great, now the world knows Terri is in Maui and she's going to flip. I figure it's better for her to hear it from me, so I turn back to the bar and finish my conversation with Angelo on the way.

"You promise you can get my driveway done before tomorrow morning?"

"Have I ever let you down?"

The answer is an unequivocal yes, and on numerous occasions, but I don't want to argue because, well, I never want to argue.

"Thanks," I reply and terminate the call.

#

I head back through the gate and notice a hose I can use to wash the sand off my feet. I do so and dry off then put my shoes on and walk back to the bar. The table where Terri and I were sitting is empty, but I return, assuming she's using the bathroom.

I order a glass of wine and notice Brenda's still at the bar with her friend. Our eyes meet and she taps her friend on the shoulder, points at me, and holds her thumb and pointer finger out about an inch apart while her friend giggles. The waiter brings my wine and I drown my sorrow with a big gulp.

After waiting ten minutes, I've exhausted all my social media feeds and start wondering where my dinner companion has gone. I decide to look up Brenda's post on Instagram and search for the hashtags that Angelo mentioned—I shake my head when I see the photo of Brenda and Terri. I get that fame comes with a price, but why does privacy have to be stepped on?

I sit alone a little while longer and finish the glass of wine and order another, and then another. While the wine takes effect, I start making notes on my phone about everything that's happened in the past 18 hours, thinking it could make for an interesting story one day.

After forty-five minutes of drinking and giving my thumbs a workout, I look up and find I'm the only person left and the bartender's staring at me, as if to suggest I'm the one roadblock between himself and something better. I get the hint, ask for the check, and charge the wine to our room, which I return to immediately after leaving the bar.

I walk in and see the door between the suite's bedroom and living area is closed and there's a Do Not Disturb tag hanging on it. I innocently assume Terri has decided to go to bed early, so I pull out the sofa bed and go to the closet for the pillows and bedsheets. I then come to the uncomfortable realization that the only bathroom in the suite is in the bedroom.

Overcome with exhaustion, I place my fear of not being able to pee on hold and get into bed. My head hits the pillow and I'm about to drift off when I hear banging coming from the bedroom. At first, it sounds like a hammer gently hitting the wall, but it steadily becomes louder and the tempo gets faster—eventually, it sounds like the background audio from every episode of *This Old House* being played at the same time. I quickly come to the realization that Terri is not alone in there and remember how she turned Ted McGinley's head at the bar. Perhaps he's her costar for the evening.

This is confirmed when I hear her screaming, "Right there. Right there! Yes. Yes. Yes." This is followed by a moan from her partner that sounds like an elephant giving birth.

I close my eyes hoping it's over, but apparently, it's just begun. This cycle repeats no fewer than four more times and each time, it sounds like they're upping the difficulty level—I hear body parts slapping against each other and Terri shouting guidance as if she's directing a porno.

After two hours of this, I have to pee so bad I can taste it. I really don't want to put on my shoes and go back to the lobby, so I consider my only other option, using the kitchenette sink as my personal urinal. Assuming Terri and Jack Hammer are gearing up for round five, I go to the sink.

There's a problem with this plan, though. The sink is higher than my waist—if I'm going to use it, I need a boost. I look around for a step stool but don't find one; as if the Ritz Carlton on Maui is going to have a step stool lying around. My only option is to kneel on the counter and aim for the sink as if I'm Tim Conway in a Dorf on Peeing sketch.

I put my palms on the counter and scramble up so I'm kneeling on the two-inch-wide stretch of counter in front of the sink. My knees want to rebel, so I balance myself, get a good base, then reach down and pull my dick through the hole in my boxers and start to pee. After I've finished, I shake it vigorously and breathe a sigh of relief.

Then I hear the door open.

A voice says, "You want a glass of water? I'm getting one."

I'd like to say I can only imagine what this mystery man thinks as he sees a man kneeling on the counter and shaking his dick in front of the kitchen sink, but I don't have to because I know.

"What the fuck are you doing, pervert?" he shouts while rushing toward the sink.

I hear Terri's voice next, "What are you talking about?"

"There's a pervert in the kitchen!"

"What?" Terri screams.

I turn around to see Ted McGinley staring at me; he's wearing nothing at all and sporting an erection that looks like it could handle a beach towel. I lose my balance and fall sideways, my head bouncing off the counter as I crumble to the floor.

"Fuck!" I scream.

"Clark, is that you?" I look up to see Terri standing in the doorway, covered in sheets.

"Who the fuck is Clark?" her companion asks.

"He's staying on the couch."

By this time, I'm up on my knees and find myself a cock's length away from Ted's penis, which is still standing at attention. The side effects of Viagra can be a bitch.

"Can you put something on?" I say as I pull myself up to my feet.

"Yeah, just as soon as you tell me why you were jerking off in the sink, fucking freak."

"I was taking a leak. The only toilet in this room is through that door," I say, pointing to the bedroom, "and it was closed."

"Hey wait," he says. "You are that fucking wack job from the bar. The guy who was giving himself a pep talk in the bathroom mirror."

"What's he talking about, Clark?"

"Nothing," I say hastily

"Yeah, it's like he had just watched an episode of Dr. Phil or something. He's a fucking weirdo."

"I think it's time for you to leave now, Andy," Terri says. Silver lining, at least now I can stop calling him Ted.

"What? I still got a few more rounds in the chamber, babe," he says with utter fucking dejection.

"I'm getting a headache. Time to go."

"What about Clarence?" Andy asks while Terri goes back into the bedroom.

"Clark," I reply, not that it's my name, but because of the principle of it all.

"This room is only big enough for two," Terri replies while handing Andy his wad of clothes. "Time to go night night."

She's managed to put on a bathrobe and walks Andy to the door and opens it before he can even get his boxers on.

"If you are not out of here in five seconds, I scream rape."

"You are one crazy bitch," he shouts while hopping out the door on one foot. I don't see it, but I'm 99% sure he falls in the hallway due to the thump I hear after the door closes.

"So I've been told," she shouts through the closed door and turns back to the bedroom. "Big boys make pee pee on the potty, Clark," she says over her shoulder. "Feel free to use it if you need to." She leaves the door ajar, crawls into bed, and I don't see her again until morning.

65

CHAPTER NINE

Clark's Gimp Suit

After all that humiliation, I'm still able to fall asleep almost immediately and don't wake up until 8:30. For a sofa bed, my accommodation is quite comfortable, but then again, I wouldn't expect anything less from the Ritz. I look to Terri's door and see that it's no longer ajar but wide open and take that to mean she's left the room. Walking through the bedroom confirms my suspicion—no Terri. I use the bathroom and see a note she's written in lipstick on the mirror. It reads, "Meet me for breakfast at 8:45." She kissed the mirror next to the time.

My first instinct is to change, but I realize my suitcase never arrived from the airline, so instead, I take the world's quickest shower and put my dirty clothes back on. I curse myself for wearing a white button-down shirt and khaki pants to the airport yesterday, both are wrinkled, and I look like a middle-aged man doing the walk of shame, which wouldn't be a bad thing except for the fact I haven't gotten laid in over ten years.

The elevator ride to the lobby is your standard,

uneventful elevator ride until the video monitor switches to entertainment news and the featured story is about Terri and how she stormed off the set of her current movie over creative differences with the director. The "analyst," if that's what pop-culture pundits are called, suggests this could be a career-ending move. The story wraps with rumors that Terri is in Hawaii with a mystery man. I suppose I can add that title to my résumé. If only they knew about the McGinley express that pulled into town last night, now that would be a real story.

I let my fellow passengers stream from the elevator while I watch the end of the segment—it concludes with a still shot of her raising absolute hell on the set of *Temporary Layoffs*. I get off and find her sitting at an outdoor table overlooking the Pacific. Her red hair is swaying with the breeze and for a moment I wonder what it's like to be Ted McGinley.

"You're late, Clark."

She says this without even turning around to confirm it's actually me standing behind her.

"How did…"

"I can tell by the way you walk. You kind of shuffle. You're always huffing and puffing like you're exhausted, too."

Oh, great. She turns around with a bright smile, and my first instinct is to apologize for being late, but she'd just tell me I shouldn't give a fuck about being late; I give a fuck about being scolded, so I hold my tongue.

The truth is, paranoia around tardiness was instilled early by my mother who would scream at me and my sister if there was even a chance we'd make her late for something. I'm pretty sure she never wanted kids, and she was never able to forgive us for making her late for her period.

I take the seat across from Terri and notice her eyes are puffy, as if she's been crying. I stare a little too long and she calls me on it.

"I've had a bad morning, okay?"

I shift my gaze but wish I didn't have to—while the skin around her eyes puts me in mind of a puffer fish, her blue irises are works of art.

"The elevator?" I ask, referring to the news segment.

"You saw that?"

"Yes. What's going on?"

"I don't really want to talk about it."

I could easily call bullshit—she's made me talk about my career and my sex life but won't say a goddamn thing about herself. But, of course, I give her a pass.

"What would you like to do today?" I ask.

"Hollywood is so fucking messed up."

Somebody apparently wants to talk about her career after all. Instead of replying, I look at her and nod, suggesting she continue her train of thought. It's a little trick we moderators use as a way of not injecting our biases by asking questions.

"This is my first theatrical film after the trainwreck that was *Girls Night In* and the goddamn director isn't taking me seriously."

I pour myself a coffee from the carafe and get the sense she wants me to ask a follow-up question, so I do.

"In what ways do you think he isn't taking you seriously?"

"I read this script five times before accepting the role, and there's nothing in there that calls for gratuitous nudity, but the fucking director wants me topless in half my scenes. I know I have nice tits—hell, I put them in—but I just don't see how my boobs move the story forward."

Last week, if you told me I'd be in Maui talking to a starlet about her boobs the day after being fired, I'd have called you deranged. But here I am.

I'm at a near loss for words and say the only thing that comes into my male mind: "Those are fake?"

She looked at me with squinted eyes and raised cheekbones, giving off the universal sign for "what's your fucking problem?"

The woman wasn't the least bit concerned about me overhearing her ride a dick bicycle for half the night, so I'm not sure why she's upset that I'm asking about her boob job, but then again, she's a redhead, and they aren't known for rational thought.

"I don't know what I am going to do. My agent keeps calling to remind me I'll be in breach of contract if I don't return to the set on Monday."

"So go back to the set on Monday."

"It's not that simple, Clark. If I do that, and they haven't conceded the nude scenes, I won't have gained anything. Plus, there's another problem with that plan."

I look at her with a raised eyebrow.

"I can't go back on Monday because I'm going to the meeting with your agent."

I raise the other eyebrow and realize I must look like Spock on crack.

"Why would you do that?"

"This is a new world for you, Clark—you need my help navigating."

The waiter comes and she orders an egg white omelet

with veggies. I opt for pancakes.

"How do you stay so thin eating carbs like that for breakfast?"

"I have a high metabolism."

"That's just not fair. I haven't had carbs in years. I'd kill for a piece of French toast."

I shouldn't give a fuck about anything—she can give all the fucks about her diet. Talk about not fair.

I'm tempted to address last night's fuckfest. If she's planning on another marathon, I need a different room. She must have read my mind because she blurts out, "Jesus Christ, my pussy hurts."

And there you have it.

"Sorry, if I interrupted anything last night."

"Please don't tell me you give a fuck about that, Clark. Look, people have sex, it's natural. I needed to blow off some steam. I'm actually happy Andy caught you wanking in the sink. It was a good reason to get rid of him. I was done with him."

"I was taking a piss."

"Whatever. It's natural to wank, Clark."

She doesn't have to tell me that. Being married to a lesbian has earned me a master's degree in masturbation. I'm a master of bation.

She changes the subject abruptly. "What do you want to do today, Clark?"

Didn't I just ask her this before she started bitching about Hollywood? In all honestly, I haven't given it much thought, but I have to call the airline to see where the fuck my bag is and arrange for a flight home tomorrow. Given the time change and the flight duration, I'll have to leave as early as possible to make the meeting. I relay all of this to Terri.

"Why don't you take care of that now and I'll plan our day. Teamwork to make a dream work!"

This is one of Pete Jackson's favorite sayings and hearing it makes me want to blow up a piano. My fantasy of instrumental destruction is cut short by the arrival of my pancakes and Terri's omelet. I excuse myself from the table, as I feel compelled to wash my hands before I eat, and when I return, I find Terri attacking my pancakes like Tom Hanks' character in *Castaway* would have if a breakfast buffet washed ashore.

"Are they good?" I ask.

"Oh my fucking god, they are amazing," she says with a mouth full of my breakfast.

I'm left with her bullshit omelet and eat it with much less ferocity than she's shown my pancakes.

The waiter removes our plates and I reach for my phone to call the airline. As it rings, I hear Terri ask the busboy about things to do in Maui, and all I hear him say is "it's not in any guidebook but..." before my attention shifts to the computerized voice on the other end of the line. After dictating my frequent flyer number and saying "representative" four times, I'm connected to someone in Atlanta manning the "Flying Colonel" service desk. I travel so much that precious metal distinctions no longer apply—I'm now a military-grade traveler. While I tend to eschew such distinctions, it gets me through customer service queues quicker than the run of the mill Double Secret Platinum Medallion flyer.

"Good evening, Ms. Carson, my name is Diane, how can I help you today?"

While I'm a Flying Colonel, no one has gotten the

memo that I'm a man. I correct Diane and she apologizes profusely.

"Well, how can I help you then, Mr. Carson?"

"Well, Diane, my flight to New York was canceled yesterday and I'm in Maui…"

"Yes, I see that right here, Mr. Carson. How's the weather in Maui?"

"It's beautiful but…"

"I bet you want to know where your bag is, don't you?"

It's the second time today my mind has been read, though unlike Terri, Diane doesn't share the state of her vagina with me.

"I would be forever in your debt if you could tell me."

"Don't you worry, Mr. Carson, I can confirm that they arrived late last night at the airport in Maui and someone will be delivering them to your hotel today."

"Well that's excellent news, Diane. You must make Jack very proud."

"Pardon me, Mr. Carson?"

Apparently, she didn't catch my John Cougar Mellencamp reference. Or maybe it's just John Cougar. Come to think of it, maybe that was John Mellencamp. Who the fuck knows—the point is, she didn't get it and I should move on.

"Sorry about that. Diane, could you help me book a flight back to New York tomorrow morning?"

"I'd be happy to help you with that. Let's see, there's a flight that leaves tomorrow afternoon at one and gets into JFK Monday morning at 8:29. You have an hour layover in LA."

My first instinct is to see if she can get me on a flight back today so I have a full day to recover before meeting my prospective agent, but I glance over at Terri, who's still engaged in conversation with the busboy, and know if I even mention that, she'll accuse me of giving too much of a fuck.

"Can you get me on that flight?"

"I can do better than that, Mr. Kelly. I can get you an automatic upgrade."

I then remember what Terri said about coming to New York with me and, against my better judgment, ask about the possibility of getting her on that flight.

"Diane, I'll have a traveling companion with me. Her name is Terri Flynn and…"

"Shut the front door!"

"Pardon me?"

"The actress Terri Flynn? I heard she was in Maui this weekend. Are we talking about the same Terri Flynn?"

"Flaming red hair and unpredictable personality?"

"That sounds about right."

"Then, yes."

"Okay, I've got her on the same flight, sitting right next to you in first class."

"Thank you, Diane."

I get off the phone and look at Terri. The busboy has just left and she has a bunch of notes written on a napkin.

"All squared away with Delta?"

"Yes. Apparently, my bag should be on its way to the hotel and I got us both on a flight back to NY tomorrow."

"Really?" she asks with a hint of astonishment.

"Really," I say with a smile. "So what's on tap for today?"

"You should do that more."

"Do what more?" I ask.

"Smile. You have a nice smile."

"I'll make a mental note of that. What's on the napkin agenda? Should I be afraid to ask?"

"Well, Rogerio our busboy just told me about a secret hike that ends near a hidden waterfall. Are you feeling adventurous, Clark?"

By now you may have put two and two together and figured out that "adventurous" and "Kelly Carson" don't exactly go hand in hand. As a case in point, my sister once wrote a dating profile for me that read, "White-collar worker with limited sense of adventure and average-sized penis seeks companionship with a woman not bothered by any of the above." But today, I'm starting to feel more like Clark than like Kelly, so I say, "Bring it on."

"I like this new Clark. Let's go upstairs and see if your bag is here."

As we leave the table and head for the elevator, she reads from Rogerio's Hiking Checklist: bathing suit, old sneakers, waterproof backpack, flashlight, Ziploc bags.

"What kind of hike is this?" I ask.

"Are you giving a fuck about this, Clark? Because if you are, you know what I'm going to say."

"No fucks given."

We get to the room, and sure enough, there's a suitcase in the foyer. It looks just like my black bag, but I have a feeling something isn't right. I see the name tag the airline put on at the gate, though, so I chalk my nervousness up to natural suspiciousness.

I wheel the suitcase to the sofa bed and lay it on its side. Terri's hovering and I give her a look to politely suggest she back the fuck up a little bit.

"What?" she asks. "I want to see what you got in there."

I shake my head and unzip the suitcase. Once I separate it, I know something's off.

"Holy shit, Clark, is that what I think it is?"

Terri pushes past me and pulls out a one-piece leather outfit replete with ball gag and riding crop.

"Ohhh, Clark, I've been very a bad girl. Come punish me."

"This isn't mine. None of this is mine!"

"I always knew there was something kinky about you. But how do you fit into this gimp suit? It would be tight on me!"

"It's. Not. Mine!" I say through gritted teeth.

"Relax there, gimporino, I'm just trying to have a little fun. Let's see what else is in here."

Terri rifles through the suitcase and finds enough kinky stuff to fill a Frederick's of Hollywood storefront.

"She's into some serious shit."

By now, I've collapsed onto the sofa bed and am ready to cry when a thought comes and I start laughing uncontrollably.

"What's so funny, Clark?"

Between gasps, I manage to say, "Somewhere on this island, there's a dominatrix who just got a suitcase full of button-down shirts and khakis. She's probably cutting a hole in the crotch of my J.Crew pants right now."

Terri blurts out a laugh. "She's going to be known as the Vineyard Vines Vixen."

"The Polo Pussycat," I add.

This causes her to actually chortle. She then has an epiphany, "I bet it belongs to that woman we saw in the airport. Do any of her clothes smell like R. Kelly?"

I don't dare do a sniff test.

"What the fuck am I going to do?" I say, shoving my palms into my eyes. A moment later, I feel her join me on the bed. I open my eyes to find her gorgeous blue eyes staring into mine.

"I have an idea," she says while biting her lip.

This makes my heart pump the entirety of my blood supply to my pelvic region.

"What's that?" I'm able to say, even though my mouth has gone bone dry.

She brings her lips close to my ear, and in the sexiest voice I've ever heard, she whispers, "I'll take you shopping."

She grabs a pillow and smacks me over the head. "Come on, lover boy, time to blow this joint. Let's get some retail therapy and some exercise and then who knows what the night will bring."

She darts from the room and I follow after, trying to think about baseball so I'm not walking around with my McGinley jutting out.

CHAPTER TEN

Walking on Air

Let's just fast-forward through some mundane matters here, but before that, a note on the Ritz Carlton—they know how to do customer service; not only do they tell us exactly where to shop, they drive us there in a fucking Bentley.

Terri buys me an outfit for the pending hike as well as clothes for this evening and tomorrow morning including a tee-shirt with a dolphin on it because she claims it's my spirit animal. I manage not to give a fuck about having such a girly spirit animal and she manages to pick up some things for herself and other hiking essentials. We change, and our driver drops us near the start of our hike, promises to take our bags back to our room, and tells us to call him when we're done.

"We have to find the cow field," Terri says.

"Hungry, are you?"

She slaps my arm and I try not to get a hard-on.

"Rogerio says our hike begins in a cow field."

I don't see any cows, but my sense of olfaction is

working overtime—I can certainly smell them.

"Judging by what my nose is telling me, we're close."

We walk through a clearing and sure enough, a number of future hamburgers are grazing in front of us.

"Does McDonald's know about this place?"

"Very funny, Clark."

We walk through the cows, who barely glance at us with their sad cow eyes and their mouths full of cud. I can't help but feel as if they are judging me for my dolphin tee-shirt and secretly hoping I step in a pile of their shit.

We leave the cows behind and Terri stops and points down the field.

"Now we're supposed to find an old riverbed."

We walk in the direction she points towards and come across what appears to be a dry riverbed. It's rocky, and I immediately understand why Rogerio was insistent we wear sneakers, not flip-flops or sandals. After a while, the terrain becomes thick with branches.

"Rogerio told me we may have to crawl under these branches."

I get down on my belly and begin to mimic the Army men my sister and I used to pretend to be. Once we clear the bushes, we're standing in front of a pond; there's a waterfall across the way and what appears to be a cave behind the waterfall. I assume this is our destination, as there's no other way to go.

"I guess this is why we needed a waterproof backpack," Terri says. She's wearing a white tank top and minuscule khaki shorts; the fact that she resembles a red-haired Lara Croft isn't lost on me. I want to start calling her Lara instead of Lois, but I don't think that will fly with her so long as she keeps calling me Clark.

Terri jumps in first and I follow. The water is warm and comes up to my waist. I'm scared of heights—are you surprised?—and was worried we might have to jump from a higher altitude, but I easily handled the three-foot hop into the pond.

We swim through the waterfall and I can't help but notice how sexy Terri looks with her hair slicked back; the fact that her nipples are poking through her white tank top isn't unfortunate.

We enter the cave behind the waterfall and Terri removes her backpack to retrieve helmet lamps. She switches them on and hands one to me.

She affixes hers to her head. I do the same and notice that each way I turn, my lamp illuminates artwork carved into the stone.

"This is amazing, Clark. I wonder who did this."

I'm pretty sure it was Hawaiian kids with nothing better to do but don't want to ruin the moment Terri's having, so I opt to keep my mouth shut.

After ten minutes of wading, the water becomes more and more shallow. Terri and I see a light ahead and realize we're almost at the end of the cave. As we exit, we see two rock walls parallel to one another with water trickling down their faces.

"Did you bring a ladder in your backpack?" I ask.

"Rogerio says there's a trick to getting up there. There are rocks that serve as foot and handholds—it may take some trial and error, but it should be easier than climbing the rope in gym class."

"That always made me feel kind of funny," I say in my best Dana Carvey voice.

"Party on, Garth," Terri replies. She moves to the wall

and scales with ease—like scaling rock faces is part of her everyday life—and once again, I follow her lead.

At the top, I look down and can't believe how high we are—we're at least fifty feet above the water. Terri removes the backpack and chucks it into the water below.

"What are you doing? That has my phone, wallet, our hotel key."

"Last stop on the hike," Terri says. "Unless you want to retrace your steps, there's only one move."

"Jump? I can't do that."

"Going back down the wall will be harder."

"Maybe, but I don't want to die either."

"You're not going to die. Just follow me."

I watch as Terri throws herself off the cliff and plummets into the water.

I immediately start pacing back and forth, and my mouth has gone bone dry from the nervousness. I feel something trickling down my leg and realize I pissed myself, just a little. I really don't do well with heights.

I look down but don't see Terri surface. I have visions of her drowning like Natalie Wood except instead of Robert Wagner, I'll be fingered for her death. Another thing to add to the old résumé—murder suspect. Wait, was Christopher Walken the suspect in that investigation, because I totally could see him killing somebody. Fuck, why the hell am I even thinking about this? Oh yeah, it's because I'm scared shitless and delaying the inevitable.

I'm brought back to reality when I hear, "Help! Help!" I look around to see if there's any other way down. There isn't. I realize what I have to do for my friend.

She's trying to turn me into Christopher Reeve's *Superman*, but I feel more like William Katt's *Greatest*

American Hero—except for the fact that I am not sporting a red pajama-like superhero suit left for me by aliens and Robert Culp isn't around to spur me into action. Nevertheless, I take a few steps back then blindly run and jump off the cliff with my arms extended like a fucking moron who's trying to fly. All anyone within earshot would have heard was some garbled variation of "fuck" being screamed by a 42-year-old idiot.

My sister was fond of slapping me for no apparent reason. It was her way of exerting power over her "little" brother. She's got nothing on this body of water I just jumped into, which I hit with a force greater than any slap I've ever received, largely because I lead with my face.

The water is cold as I float back to the surface, and while I'm still terrified, I also feel exhilarated. I look around for Terri and see her laughing on the rocks by the edge of the water.

"Are you okay?" I scream.

"You should have seen the look on your face!"

It dawns on me—I've been had.

"Fucking trickster asshole. You're crazy, you know that?"

"It comes with the hair."

I swim to her and pull myself onto the rock beside her and see her eyes go wide as I exit.

"How did they miss that on an ultrasound?"

"Miss what?" I ask, not realizing my shorts came off when I hit the water.

"That!" she says, pointing at my penis.

I look down and put my trembling hands in front of my dick.

"I'm impressed, Clark."

I look back and see my shorts floating on the surface. I

dive back in, retrieve them, and awkwardly put them on in the water before swimming back.

"The show is over I guess," Terri says.

"Nobody rides for free," I reply, getting out of the water for a second time. "Where do we go from here?"

"Through that clearing." Terri points to a dirt path about 30 yards away. "There's apparently a drug addiction and recovery center on the other side of the woods. We can stroll the grounds and call the hotel to get us when we're ready."

"Do you remember the name of the center by any chance?"

"Ball or Stall or something like that."

Terri confirmed what I suspected—we're going to have a walk through my old bat shit boss's recovery center before making our way back.

I jump off the rock and extend my hand to help her down. Then, for the first time since meeting Terri Flynn, I take the lead and she follows me as I make my way toward reacquainting myself with an old friend.

CHAPTER ELEVEN

The Stahl Center for Peace and Balance

We reach a clearing and suddenly a large glass pyramid that looks plucked from Paris and planted in the middle of Maui looms before us—I remember my former boss's fascination with the City of Lights. She spent her junior year in Paris and fell in love with a Frenchman who broke her heart, but not before introducing her to Colombian marching powder.

We walk to the entrance and I pull on the door, but it doesn't budge. Terri taps me on the shoulder and points to a call box. I push a button and a second later, a soft Hawaiian voice says, "Aloha. Welcome to Stahl Center for Peace and Balance. Are you visiting a guest or here to inquire about our services?"

"I'm here to see Michele Stahl. Is she available?"

"Do you have an appointment with Ms. Stahl?"

"No, but I'm an old friend from New York."

"I'm sorry, but she sees people by appointment only. You will have to call her assistant and make an appointment."

That's when I have an epiphany. I turn to Terri and mouth, "I'm about to throw you under the bus."

I don't know if she got a word of it, but she responds with, "Whatever, I really have to pee."

"I was trying to be discreet before," I say, "but I am here with actress Terri Flynn. Do you know who she is?"

"Of course. *Our Boy Roy* is my favorite show and always will be."

"She is looking to inquire about rehabilitation services but will only speak with Ms. Stahl."

"In that case, come on in."

I hear the door buzz, but when I pull it, it still doesn't budge.

"Try pushing it, Clark."

I push it and it opens right up. Terri smirks as I hold the door open. From the corner of my eye, I see some ruffling in the bushes about 25 yards away. I just assume it's an exotic bird or something and follow Terri through the door.

We enter a lobby that feels more like a family room than the front office of a rehabilitation center.

"Aloha," says a large Hawaiian man sitting on a couch in the center of the room. "How may we be of service, Ms. Flynn?"

"I really have to pee."

"The bathroom is down the hall on the right. But before you go, I have to frisk you to make sure you have not brought drugs."

"Do you see what I'm wearing. Did you notice that I'm soaking wet?"

"It's the rules."

Terri groans and raises her hands above her head, and I

watch as the large Hawaiian man pats her down. She turns and gives me a dirty look and asks for the backpack; she takes out a brush and hands the bag back to me.

"You may proceed," the man says.

I watch Terri's attractive backside as she walks to the restroom, and for a minute, I allow myself to daydream about what it would be like to caress it, but my dream ends when my new Hawaiian friend asks to see the bag, as well.

He has a look through our Ziploc bags, then asks, "Did you just do The Hike of Destiny?"

"The what?"

"The Hike of Destiny. Start through a cow field, crawl under brush, swim through a cave, big fucking drop at end?"

"That sounds about right."

"And you fucking lived! We lose a lot of tourists every year—don't survive the drop when the water is low. You lucky, my friend. They say if you live through that hike, you come out a changed man."

"Believe it or not, I'm walking on air."

Terri returns looking refreshed. Her red hair is brushed out and starting to curl—just when I thought she couldn't get any sexier.

"I just have some paperwork for you to fill out, Ms. Flynn."

"Hold on a second," I interrupt. "But we don't even know your name."

"Ahh. My name is Saffron."

He's named after a fucking spice, not that I give a fuck.

"Saffron, Ms. Flynn will only speak with Michele Stahl. Can we see her now?"

"This is highly unusual, but let me see what I can do."

He taps buttons on his phone and puts it to his ear.

"I need to speak with Vanilla; is she in? Uh huh. Okay. Can she spare a few minutes to come to the lobby and meet a potential guest? Yes, celebrity. Good. Good. Okay. Thanks."

While I'd like to have heard the other end of that conversation, I'd love to know why he referred to my old boss as Vanilla. Is everyone here named after a spice?

"She will be down in ten minutes. She says to enjoy the artwork while you wait."

Saffron leaves and Terri and I enter a warmly decorated room off the lobby that's covered with artwork from the Baroque period. We wind up in front of a painting called Triumph of the Immaculate by Matteis; don't think for a minute I'm some art snob—the title and artist's name are on a plaque underneath.

As I study it, I notice something funny—instead of the artist's original painting of the Virgin Mother, my old boss's likeness is included. I look around the room and see the same change has been made to all the other replicas hanging in the room.

"What are we doing here anyway, Clark? Can't we just go back to the hotel? I'm starving after that hike."

"I am here to see an old friend."

"Who's this old friend of yours anyway?"

"My old boss."

"The one who fired you over the phone? This should be interesting."

"No. The one who sold her company to the douchebag who fired me over the phone."

"Then this should be even more interesting. It sounds

like there might be some conflict here, Clark. I'm impressed."

"I know, it's a bit out of character, but I got some questions and only she has the answers."

"Oh, I see—you still give a fuck about your old job. I thought you were evolving."

"I just went on a suicidal hike and lived to tell the tale. To get back to our hotel, we have to cross the grounds of my old boss's new place of business. I'm taking it as a sign from above that I'm supposed to see her."

"I thought you didn't believe in God," Terri mutters.

"I'm converting," I say loudly.

"Well, as I live and breathe, Kelly Carson in the flesh."

Terri and I turn and there's Michele Stahl, standing in the doorway. She's dressed in white from head to toe, and her platinum hair is cut at chin length. It's been three years since I've seen her, but she really does look younger —I guess that wasn't movie magic in the commercial. She comes over and gives me a big hug and kisses both cheeks —European style—and I'm immediately hit by the scent of vanilla. She gives Terri the same treatment.

"To what do I owe the honor of a visit from my favorite former employee? You don't expect me to believe this beautiful specimen is an addict?"

"We happened to be in the neighborhood. Is there a place we can meet in private?"

"Absolutely. We shall go to my private residence on the third floor. Are you hungry?"

"Starving," Terri says.

"Then I shall have my chef prepare something." Michele raises her wrist to her mouth and says, "Sumac, prepare a meal for three. We'll take it on the balcony.

Love, love, kiss, kiss."

This exchange supports my spice hypotheses and now I feel like I'm in the Twilight Zone.

"Follow me to the lift," Vanilla, I mean Michele, instructs, and Terri and I follow.

We head to the third floor and stop in front of a purple door that looks like it could be the entrance to Barney's Playhouse.

"This is modeled after Eglise Saint-Étienne-du-Mont in the fifth arrondissement. I almost got married in that church, but it didn't work out. C'est la vie, as the French say."

She pushes the door open and we walk into a spacious, open foyer decorated all in white.

"White is the symbol of purity—I surround myself in white these days."

I remember the old Michele also surrounded herself with a lot of white. It caused her to stay up all night and make bad choices. I'm curious to hear how she turned her life around.

"Follow me to the balcony. Sumac," she shouts, "bring some Evian for my guests."

"Right away, madame," I hear a voice shout from what I presume is the kitchen.

We follow her to the balcony, where she proceeds to tell us what it's a replica of.

"The Café de Flore is one of the oldest coffeehouses in Paris. This balcony is a replica of the one right above it. Please sit down."

We do as suggested, and we are met on the balcony by a tall, trim man with dark hair and a thick Tom Selleck 'stache—if I didn't know any better, I would have sworn

Magnum P.I. himself was standing before us. He places a bottle of Evian and three glasses on the table.

"Shall I pour for you, madame?"

"Please, Thomas—I mean, Sumac."

"My pleasure."

After he pours us each a glass, Sumac informs us that lunch will be ready in twenty minutes. He leaves, and Vanilla wastes no time asking questions.

"Are you still married to that lesbian?"

Terri, seated to my left, chokes on her water and goes into a prolonged coughing fit. When she finally stops, she turns to me and says, "Clark, you're married to a lesbian?"

Vanilla picks up on my nickname.

"What? You swapped Kelly for Clark?"

This is coming from a woman who changed her name to a spice.

"It's a long story," I reply.

"I need to hear about the lesbian," Terri chimes in.

"Kelly over here came home early from a business trip and found his wife face deep in their handywoman's va jay jay."

"Is that true, Clark?"

"Yes," I say through my teeth.

"Who hires a handywoman?" Terri asks.

I'll admit I'm not the world's handiest guy, which actually put a big strain on my marriage because my father-in-law was a mechanical engineer. The guy could do it all—install a ceiling fan, hang sheetrock, unclog the shit out of a shit-clogged drain. So that was my wife's frame of reference when it came to men, and I can't even hang a fucking picture without screwing up. As such, we hired a handywoman named Ella to help with simple household duties. So my ineptitude with tools pretty much led to the cunnilingus that ended my marriage.

I simply defend myself by saying, "I'm just not… handy."

"And you didn't divorce her?"

"Your friend Kelly, I mean Clark, over here hates conflict so they agreed to an open marriage. Clark agrees to support his lesbian wife and she agrees to…well, what does she agree to?"

"Can we please get off my wife?"

"You apparently haven't been on her in a while," Terri jokes.

"Ohh, I like her," Vanilla pipes up.

Thankfully, we are interrupted by Sumac, who has returned with lunch. His white-gloved hands present a covered plate to each of us.

"Today I have prepared fish native to these waters. It is called opakapaka, sometimes referred to as pink snapper. Bon appétit."

Terri giggles and doesn't even try to suppress it. "I bet it's been a while since you've had some good pink snapper, huh Clark?"

I drop my knife and fork onto my plate and the noise silences my lunch companions. Vanilla takes the hint and changes the topic.

"So why are you here, Kelly?"

"Well, yesterday I was in the Delta lounge at LAX and Pete Jackson fired me over the phone."

"Good for you!" Vanilla shouted. "You were too good for that place."

"Good for me? How can that possibly be good for me?"

"Do you know why I hired you when you were just a

green twenty-five-year-old kid who knew nothing about the business?"

"Enlighten me."

"Because you were curious, and you can't learn curiosity. You wanted to solve puzzles and you soaked up everything I taught you. There is nothing left for you to learn at that place. You have more than enough talent to be your own boss. Embrace this change."

"But why did you sell your company to a behemoth like Omnivore? You had to know they were going to change everything you worked so hard to build."

"I can give you twenty million reasons why I did that."

"So it was all about the money?"

"Yes and no. I needed out of the corporate world—it was killing me. I had to snort a mound of blow every day just to keep going, and sooner or later, that life was going to kill me. So I came to Hawaii, went to rehab, saw what was wrong with most rehab facilities, and decided to build this place as an oasis for peace and balance."

She says this with her arms folded in stereotypical "Namaste" fashion.

"It's a beautiful place," Terri adds.

"It's also one hell of a tax shelter," Vanilla admits.

There's the Vanilla I know and love.

"So the big question is what are you going to do with this opportunity in front of you?"

"Tell her about the book," Terri says.

I sigh loudly, as I really don't want to talk about it at the moment.

"What book?"

"Clark here has written a book, and he has an agent interested."

Vanilla's eyes go wide and she grabs my wrist. "There are no coincidences in life, Clark."

Great, now she is going to lay some *Celestine Prophecy* shit on me. No offense to author James Redfield, but one year, in lieu of bonuses, we all got a copy of that book with a handwritten note from Michele about how it would change our lives and ways of thinking. Clearly, it didn't work on me.

"I know you never believed in my new age spirituality, but hear me out. You lose your job and on the same day get a call from an agent who's interested in your book. It's a sign."

We are rejoined by Sumac, who clears away our dirty plates.

"Would you care for some herbal tea?" he asks.

We all nod.

"I'll bring some right away."

"The book has real potential, too," Terri says. "It's about a former soap actor who was big in the 80s and is looking to reignite his career in the present-day entertainment industry. He hates reality TV, but after stumbling onto a reality shoot, he's thrust back into the spotlight."

"That's a great premise, and everything 80s is in these days, but where's the tension?"

"Exactly!" Terri says. "The book is laugh-out-loud funny and the overall story is quite original, but there's almost no tension."

Sumac returns with a pot of hot water and three ceramic mugs. We each take a teabag from a wooden box and I notice what look like buds of cannabis filling one of the spots for tea.

"I thought this was an addiction and recovery place."

"It is, but marijuana is used medicinally here. It's quite legal really."

I'll have to take her word for it. After we steep our teabags for a few minutes, the conversation about my book picks back up.

"At some point, my dear, you have to get comfortable with tension. Embrace it and work through it. It must be used to take your readers on a journey."

"That's pretty much exactly what I told him," Terri says.

A sound emanates from Michele's wrist and she turns it to see what her watch wants her to know.

"I'm sorry, but I have to run a meeting downstairs."

She gets up and reaches into her pocketbook to remove what looks like a valet parking ticket and hands it to Terri.

"Hand this to the gentleman in the lobby and he will have someone retrieve my car. Take it for a spin around the island and leave it parked at your hotel. I can have someone come and get it tomorrow. Have a little fun."

She then pulls Terri close and whispers, "There's a little gift for you guys in the glove box. Should make the long flight home go by a lot easier."

I hear because my former boss is unable to actually whisper.

She leaves, but the scent of vanilla lingers for a moment. The two of us finish our tea in relative silence before Sumac comes to show us out.

CHAPTER TWELVE

Papparazi Ambush

I hand the ticket to Saffron and he takes out his phone and scans the barcode.

"I see Vanilla is letting you borrow her car. Take care with it, my friend—it's a mean machine."

Terri and I walk through the main doors and back into the warm Maui air. A few minutes later, we hear an engine revving and then see a candy apple-red Ferrari whipping toward us.

"Holy shit, Clark," Terri says. "Is that what I think it is?"

"Yep," I reply.

As the Italian sports car gets closer, I see that the vanity plate reads Higgins.

"She's still as crazy as ever," I say under my breath.

The car stops in front of us, but my attention is again drawn to those same ruffling bushes. This time, my curiosity gets the better of me and I walk toward it.

"Clark, where are you going?"

"I'll be right back—get in the car."

As I get closer, I hear what sounds like a man on his phone. Ten more steps, and I hear him clearly.

"It looks like Terri Flynn is considering rehab." Pause. "Yes, I saw her with my own eyes. I have pictures." Pause. "No, she looked all disheveled, like shit really." Pause. "No, she had some middle-aged guy with her." Pause. "Could be a bodyguard. Didn't look strong, though. Goes by the name Clark." Pause. "Yeah, well that shotgun mic works well." Pause. "Yeah, I'll send the pictures now." Pause. "Always a pleasure doing business with you too."

As a non-celebrity, I always thought famous people who complained about paparazzi were just crybabies. I never thought to consider it from another point of view, but my friend Terri has just had her privacy violated by some scumbag looking to make a few dollars off her story, not even caring if his assumptions were correct. I'm not sure what comes over me, but I have an urge for conflict.

"Can I help you?" I say, sneaking up behind him.

"What the fuck? Jesus Christ, you scared me."

I feel like a completely different person from the man who woke up today—I'm confronting this guy head on without thinking twice.

"How about you give me the SD card those pictures are on and show a little respect to my friend Terri."

The photographer, whose short stature and thinning hairline have undoubtedly contributed to a Napoleon complex, laughs in my face.

"How about you go fuck yourself? It's a free country and I haven't broken any laws."

He tries to walk past me, but I extend my right arm and it meets his shoulder. I like this new me.

"Don't put your fucking hands on me, motherfucker. I

am Todd Fucking McKay."

"You may want to get your facts straight, Todd Fucking McKay. Terri wasn't here to check out rehab—we were here to visit my old friend, Michele Stahl, who happens to own this center."

"Let's just pretend I give a flying fuck about the facts. Now get out of my way before I call the cops."

I remove my hand from his shoulder but stick out my left foot and trip him; to help him down, I grab him by the neck and give him a little push until his face is in the dirt. Seven years of martial arts have finally paid off.

"You've got a dirty mouth," I say. "It's even dirtier now." I'm not even quoting a movie—that's just some original badass shit.

"You goddamn motherfucker. I know some powerful fucking people and am going to ruin your career. No one does this to Todd McKay."

What career? I'm not sure how I've become a goddamn daredevil, but perhaps, as Bob Dylan sang, "When you ain't got nothing, you got nothing to lose."

"One more chance—give me the pictures."

"Suck a dick," he replies with his face still in the dirt.

I place a knee into the center of his back and remove the camera from around his neck.

"That's mine, asshole!" he says.

I remove my knee from his back and proceed to take a number of pictures of Todd Fucking McKay attempting to get up, paying particular attention to the dirt around his mouth. I then pop the SD card out of the camera and put it in my pocket.

"I can't wait to see what else you have on here."

"Give that card back!"

He takes a step towards me and I raise his camera over my head as if I'm about to smash it to the ground.

"Come any closer and the Canon gets it."

Cliché, I know, but it's the best that the new Clark could come up with.

"If there's anything wrong with that camera, I'll sue your fucking pants off, asshole. It cost more than most cars."

I pretend as if I'm going to toss it to him and he darts in the direction he thinks it will land. In truth, I hold onto it, but this puts a comfortable amount of space between us. I set the camera down gently in front of me and sprint back towards the car. He's overweight and I'm not afraid of him catching up.

"This isn't the last you'll hear of me, asshole."

"Go fuck yourself," I say mid sprint, concluding the coolest sequence of my life.

#

I get to the Ferrari and find Terri sitting in the passenger seat. I anticipated finding her behind the wheel but guess that, because of her age, she never learned to drive stick.

"Where did you go, and why are you out of breath?"

I relay the story of the photographer, and she's incredulous.

"You got his SD card? Are you serious?"

"Quite," I say, pushing the clutch down with my left foot and putting the car into first gear. I give it a little too much gas and remove my foot from the clutch a little too quickly, causing the car to jump forward and spit gravel.

"And you did this all for me?"

"The guy was an asshole—he kept calling me an asshole, though."

"They are all assholes. I just never had anybody stick up for me before. The first thing a manager or agent tells you is to ignore them and not engage. I secretly think all they care about is the free publicity."

We pass the photographer, who's screaming into his cell phone. I honk and wave and Terri flips him the middle finger. I roll down the window.

"Oh, and if you want to add my name to your story, it's Kelly Carson. That's K-E-L-L-Y C-A-R-S-O-N." I say each letter slowly, still unsure where this asshole side of me came from. I peel away.

Terri's laughter is interrupted by her phone.

She looks at the display and says "Fuck."

I tend to have the same reaction every time my wife calls.

"Is that my wife?" I say jokingly.

"It's Woody, my agent—he reminds me of Woody Allen. I better take it, though. I'll put it on speaker so you can hear how neurotic this guy is." She taps the accept button. "Hi Woody."

"Don't 'hi Woody' me, Terri. First, you walk off a film set, and now I find out through Instagram that you're in Maui with some new fling—what the fuck are you doing in Maui?"

"Didn't you hear? I'm going to rehab."

"Wait, what?"

Terri relays my scuffle with the photographer in the bushes, and that just makes him even angrier.

"Jesus H Christ, how many times have I told you not to engage with those vultures. It only fuels their fire."

"My friend Clark didn't know," Terri says and then starts rubbing my leg. It's a genial rub, not a your-cock's-next rub, but it feels good, nonetheless.

"Actually, a rehab story I can work with," Woody says. "That could possibly solve our problem."

"And what problem is that?"

"Um…the one where you walked off set."

"Did you address my concerns with the director and producer?"

"Look, Terri, they are not budging. They want boobs."

"Then I'm not going back. That part of my career is over, Woody, and there's nothing in the story that calls for skin."

"This isn't your first trip around the block, babe," Woody says dismissively. "Why do you think you got this part, because of your acting chops?"

"I'd like to think so."

"Well you are wrong. Your sex appeal got you this part. It's a goddamn skin comedy, play ball."

"And what if I don't?"

"Then you need to find a new agent, but don't expect anyone to take you on. Your reputation will be ruined. You'll be too much of a risk."

"Well maybe that's a chance I'm willing to take," Terri shouts.

"Why don't you call me back when you can be reasonable,"

"Do you know why you've been divorced four times, Woody?"

"Enlighten me," the agent shouts.

"Because you have not learned to never tell a woman to be reasonable."

She hangs up and throws the phone to the floorboard.

"I need a drink," she says.

"I need a shower after hearing that guy. Is that how things work in Hollywood?"

"Welcome to my world."

I downshift to third gear from fourth to pick up speed and we hightail it back to the Ritz.

CHAPTER THIRTEEN

1974

We pull up the main driveway to the Ritz Carlton just a little after five p.m. Before exiting the car, Terri opens the small glove box and retrieves a plastic bag; knowing my old boss, I'm scared it's blow, but it turns out to be gummy bears.

"Looks like someone has a sweet tooth," Terri says and puts them in her backpack.

I get out and hand the keys to the valet, who asks for my name and room number. I tell him to put it under Vanilla Stahl and that someone will be by to pick it up tomorrow. He gives me a confused look. Fuck, does he think I'm Vanilla Stahl—wait, fuck it.

As he pulls away, scenes from *Ferris Bueller's Day Off* flash before my eyes—I just hope the car doesn't wind up crashing into the woods from a two-story window.

It's only after he takes the car that I notice a familiar face staring at me; Eva, the attendant I pissed off on our flight to Maui, is standing just inside the front door, as if waiting for a ride. That's when I remember the reason we got into the Ritz in the first place—that's where the airline puts up its flight crews in Maui. Their union must have some powerful negotiators.

Eva is much more attractive than she looked on the airplane. Her blonde hair is down and she's not sporting the requisite blue blazer/polyester pantsuit. I open the door for Terri and am surprised when Eva smiles at me and says, "Nice ride."

I'm not sure where it comes from, but "drink later?" leaps from my mouth.

She replies, "Ballsy move asking another woman for a drink in front of your companion."

"Terri? She's just a friend. Isn't that right, Terri?"

"Yeah, just a friend," she says, but I detect a hint of disappointment in her voice.

Terri keeps walking, and I realize I don't know Eva's real name, so I ask.

"It's Madeline, but everyone calls me Maddy."

"Well my name is Kelly, but everyone calls me Clark. Eight p.m. in the lobby?"

"Looking forward to it," she says with a smile.

I turn and catch up with Terri, who's waiting for the elevator.

"Wait up," I call out.

"Nice move back there, Casanova."

"Yeah, I'm surprising the shit out of myself right now."

The elevator opens and before we're reach the second floor, the entertainment news comes on the video monitor.

"Rumor has it Terri Flynn, starlet on her second comeback, has checked herself into a rehab center in Maui. This could certainly explain why she walked off the set of *Temporary Layoffs*, a comeback comedy for 70s icon

Jimmy Walker. And everyone wants to know, who is the mystery man she was photographed with in Hawaii? Bodyguard? Sponsor? Life coach?"

"Fucking vultures," I say as we pass the thirteenth floor.

"You know what, Clark, I really don't give a fuck. My agent will likely spin this into something that helps my career."

The elevator opens and we walk in silence to the room. I start to wonder whether she really enjoys her chosen career.

"I call first shower," she says.

"Fine by me."

I see the chambermaid has transformed the sofa bed back into a couch. I also see something familiar, my suitcase. On top is a hand-written apology and a voucher for 15,000 Delta points.

I open the suitcase and instead of bondage gear, I find my collection of khaki pants, button-down shirts with whale logos, and argyle socks.

"There's maybe a God after all," I say.

"What's that, Clark?" Terri shouts from the bathroom.

"Nothing."

I feel my phone buzz and take it out to see an image of my sister's TV with yours truly dead center. Another buzz: "WTF?"

I tap a reply "I'll explain later. Dinner Monday?"

She replies with a brief "Sure."

I hear the door to the bathroom open and Terri shouts, "All yours, Clark."

I put down my phone and walk into Terri's bedroom to find her standing in the middle of the room wearing nothing but a towel. I have the urge to walk over there and release her from the terry cloth that binds her, but something stops me.

"Don't take too long, Clark. I'm hungry."

I walk into the bathroom and leave the door ajar as an invitation for Terri to join me. She doesn't. After a quick wash, I dry off, wrap a towel around myself, and head back to my suitcase. Terri is sitting on the couch watching TV.

"I see you got your suitcase back," she observes without taking her eyes off the boob tube. "You must be happy."

"Thrilled," I say, grabbing a pair of boxers.

"Do you want me to leave while you get dressed?"

"No. I don't give a fuck if you see me or not."

A wry smile comes across her lips, but her eyes don't move from the TV.

I dress in a white tee-shirt and jeans, and somehow, I don't realize I look like a reject from a John Cougar Mellencamp video until we're walking to the elevator.

"You seem different to me, Clark."

"I'm not sure what it is, but I feel different. Must have been that hike."

"Must have," Terri says, somewhat dismissively.

"What's the matter?" I sense she's upset.

"I'm just hungry."

I am not buying this. My guess is the bullshit news coverage is eating away at her. We stop at the ninth floor and are joined by a family of four, including a pair of seven- or eight-year-old twin boys.

"The thing is," she speaks up, "no one is ever going to hear my side of this. It's easier to believe a story about me going to rehab than one about me walking off the set for not wanting to show my tits gratuitously."

Terri apparently isn't aware we have company in the elevator until the boys start to giggle.

We make it to the lobby and the mother rushes her boys out while the father lingers to get a better look at Terri.

"Howard!" the mother calls.

"Coming, Jara." As he walks out, he's hunching over a bit—something tells me Howie doesn't get out much.

We head through the lobby to the restaurant, and the hostess informs us there's a fifteen-minute wait, so we go to the bar—history repeats itself.

"What would you like?" I ask Terri. My sense is she'll want the entire left side of the drink menu, but she surprises me with her choice.

"Just a white wine, sauvignon blanc from New Zealand if they have one."

She sits at a high-top and I go to the bar, which is hopping on this Saturday night. Unfortunately, the only open spot is next to Ted McGinley. I know his name is Andy, but I don't give a fuck about that, to me he'll always be Ted.

"Well, if it isn't the sink pisser."

"Hi Ted."

"My name's not fucking Ted, freak."

"Aloha! What can I get for you?" Carl the bartender says in a friendly tone.

"Do you have any sauvignon blanc from New Zealand?"

"Fucking fairy," Ted whispers.

"Yes, sir. Kim Crawford okay?"

"Fine."

He gives a generous pour and I also ask for a "Ketel One Vodka with club soda and a splash of cranberry."

"Right away, sir."

Ted repeats my order in a mocking, effeminate tone. I'm in such a good place right now I actually get a kick out of it.

Carl comes back with my drink and the bill.

"Sign to the room, sir?"

I nod and tell him the number then get up.

"Enjoy my sloppy seconds," McGinley snickers while I leave.

I turn back with a smile and suggest he "go kill a sitcom."

The look on his face tells me one of two things—either he doesn't know he looks like Ted McGinley or he doesn't know McGinley's history of killing shows.

"I ran into your friend from last night," I say, handing Terri the wine. She takes a big gulp, almost finishing it in about one second.

She looks toward the bar and finishes the glass.

"He served his purpose. What are you drinking?"

I tell her.

"Vodka, huh?" she says, remembering what I told her yesterday about my love-hate relationship with the spirit.

"What can I say, I'm feeling dangerous."

"Dangerous, Ice Man?" she replies and clicks her jaw— not one but two *Top Gun* references. I almost pinch myself.

She's the first woman I've ever met who not only appreciates 80s and 90s pop-culture references but also introduces them in daily interaction. If she wasn't so crazy, and if I weren't still married, I'd propose to her right now.

We end up at the same table as the prior evening, and Terri orders another glass of wine. I'm still working on my cocktail, so I pass on ordering another.

"Is there something you want to talk about?" I ask while taking a sip. The vodka is loosening my lips and making me feel warm and extra confident.

"What are you going to do about your wife, Clark?"

And there's the Terri I've come to know. She'll do anything to deflect talk about herself.

"Right now, I'd rather not think about her," I say, pointing the bottom of my glass toward the moon.

"Why do you stay with her?"

"Because at one point I loved her, and part of me still does. And if I don't take care of her, who will?"

"Look, Clark, it's a totally one-sided relationship, and that isn't sustainable. You've got to cut the cord."

The waitress returns with Terri's wine and we order dinner; Terri throws a curveball by ordering pork and I get the filet of pompano. I also order a glass of what Terri's drinking—I fear another vodka might not be such a good idea.

"I know you don't like talking about yourself, but I'm not discussing my wife all night, so unless you do some talking, it's going to be a quiet dinner."

Terri takes a sip of her wine.

"I'm 42."

In my mind's ear, I hear a needle scratching across a record. My bafflement encourages Terri to talk.

"The internet will tell you I was born in 1980, but it was actually '74."

This certainly explains why she gets all my references; we're the exact same age.

"Do you know how much pressure there is on actresses to look young? Men can grow old naturally, but we have to fight it every step of the way."

She never disappoints—now she's paraphrasing an Oil of Olay commercial from over twenty years ago. The moderator in me kicks in and I allow my curiosity to lead the conversation.

"What would you do if you weren't an actor?"

"Excuse me?"

"Can't even imagine it, huh? If you weren't an actor, what would you do?"

She pauses and takes a sip.

"Teach. I've always enjoyed working with kids."

"Okay," I say. "What about combining the two, teach acting to kids?"

"Do you know how evil kids are in LA? I'd want to smack them all."

"Who says it has to be in LA? Why not somewhere far away from California?"

"Like where?"

"Deerfield, Illinois."

Her expression suggests she's had a bad experience there—or she's about to throw up.

"What's wrong with Deerfield?" I ask.

"That's where my father lives. How could you possibly know that?"

"I didn't. I just go there often for work."

"Believe me, that's the last place you'd find me."

"Don't get along with your dad?"

"I haven't spoken to that man in fifteen years."

I want more, but in this case, I know silence is the best way to get it. I don't say a word. We both take a drink, and then my tactic pays off.

"He's a career military guy and a lawyer to boot. Nothing we ever did was up to his standards, and he hated that my mother got me involved in acting, which he considers a dishonest way to make a living. She moved for him no fewer than fifteen times over the course of their marriage and he never once showed any appreciation for her sacrifices."

"A real lifer, huh?"

"Wasn't supposed to be. He wanted to go to law school after college but didn't have the means to pay for it, so he joined the Navy and was going to do a few years and then go back on the GI bill. Well, he did that but then sat in on a presentation about the JAG corps when he was in law school. After graduating, he joined up again, this time as a lawyer in the reserves."

"Kaffee?"

"Yes, but he looks nothing like Tom Cruise."

"So where did you grow up?"

"After my mom started having kids, she told my dad he could move all he wanted but she was staying put in San Diego, so that's where I grew up."

"And that's where you got into acting?"

"Yeah, and it kind of started to take off when the guy who ran my middle school theatre department said I had a knack for acting and put my mom in touch with an agent who arranged auditions in LA."

"What did your dad say about that?"

"He dismissed it, of course, but that didn't stop my mom. I started getting commercials and the occasional role on evening dramas; I was very good at playing a sick child. I died on *Hill Street Blues*, *L.A. Law*, and *Hooperman*."

"That's like a Steven Bochco trifecta."

"Very good, Kel…I mean, Clark."

"What would it take for you to get in touch with your

father?"

"I don't know, maybe Hell freezing over."

"Fair enough."

Our food arrives, and we dig in like savages who haven't eaten in days.

CHAPTER FOURTEEN

End of an Era

Terri takes care of the check while I note the time.

"Shit!" It's just past eight and I'm late for Maddy.

"What's the matter?"

"I'm late for my damsel in distress."

"Don't sweat it, Clark. It's better to show up a few minutes late—you'll seem less desperate. Think you'll need the room tonight?"

I'm flattered Terri assumes I'll be McGinley'ing the flight attendant but shrug it off as wishful thinking.

"We're just having a drink."

"Sure, Clark, just a get-to-know-you drink in Maui with someone you'll never see again. But if you don't need the room, I'm calling it an early night."

"Go on up. I'll see you in a bit."

We part ways in the lobby—she toward the elevator and me toward the gorgeous blonde standing at the fountain just past the concierge desk.

She's wearing a red dress so short that, should she need to bend over, everyone in the lobby would see the entirety of her entirety. I'm secretly praying she drops the small handbag she's carrying.

She looks up from her phone with a scolding gaze that suggests my lateness is a major fuck-up, but I don't want to double-down on the fuck-up with an apology—that may come across as nice, and Terri made it clear that women don't fuck nice.

"Let's skip the drinks and go back to your room."

Okay, so I think that but don't say it—maybe I'm gaining an edge, but I'm not there yet. Cut me some slack.

Instead I say, "There you are, I've been looking all over for you."

"I've been here for ten minutes, I didn't see you come by."

I smile and shrug—she realizes I'm messing around.

"Well played, passenger Carson."

"Please, call me Kelly."

"Kelly Carson, huh?"

I'm waiting for the inevitable comment about my name, but she surprises me. "I like the sound of that. Rolls off the tongue."

I have something in my pants I'd like to roll off her tongue. I'd love to get out of the hotel and deeper into Maui, but Maddy suggests grabbing a drink at the hotel bar and then seeing where the evening will take us. If I were a betting man, I'd bet my forthcoming severance package that she's got a backup plan.

"What would you like to drink?" I ask as we take a seat at a high-top table.

"Tequila on the rocks with lime. Don Julio Blanco if they have it."

There's a country song called "Tequila Makes her

Clothes Fall Off"—I'm hoping it's prophetic.

I walk to the bar, somewhat fearful of leaving Maddy among the circling sharks, and wind up next to good ol' Ted, who isn't looking so hot. I'm worried that history will repeat itself and he'll try to bone Maddy, then again, he's probably too drunk to get a boner. I call for Carl's attention and order Maddy's tequila and a glass of wine. And then I hear the slurring.

"Hey, hey, hey. Thisssss is the motherfucker I wassss talking about who pissssed in the sssink lasssst night. I wasss plowing his old lady and hesss pissssing in the motherfucking sssssink."

"Carl, I think Mr. D'Arcy over here has had enough to drink."

Lest you think I'm a reader of highbrow fiction, I'm not referring to a character from *Pride and Prejudice*—D'Arcy was Ted McGinley's character on *Married with Children*.

"My name issssn't D'Arcy, asssssshole. And tell that crazy redhead you're with not to call me tonight."

"Carl, does my date look like she has red hair?" I point to Maddy.

"No sir," he says, handing me our drinks.

He then turns his attention to Ted, "I'm sorry, sir, but the bar is closed for you tonight."

"One for the road?"

"I'm sorry, sir, no can do."

"Fuck this fucking place."

Ted dismounts his barstool and ambles out the door, bumbling around as if he spent the day riding a dick bicycle. Should I ever meet them, remind me to thank Ariana Grande and Nicki Minaj for that line—I've been able to use it twice today.

"What was that all about?" Maddy asks.

"A man's got to know his limitations," I say, quoting Clint Eastwood from the first *Dirty Harry*.

"Huh?" Maddy doesn't pick up on the reference and I suddenly miss Terri, who would have undoubtedly replied with, "Make my day"—it's from a different *Dirty Harry* movie but would have been an appropriate response, nonetheless.

After an awkward silence, I sense she's looking for me to take charge of the conversation. As a moderator, I've learned that, apart from the cash, people participate in marketing studies because it's about their only chance to have someone actively listen to them. For the most part, people love to talk about themselves and, given the chance, will do so in a heartbeat.

"Tell me, Maddy, when did you know you wanted to be a flight attendant?"

Her eyes light up. I'm guessing she's used to guys opening with basic small talk, but I sense that my instinct to ask about her career is about to pay dividends.

"When I was a little girl, my mother took me on a flight from the small town in Florida where I grew up to New York, where my grandfather was in the hospital. I couldn't have been more than five or six at the time, but I remember being welcomed onto the plane by a beautiful woman who was all smiles. She looked so happy and in love with her job. Right then and there, I knew that's what I wanted to do when I grew up."

Maddy has a very soft southern accent which, no doubt, she tries to hide in order to appear more sophisticated. One thing I've learned, though, is that when people start talking about their childhood, hidden accents come out in earnest.

"Just like that?" I ask.

"Just like that," she says with a smile.

She's given me a few avenues for follow-up questions. I choose not to ask about her mother or her grandfather, fearing family talk could bring up sad, vibe-killing memories, so instead, I ask about her hometown.

"Tell me about this small town in Florida," I say, moving a little closer.

"Well, it's not so little anymore, but in the 70s, Plantation was mostly farmland, all horses and cows and open space. Today, it's all strip malls." Her accent is in full effect.

"I've been to Plantation. Just west of Fort Lauderdale, right?"

"Yep. A great place to grow up. What brought you down there?"

"I was hired to run focus groups for a pharmaceutical company. They wanted to be in South Florida, but Miami and Fort Lauderdale had too many Northeast transplants. We settled on Plantation as a place to find native Floridians."

"Focus groups? I thought you were an actor or something."

She clearly remembers my "I'm on with my agent" defense on yesterday's flight.

"Nah, but I'm also a novelist. Yesterday, I was talking to a literary agent who called at an unfortunate time."

"Have you written anything I may have read?" she asks, sucking the slice of lime between her lips.

"Ask me again next year."

"So that chat was about your first book?"

"The first anyone has shown interest in."

The truth is, I have three other novels but don't feel strongly enough about those to pitch them to a bum, let alone an agent.

"Here's to you," she says, raising her glass.

"Here's to me." I raise my glass and we both drink—I'm almost entirely certain I'm doing a pretty fucking great job so far.

"What's the craziest thing you have ever focus grouped?" she asks, turning the focus of conversation to yours truly.

The truth is, most of my work is pretty boring. I'm often asked to run discussions on topics that might serve as a cure for insomnia. I do have one client, though, that is not your run-of-the-mill packaged goods product, so I respond with, "Sexual lubricants."

It's true. I have an Australian client named Natasha who leads up marketing for a company that makes condoms and a variety of lubes.

"Wait, what?" Maddy says.

"I was hired by a lube company to field the research that would inform advertising for a new line of lubricants targeted towards young couples. Let me tell you it wasn't a dry conversation."

Maddy snorts at my joke and asks, "Did you have to watch them use the product?" when she regains composure.

"Not exactly. I had them keep a sex diary on their mobile phone and write down their experiences with the product over a few weeks. Then I invited them to a group discussion where we talked about the product in more detail."

"Sounds like you may have had to go down a slippery slope," Maddy says and lets out a loud cackle at her own joke. As hot as she is, that cackle is definitely a deal breaker for her long-term prospects. I'm tempted to tell her about the woman who kept referring to the product as fuck cream but am afraid to hear that cackle again, so I hold my tongue.

"So Kelly Carson, where will you be focus grouping next?"

"As a matter of fact, my schedule just opened right up. I got fired yesterday while I was in the Sky Club at LAX."

"Oh my stars, I am so sorry," Maddy says, grabbing my arm and dialing up the southern charm.

I then tell her about meeting Terri Flynn and this spur-of-the-moment trip to Hawaii.

"You have an adventurous soul," she says, and I feel her toes trailing up the length of my calf. I wonder how she removed her shoe so artfully, but then realize this isn't her first rodeo.

"I like a man with a sense of adventure."

She catches me glancing at the path that leads down to the beach. I nod toward it and ask, "How would you like a little adventure right now?"

As the words leave my mouth, I wonder who is this stranger living inside me? It was the most bizarre thing to hit my ears since an extremely drunk focus group participant decided to answer every question by saluting me and saying "Aye aye, captain." The sad thing is, that was a study involving airline pilots.

Maddy's naughty smile is her way of accepting my brazen invitation. We leave our glasses on the table and walk down the path to the ocean. Maddy is carrying her shoes, and I remove mine to do the same. We're strolling with the ocean to our left, the full moon illuminating the calm water.

"I've been flying for the airline for over twenty years and finally got the LA to Maui route. I come here at least three times a month and it never gets old."

"How could this possibly get old? I'm dreading going back to New York tomorrow."

"Are you flying through LA on the one p.m?"

"Yes ma'am."

"Then I'll be sure to take special care of you."

We walk to a cabana that has two chaise lounge chairs draped with towels.

"Come here," she says. She pulls me close and whispers into my ear. "I have a secret."

"What's that?" I whisper back. My heart rate has jumped by perhaps 40 beats per minute.

"I really have to pee!" She giggles.

"I don't see a ladies' room around here?" I say, and she catches the disappointment in my voice.

"Oh, I do," she says and pushes me away gently. She then takes another step back, reaches to the bottom of her dress with both hands, and pulls it up over her head. She's completely nude—the perfections of her northern and southern hemispheres convinces me that, without the shadow of a doubt, God does exist and is almost certainly a man. Wearing nothing but a devilish smile, Maddy asks, "You going to join me, Mr. Writer?"

I assume this really isn't about urination. I've never done anything like this before, but I can tell you one thing, she doesn't have to ask me twice. I'm down to everything but my boxers in seconds. I hesitate before removing them but then remember not to give a fuck, and then just like that, there's my entirety for her.

Maddy glances down and smiles, then turns and runs toward the water, showing me one of the most perfect asses I've ever laid eyes on. I sprint to catch up.

We splash into the water and she dives in with a few freestyle strokes to go farther out—I don't hesitate to follow. Once I catch her, I plant my feet and the water is up to my chest. She disappears under and I feel her hands on my legs, as if she's asking to swim between. Who am I to stop her? I widen, and as she passes through, she blows bubbles that reach me below the waist—it's not an altogether unpleasant sensation.

She comes up with arms extended. I grab her and pull myself close, my heart now chugging at a million beats per second.

She reaches behind my neck and pulls me close; she bites my lip and inserts her tongue. I feel a warm sensation around my waist and try to forget that she might in fact be peeing. She reaches under the water like a doctor checking for a hernia, though I decide not to cough.

"What are we going to do about this?" she says, her teeth now around my earlobe.

Before I can respond, she lets go of me and swims back to shore. I follow behind, swimming freestyle until my arousal starts dragging against the sand, at which point I stand and join her at the water's edge.

"Get on your back," she commands. Now as a rule, I hate the feeling of having wet sand on me, but I'm willing to make an exception tonight. I lie down and before I can take a breath, she positions her hips over my head and rests the junction of her thighs right on my mouth; she leans over my head, placing her hands on the sand for balance.

I begin by offering small kisses around her inner thighs, grazing her center teasingly as I pass from thigh to thigh. After I've tortured her long enough, I point my tongue and start massaging her slowly at first and then build up speed—if there's one benefit to having a lesbian twin sister, it's all unsolicited advice from her girlfriends; if there's one benefit to having a lesbian wife, it's that I can put those lessons into practice on a flight attendant without feeling the least bit guilty.

After a few minutes of this, Maddy repositions herself so that her gift-from-God perfect ass is in my face and her head's below my waist. She then takes me inside her mouth and rocks her hips back and forth while I continue to explore her with my mouth.

Now it's been a very long time since I've been in a position like this and I am trying my hardest not to finish too soon. The alcohol is certainly helping, as is the fear that we might get caught, but that's not enough. If I don't get her to stop, she's going to add some unintended calories to her diet.

"Slow down, baby."

She removes me from her mouth and slithers around until she's positioned right on top of me. She places one palm on my chest, for balance, and uses the other hand to guide me inside her.

By now, I'm so incredibly turned on that a strong breeze might finish me. She starts rocking back and forth slowly at first and increases the pace to an unbearable degree—I can't hold out any longer. She lets out a long moan and that's all I need to push me over the edge. I cum so hard

I'm surprised I don't push ten feet into the sand while she goes flying into the ocean like a rocket. Somehow, we stay affixed and she collapses on my chest. After a few deep breaths, she whispers in my ear, "Put that in your book."

She gets up and walks back into the ocean to clean herself. I do the same—I feel like I've been double-dipped in sand and sex juices. Maddy is kind enough to rub the sand off my back as we slow dance in the water, and I do the same for her. Once we're as clean as you can get in the ocean, we walk back to the cabana, dry ourselves with the towels, and dress. Then Maddy's purse starts vibrating.

"Fuck," she says, taking out her phone. "It's my husband."

"Husband?"

"Yeah," she says without remorse. "Our sex life has been dead for years, but I have needs." She lets out a cackle so loud I'm afraid it will call unwanted attention.

"Same here," I say.

Huh, what do you know, a couple of adulterers.

She groans and answers the phone. "Hi, baby. I'm sorry I couldn't call earlier—Charles and I went to the movies."

I can't hear his reply, but he must want some clarification on Charles. "Yes," Maddy responds, "he's the gay one—they're all gay ones."

While Maddy tries to mollify her husband, I walk ahead and begin rinsing my feet in the spigot at the entrance to the resort. I feel like I'm high, not that I know how it feels to actually be high, but if this is what it feels like, I'm going to begin smoking weed. A few minutes later, Maddy comes sauntering up, looking like she might feel a little high too.

"Everything okay on the home front?" I ask.

"Nothing I can't handle. Move over, my turn." She hands me her purse and shoes and begins rinsing her feet.

When she's done, we walk back to the Ritz barefoot, passing through the bar area where Carl gives me a surreptitious thumb up.

"I need to shower the rest of this sand from my hair," Maddy says. "Could I use yours?"

"As tempting as that sounds, I'm sharing a suite with Terri, and in this case, I think three's a crowd."

"Damnit. I'm sharing a room, too—the airline makes us. Looks like this is the end of our night then."

"Looks as if," I confirm.

We head to the elevator—I push 38, she hits 16—and then we make out like high school kids until her stop. Luckily, we're alone, though we probably would have done it anyway.

"Last chance to invite me up," she says as the door opens.

"I wish." I reach in for one last kiss while holding the door open, which I do until the elevator starts beeping, informing me I'd better stop.

"See you tomorrow, Kelly Carson."

"Goodnight, Maddy."

The elevator closes, and I ascend to the 38th floor. In the room, I find Terri on the couch watching TV. She looks me up and down and smiles approvingly—she knows there's a story to tell.

"You look like hell," she says. "Cheer me up and tell me everything."

CHAPTER FIFTEEN

An Intimate Moment

I take a quick shower and am amazed at the amount of sand rolling off my body—it's like I had a sandcastle pressed between my cheeks. I wrap myself in a towel and go back into the room, where Terri's still watching TV. I dig out clothes suitable for sleeping and am amazed at how comfortable I've come to feel in front of a woman I only met yesterday.

"I can't wait any longer," she says. "Tell me every damn detail."

I sit down and share everything about my escapade with Maddy on the beach.

"Good for you, Clark. You deserved that."

"There's only one catch, she's married."

"Um, so are you. Do you seriously give a fuck that she's married?"

I search my feelings and recall that orgasm—I'm having a tough time finding remorse.

"I guess not," I reply.

I see Terri has gotten into the bag of gummy bears that

she removed from the Ferrari, but it looks like she's only had a couple. Since it's a near impossibility to have just a few of those tasty little bastards, I assume she's watching her weight.

"I'm insecure," she blurts in a trance-like fashion, knocking me off balance, leaving me to wonder, what happened to the impulsive redheaded starlet I've spent the past two days with?

"What?"

"Ever since I was little. That's why I act so crazy. The flirting, the sex, the risky behavior, all because I don't feel the least bit confident inside."

Um, I'm not sure what is making her open up to me— maybe those gummy bears are laced with truth serum.

"I'm sorry for dragging you all the way to Maui, Clark. Maybe it would have been better if you didn't meet me."

"What?" I say. "In the past 36 hours, I've jumped off a cliff, beaten up a photographer, and got some bush for the first time since there was a Bush in the White House. I feel more alive than I have in years."

"Just don't let it get to your head, Romeo," she says. "Either of them."

"What's gotten into you?"

"I just fucked up my chance at a comeback and am feeling down in the dumps, okay?"

As someone who talks to people for a living, I know when to push for more and when to let a topic die. My Spidey sense tells me to do the latter, so I don't push her anymore.

Terri gets up from the couch and walks to the desk where the hotel has left its folio of services. "These gummies aren't doing it for me. You want room service?"

While the fish I had at dinner was filling, the workout I had on the beach did take its toll.

"I could eat."

"Good. Order us a pizza. Just cheese, no extra shit." She says this while throwing the menu at me.

Interesting choice for someone concerned about carbs, I think, but whatever.

"Pizza it is."

I call downstairs to place the order, and she pops another gummy into her mouth.

"Let's find a good pizza-eating movie," she says as she navigates to the Adult category before settling on *Star Trek: In Erection.*

"Seen this one? Jusssst kidding, Clark."

"And here I was wondering what the Vulcan Dirty Mind Meld would be."

"Good one."

She switches from porn to Classic Comedies and stops on *Airplane!*

"Surely, you can't be serious?" I ask.

"I am, and don't call me Shirley," she says without skipping a beat. Now that my decade-long dry spell is officially over, my penis is telling me it wants more, and movie quotes are my Viagra.

Fifteen minutes into the movie, during a joke about being in a Turkish prison, room service is at the door. I get up to retrieve the pie, tip the dude five bucks, and set the steaming pie in front of Terri. She lunges for a slice—I do the same.

"Fuck!" she screams.

"Too hot?"

"Africa hot!"—a *Biloxi Blues* reference, and my dick is

back to standing at attention. This woman just might be my soulmate. For this, I can handle some crazy, maybe even a lot of it.

We spend the next ninety minutes reciting the movie word for word, regardless of whether we have mouths full of pizza. When it's over, we're tempted to start *Airplane II: The Sequel*, but it's well past midnight and we're both exhausted—Terri looks mellow enough to fall asleep right here and now.

"I'm gonna call it a night, Clark. We have a long flight tomorrow and I want to get some exercise in the morning so I don't cramp up on the plane."

"Sounds good to me."

"Can I ask you a favor?"

"Sure."

"Will you sleep in the bed with me tonight?"

Did she just say what I think she said?

"Ummm…" is all I can muster.

"Don't get the wrong idea. I'm just anxious from that chat with my agent. It feels like my career's on the ropes. I just want to fall asleep in someone's arms."

"How can I say no to that?"

She goes into the bathroom to pee and wash up. When she's done, I do the same, although I have to wait for my erection to subside. The old Kelly would be anxious about Terri thinking I'm taking a dump, but tonight I don't care. I crawl into bed next to her.

"Just spoon with me until I fall asleep, Clark. Then you can go to your couch or stay here—your work is done."

"Okay," I say. But it doesn't feel like work. I tuck myself beside her and pray my male biology doesn't awaken and cause an awkward moment.

It doesn't matter, though, she falls asleep quickly, as is evidenced by the faint, adorable sound of her snoring.

I replay the last 48 hours of my life: getting fired, meeting Terri, the agent, the cliff dive, the fight, the fucking on the fucking beach. I start to wonder when reality will come back to pay me a visit, because if there's one thing I know with certainty, it's that extreme highs are followed by extreme lows.

Sleep comes over me like a warm blanket and the next thing I know, the sun's up and I'm alone in Terri's bed.

CHAPTER SIXTEEN

Breakfast of Champions

I put on my workout clothes and go down to the fitness center expecting to find Terri. She's not there, but I do forty-five minutes on the elliptical and a series of pushups, squats, and abdominal exercises before going back to the room and taking a shower. When I come out, dressed only in a towel, I hear "hi, Clark" and almost shit.

"Jesus Fuck," I say. "When did you get back?"

"A few minutes ago," Terri replies. "You have a lovely singing voice. Was that Pearl Jam?"

I admit to singing "Yellow Ledbetter" in the shower.

"You have no idea what the real lyrics are, do you?"

"Nope," I say as I start to get dressed. "Where were you anyway? I thought you'd be in the fitness center."

"I went to Mass," she says nonchalantly.

I look at her with a raised eyebrow.

"What? I got up early, remembered it was Sunday, and went to Mass. There's a beautiful little mission church that has an open-air service at eight."

"You are full of contradictions," I reply.

"I'm a woman and a natural redhead. Want proof?"

"That you're a woman or a natural redhead?"

"The proof would be the same, Clark."

As much as I'd love to see the fire down below, my instinct tells me this is one of her tests—showing too much eagerness would almost certainly backfire.

"Raincheck," I reply coolly.

"Your loss, Superman. When do you think we need to leave here?"

"We should be packed up and in the lobby by 11:15."

"And what time do you have now?"

Terri doesn't make a habit of wearing a watch—there's something about that I admire. I look at mine and tell her, "Quarter to ten."

"Enough time for a workout. I'm going to hit the fitness center for a bit."

My stomach grumbles, reminding me I could use breakfast.

"I'm going to grab something to eat."

"All right, I'll be back up here by quarter of eleven. Oh Clark," she says.

"What?"

"Try the pancakes. They are wonderful."

"You would know."

In the elevator, the entertainment news is playing, and I'm surprised to see my face looking back at me.

"Who is this mystery man accompanying Terri Flynn in Maui?" the stupidly bubbly anchor is saying over grainy footage of us walking from the Stahl Center. "Photographer Todd McKay was up close and personal with the man in question yesterday."

The story cuts to the short and round photographer

with the valuable camera. He's talking to a local policeman and the microphone picks him up.

"His name is Kelly Carson and he assaulted me. You better know I'm filing charges against that wanker!"

The segment cuts back to the anchor who says, "We've looked up this Kelly Carson and he appears to be a marketing consultant, which simply inspires more questions, the most prominent being this: Are things so bad for Terri Flynn that she needs a marketing consultant? We will keep you updated on this story as it progresses. Now onto your local forecast…"

I exit the elevator and take an outdoor table at the restaurant. I recognize some of Maddy's colleagues at another table, but she's nowhere to be found and I can't help but wonder if she has a sore pussy. Maybe I'm more McGinley than I thought.

My phone starts buzzing while I'm ordering banana pancakes from a waiter named Isaac, whose mustache and small afro suggest he's sick with nostalgia for *The Love Boat*.

"What's up, sis?"

"What's up? Holy fuck nuts, you're what's up! You're all over the news, dear brother. Between the fling with Flynn and scuttle with the photographer, I have people calling me left and right wondering what happened to my mild-mannered research geek of a twin."

I want to argue the geek comment but fully admit it's rooted in truth.

"That guy was an asshole."

"He had to be the world's most gaping asshole. I can't imagine you getting mad enough to fight someone."

I tell her about how he was hiding in the bushes and concocting bullshit.

"Plus, I'd just gone cliff jumping, which I think is the term for it. I don't know, I was just feeling unstoppable, unfuckwithable."

"You're kind of falling for this chick, aren't you?"

"It's complicated. But you want to know something that's not in the news yet?"

"What?"

"I got laid last night. On the beach."

"No fucking way!" Jo screams. "With the actress?"

"No, the stewardess!"

"Exsqueeze me? Baking powder?" Jo says, quoting our favorite movie, *Wayne's World.*

I tell her the story, from cock-cup to beach fuck.

"And she's fucking married?"

"Apparently."

"Please tell me you used protection."

Until this point, it hadn't even crossed my mind.

"Funny thing about that…"

"Jesus fucking Christ, Kelly, the first woman you fuck outside your marriage is a flight attendant and you don't even use a rubber? Fuck going to hat meeting with the agent—your first stop after landing should be a goddamn clinic."

I'm not sure if it's psychosomatic or not, but my groin is suddenly itchy.

"And what if she gets fucking pregnant—did you think of that?"

"Not really. Look, I'm sure she's on birth control."

"Well, I'm glad you're so sure. Your judgment is impeccable these days!"

I see what looks like a stack of pancakes coming and assume it's mine.

"Look, my food's here. Can we pick this up tomorrow night at dinner?"

"Whatever, just realize you've met your stupidity quota for the year. No more fuck-ups, okay?"

"Scout's honor."

"You were never a scout!"

It's true, I was never a Boy Scout or even a Cub Scout for that matter. It's just not my thing and never was. My idea of roughing it in nature is a low-end motel on moderately wooded property. Jo, on the other hand, lobbied the Boy Scouts of America to let her in, even though she's just a girl with a boy's name.

I'm about to dig into my pancakes when Terri sits down and pulls my plate over.

"Not fucking again."

"Do you give a fuck that I'm going to eat your pancakes, Clark?"

"Yes, I give a fuck. Do you give a fuck that I give a fuck?"

I catch ol' Love Boat as he passes and put in another order of pancakes before turning my attention to Terri, breakfast thief.

"What happened to the gym?"

"Running in place is too boring. Plus, my fucking manager called and put me in a bad mood."

"What now?"

"Well, I'm not going back to *Temporary Layoffs,* which is going to bring on a flood of negative stories, which he'll respond to by issuing a press release about how I'm entering rehab."

"So that's it, no more feature film comeback for Terri Flynn?"

"They are not budging on my boobs."

"And the rehab story helps how?"

"Well, according to my people, Americans love a comeback story. If in thirty days they hear I've successfully left rehab, all that *Temporary Layoffs* damage will be minimized."

"And you're okay with that? You don't think it's better to simply stand up for yourself and say you aren't doing unnecessary nude scenes?"

"I don't have a choice, Clark."

I guess the truth has no place in an industry that has its roots in make-believe.

"You know better than I," I say as the second stack of pancakes arrives.

"So what's your strategy with the agent tomorrow?" Terri asks, switching from herself to her favorite topic, me.

"What do you mean strategy? I'm going to talk to her about my book."

"Clark, don't be so naïve. You have to have a strategy; the hardest and most critical part of the entertainment business is finding a reputable agent."

Tell me something I don't know; I could wallpaper my entire bedroom with rejection letters.

"Since you're the expert, can you give me some advice?"

"Well, I'm glad you asked," she says, extending her fork across the table to steal a bite of pancake—breakfast thieves are only content when thieving. "The best thing you can do is to show her you're coachable."

"What does that mean, coachable?"

"Look, they will be taking a risk because you're an unknown. True, it's not a financial risk at this point because they only make money when you make money and they have no cash outlay otherwise, but even so, their reputation is at stake. So tomorrow, they'll try to determine whether you're coachable—do you take direction well, will you follow her advice, that sort of thing."

"And how do I show her that?"

"Well, she'll likely give you some sort of test."

"Like what? My willingness to do a nude author photo?"

"No jokes, Clark. I assume you had to give her a writing sample?"

"She's got the whole damn thing."

"Right, well, expect her to have some comments. Listen to her criticisms with an open mind."

"Makes sense."

"But you have to be careful!" Terri says, simultaneously managing to pound her fist while pilfering another portion. "You can't come across as a pushover. You have to know when to hold 'em and when to fold 'em, so to speak."

And here we have a Kenny Rogers quote and the stirrings of an uncomfortable breakfast table erection.

"Watch out for traps. She might offer a suggestion that changes the entire tone of your work—that would be a trap. If you fall for it, she'll think you lack integrity."

"So appear open, but not wide open to everything."

"Exactly," she says and chugs my orange juice and then my ice water. "Time check."

"Eleven."

"We gotta get moving. I better help you finish those pancakes." She reaches across the table and completes the heist.

I call for the check—and I realize I'm still fucking hungry. Looks like the old Terri is back.

CHAPTER SEVENTEEN

Hunter Carson is Born

Ten minutes later, we're all checked out and sliding into the backseat of a cab. We're both quiet on the ride, enjoying our last glimpses of paradise—cabs invariably make me a little anxious, but if you're going to be anxious in a cab, it might as well be in Maui.

We get to the airport and breeze through a special security line—premium cabin perks—and park ourselves at the Delta Sky Club.

"This is all too easy," I say as we sit down.

"I've got a bad feeling about this," she replies in her best Harrison Ford voice.

And then we hear a voice boom over the loudspeaker: "Attention passengers on Delta flight 2169 with service to Los Angeles"—here it is, the bomb's about to drop—"we just want to let you know that your flight is on time. The plane is at the gate and will begin boarding in twenty-five minutes."

Terri and I exchange glances and start laughing as we realize we were thinking the same thing.

"Clark, would you be a love and get me a glass of water?"

"No champagne this afternoon?"

"Well, if you insist."

I go to the bar for two glasses of champagne and ask the bartender to put some cassis in one for Terri.

"Oh, you remembered! How sweet," Terri remarks as I hand her the flute.

Since she ate half my breakfast, I'm forced to scavenge the Sky Club for snacks and come back with a bowl of peanuts. When I return, she's on the phone, and she doesn't look happy.

"Unless they're cutting the nudity, I'm not going back."

She pauses for a few seconds, listening to the argument on the other end of the line.

"Yes, I know I don't have a nudity clause in my contract—I'm fucking fine with nudity so long as it helps to move the story forward. This is just gratuitous."

Another long pause—Terri rolls her eyes.

"You're supposed to be my agent. Whose side are you on?"

She presses her middle finger against the phone.

"Well, I don't know, Woody, would you wave your dick at a camera if it didn't move the story forward...yeah, that's right. I didn't think so."

She angrily terminates the call and finishes what little champagne is left in her flute.

"Would you care to get me another, Clark?"

She's having a frustrating time, so I oblige...and when I return, my peanuts are gone—is nothing sacred?

Terri downs her champagne and gets up.

"All right, Clark, let's go to the gate. I know how you

are about your bags."

This makes me so happy I could hug her. We head directly to the gate, no checking our bags, and board immediately. The amount of satisfaction I derive from this is probably ridiculous, but I'm not embarrassed to admit it, which is also probably ridiculous.

We walk down the jet bridge to the plane, and I'm surprised when Maddy isn't there to greet us. Instead, we're met by an attendant named Michael who's nearly desperate to help with our bags after learning we're first class.

"Will Maddy be on this flight today?"

"She decided to spend one more day in paradise," Michael quips. "She must have left quite the impression on you during your flight down here."

"Well, Michael, she's the only woman I've ever ejaculated inside of on the beach." Listen, you know me pretty well by now—I don't actually say that; I just smirk at the thought.

"Quite," I merely reply as I take the window seat.

"Can I get you anything to drink before we take off?"

"Champagne," Terri says.

"Just water for me."

"I'll take his champagne."

Michael nods and practically races toward the galley at the front of the plane.

"Clark, I hate to be a party pooper, but all this drama with my agent has given me a headache—I'm sleeping on this flight."

Terri goes into her purse and fishes out a gummy; perhaps the sugar will help her headache, temporarily anyway.

Truthfully, I'm happy she doesn't want to chat—it'll give me time to work on my manuscript; the flight to LA is a little over five hours and I am planning on using it to punch up my story so I'll have something new to share with Pam Hart, literary agent extraordinaire.

Michael returns with my water and Terri's two champagnes and she throws them down like a pro.

"Are you going to use your pillow?" she asks.

"All yours."

She wraps hers around her head, hugs mine to her chest, and is out cold in a matter of seconds.

I take out my laptop, fire it up, and stare at the title page for a full minute before deciding that something's wrong; the title, *Return to Casa Grande*, isn't the problem— the author's name is. Kelly Carson doesn't seem right anymore. But you know what does? I have a flash of inspiration, highlight my first name, and replace Kelly with Clark.

Clark Carson—that's more exciting. But can we do better? Hmmm? I'm a visual thinker, and I know inspiration is nearby. I look outside and watch as the crew loads baggage into the belly of the plane then turn my attention to an airline magazine featuring exotic travel destinations.

I thumb to an article on South African safaris entitled "Die Hard the Hunter." That's it. My nom de plume is born. I go back to my computer and alter the name to Hunter Carson. It not only seems strong but established. I save the document and close my laptop as we get set for takeoff.

I'm Hunter Carson now. And I think I like it.

My eyes are glued out the window as the plane lifts off

and the island gets smaller and smaller. It feels like I'm leaving something behind, an old, wimpier portion of my being who was too often willing to take shit and get trampled on by the likes of the Pete Fucking Jacksons of the world. **RIP** buddy.

Once we pass ten thousand feet, I get in a zone and write for four and a half straight hours, waving off meal and beverage service. I couldn't be happier with the alterations I made to my manuscript—I'm more ready than ever to meet Pam Hart.

CHAPTER EIGHTEEN

An Unintended Detour

Thanks to a strong tailwind, our flight lands thirty minutes ahead of schedule. Terri, world-class airplane sleeper, continues to doze through all of it. I watch outside as a crew member extends the jet bridge to the main door and can't help but liken this action to intercourse; apparently Terri's dirty mind is rubbing off on me—pun totally intended.

It pains me to do this because she looks so peaceful, but I tap her on the shoulder to wake her.

"Where are we, Clark?"

"LAX."

"So soon? I'm starving."

"Me too. Let's get off this thing and grab a bite."

We find a place that sells quick serve Asian food nearby, so we line up for chicken teriyaki bowls. After waiting ten minutes in line and fifteen minutes for our food, we take our grub to our gate just as the plane starts boarding.

Terri reluctantly agrees to eat on the plane, but only because we're first class and get to board almost immediately. This time, instead of champagne, she asks for water and I do the same. The two of us then attack our bowls as if we're in a Teriyaki eating contest. She wins.

At least she didn't get any of mine, though. Even so, I'm still hungry and want sweets. Even though I'm not generally a sweets guy, the craving often hits me on long trips—I usually pack a little something, but this time I'm unarmed. And then I look over at Terri just as she's popping a gummy bear into her mouth.

"Can I have one?"

Terri laughs, as if I've made another hilarious joke.

"Are you sure you can handle it, Clark?"

"How big a bitch do you think I am? I'm no stranger to refined sugar."

"Me casa su casa."

I pop a few into my mouth and wonder why she's quoting a line delivered by a drug dealer in *Pulp Fiction*. Eric Stoltz came a long way from *Mask*.

"Slow down, cowboy. Them's some powerful things."

I'm not getting the joke and she doesn't explain. Instead, she rests her head on my shoulder and starts to snooze—like I said, she's a premier plane-sleeper.

I'm hoping to do my best Terri impersonation and sleep as much as possible on the flight. Terri stressed the importance of coming off as coachable during meetings with agents, and though she didn't mention it, it's probably a good idea to come off as sane, too. And if I don't get a nice bit of sleep, I might blow that one.

Reading's often a sedative for me, so I look through the library of novels on my tablet and settle on one my sister recommended. It's a who-done-it about a lawyer turned podcaster who stumbles onto a case of wrongful imprisonment. For a thriller, it has a dark sense of humor and I find myself laughing frequently.

There's a problem, though—I get so caught up in the story that I don't want to put it down and sleep. Instead, I settle in and work my way through the rest of the gummy candy Terri put in her seat back.

Ninety minutes in, I find myself losing focus. I think I'm still enjoying the book, but I can't pay attention for a whole damn sentence. I keep reading and rereading and rereading. Then, for no reason, I just start giggling, loud enough for the undisturbable Terri to stir.

"What's the matter, Clark?"

"I don't know."

She bolts up and starts looking around frantically.

"Where's the candy, Clark?"

I point to my belly.

"Uh-oh," she says and rings the flight attendant button. Bonnie, a perky blonde, is there in seconds. It's hard to overstate how much of a shit Bonnie seems to give.

"How can I help you?"

"One of your kidneys, please." Fuck, I meant to think that.

"Forget him," Terri says. "We're going to need a lot of water."

Bonnie nods and takes off—it's a damn wonder she doesn't salute.

"Clark, listen to me. Those gummies weren't plain old gummies; they were edibles."

"No shit they were edible."

That word sounds so funny. I say it over and over.

"Edible. Edible. Hey, did you ever see *The Facts of Life*

when Mrs. Garrett started Edna's Edibles?"

"This is bad, Clark."

Her voice sounds slow, like an old cassette player that's running out of batteries.

"How do you do that thing to your voice?"

Her lips are still moving, but now I can't hear a word of it. She hands me a glass of water and I see her mouth say, "Drink this."

So refreshing. I drink it down and Terri hands me another. The sense of calm that's wrapped my body like a blanket begins trickling to my head, which feels so tingly, now that I think about it.

I watch as she pulls a pair of headphones from her bag and stuffs them in my ear. A moment later, I'm treated to the sounds of Pink Floyd and let myself sink into the euphoria. I've always hated Pink Floyd, but for whatever reason, I don't mind them so much right now.

I lose count of how many songs I hear, but I suddenly have to pee so badly I don't understand how it's not spouting from me. I reach for my seatbelt.

I look to Terri, and her mouth is moving, but I still can't hear her. Besides, I have a much more important message. "Time to go make pee pee," I say, perhaps shout—who knows.

Terri undoes her seatbelt, somehow in super-slow motion, and I'm surprised when she follows me to the restroom. It's unoccupied, which makes it so I don't have to pee all over everyone, and I'm pretty sure I hear Terri tell Bonnie that "my friend is not well." That doesn't make sense though because I'm feeling way beyond fine.

"You can't go in there with him," I think Bonnie says to Terri.

"You better sit down then," I think Terri says to Kelly.

"Sit down? I may have a girl's name, but I still gots me a dick," I think I say out loud. And apparently I do, because we are joined by another two flight attendants who look mildly to moderately terrified.

I turn around, push in the lavatory doors, and lift the toilet seat. I pull out my dick and start to piss perfectly and say it: "I'm pissing perfectly." But as I'm saying it, I turn my head to take a look in the mirror, and that's when I start screaming.

I don't recognize the face staring back. Or I do, sort of —it looks like someone dressed as me for Halloween. I avert my gaze and realize I'm hosing down pretty much everything in the bathroom. I'm no longer pissing perfectly.

This pissing comedy is interrupted by a knock. Luckily, I'm out of piss. I manage to zip up and instinctively turn to the sink; that's when I make the mistake of looking in the mirror again. Now, not only do I not recognize my face, it's crawling with bugs. How the fuck do so many bugs get on a plane? Naturally, I scream again.

The pounding becomes louder, much more insistent. I wash my hands with my eyes closed and then manage to unlock the door and step back out, where I'm greeted by five flight attendants and a security guard? I think one's a security guard. I'm escorted back to my seat and I'm starting to doze, and I think I'm getting handcuffed.

CHAPTER NINETEEN

Hell Freezes Over

I don't recall much of what happened after takeoff, but now I'm in a hospital room, so it's a safe bet there's not a lot of glory in the forgotten moments. I look around the room expecting to see Terri—instead, I find an older man with close-cropped gray hair and a jaw cut from stone. He's in a chair across the room, reading the *Chicago Tribune*; I put two and two together and figure we didn't quite make it to New York.

"Where's Terri?" I ask.

The man looks annoyed, as if I've interrupted something important. "Getting something to eat," he says through clenched teeth.

My mind is foggy, but I'm not in pain, except for my wrists. I look at one wrist and see it's encircled in red. I look at the other and see an IV sticking into my arm.

"What time is it?" I ask the gruff older man.

He nods to a clock on the wall above his head—9:32.

"Fuck!" I say. "I need to make a phone call." Why is my mouth so fucking dry?

"Son," the man across the room says, "a phone call ain't gonna happen. There's a few gentlemen who wanna talk to you first."

"But I have to call my…"

Sgt. Slaughter interrupts me before I can say "agent."

"You ain't saying a thing to anyone until those patient gentlemen, who've been waiting outside your room since 6:30, get a chance to ask you some questions. Now shut your pie hole until they come in. Got that?"

I'd say his tone is militaristic, but that would be an understatement. He makes George C. Scott's Patton seem like Patton Oswalt.

A moment later, the door opens and I'm expecting military police but am relieved to see Terri with two cups of coffee.

"Oh good, you are awake."

"Aren't you a sight for sore eyes. Any idea who he is?"

"Him?" Terri says. "Well, I guess you could say Hell froze over."

"Clark, meet Captain Kevin Flynn."

"What in the fucking fuck is going the fuck on?" I'm lucid enough to prevent myself from saying it.

"Why did you just call him Clark?" her father asks. "Says on his admitting form his name is Kelly."

"I'll tell you later, Dad."

"Probably some Hollywood bullshit," he says. He gets up and retrieves the aforementioned patient men from the hallway, who turn out to be a couple of fatties in bad brown suits.

"Gentlemen, Mr. Carson here is alert. I've not spoken a word to him about why he's here. Neither has my daughter. He's all yours, but as his attorney, I'm going to stay in the room while you question him."

My attorney? I must be in a big bag of shit if Terri called her father to act as my attorney.

"Mr. Carson, I'm Detective Nick Thomas and this is my partner, Detective Chris Roberts. We're hoping you can answer a few questions about your flight last night."

These two look like they would tie for first in a Mike Ditka lookalike competition. The only distinguishing factor between them is a slight difference in height.

"I'll do my best, but honestly, I don't remember much."

"Did you have anything to drink last night?" the shorter one asks.

"No. I don't drink on airplanes."

The taller one writes something in his notebook.

"I see."

"Did you smoke any marijuana before getting on the plane last night?" Short Ditka asks.

"No. I've never touched the stuff. Not once in my life. Besides, I'd just come off a five-hour flight from Hawaii—where would I have lit up at LAX?"

"A junkie will find a way, Mr. Carson. We aren't dumb—and there's dabs, waxes, vaporizers…you name it. There's always a way to get high."

That last part sounded like it came from a weed coach's pep talk.

"Okay, but no, I didn't smoke anything, and I didn't pop any pills or sniff any powders either. I'm just about as square as they come."

Tall Ditka writes something else on his notepad.

"Can one of you tell me why I am here? I should be in New York."

"Sure," Short Ditka says. "Approximately four hours

and twenty minutes into your flight from LA to JFK, the pilot made an executive decision to divert the aircraft to Chicago O'Hare due to an unruly passenger on board. Do you know who that unruly passenger was?"

"Me?"

"Ding, ding, ding, Thomas, he got a question right. Tell him what he's won."

"Well, our contestant may have won a ten-thousand-dollar fine and a prison vacation."

"Are you kidding me?"

"Do we look like we're kidding?"

They don't. Mike Ditka clones don't kid.

"Pretty much all I remember was reading a book and eating a bag of gummy bears."

Short Ditka scribbles another note, and I'm getting unnerved.

"Where did you get these gummy bears?"

Why the hell do they care about my candy habits? Is it a crime to dine on Haribo Gold's gift to the world?

"My old boss gave them to me. She runs a drug treatment center in Maui."

The Ditkas start laughing—I'm shocked they have that function.

"What's so funny?"

"I just want to clarify something, Mr. Carson. For the record, you had no idea what was in those gummy candies?"

"No. Why?"

"Have you heard the term edibles, Mr. Carson?"

Edibles. Edibles. I remember laughing at that term last night, but don't remember why.

"Edibles are a way to eat marijuana. Based on what

you're describing and the cleanliness of your record, or more accurately, lack of one, we're inclined to believe you weren't aware you were ingesting enough pot to fuck up an elephant."

"Will that be all, gentlemen?" Terri's father asks.

"Yes, Captain Flynn," says Tall Ditka.

"We'll be in touch," says Short Ditka.

The mustachioed detectives leave, and Captain Flynn waits until they're out of earshot before giving us a tongue lashing that fits perfectly within the father-daughter estrangement narrative.

"Look, Dad, I'm sorry but…"

She's immediately cut off.

"I'm sorry? I'm sorry? This is the first I've heard from you in ten years."

"I'm sorry…" She cuts herself off this time.

"And you," he says, pointing at me. "I don't know who the fuck you are, but you'd be wise to thank the fucking maker that your story meshed with my daughter's or else you'd be looking at a five-figure fine and jail time."

"Sir, if I had any idea those candies were spiked, I would never have taken them."

Terri knew, though, but I'm smart enough not to call her on it in front of her dad.

The clock now reads 10:30, which means I'm already a half hour late for my meeting with literary agent Pam Hart. Surely, I'm fucked. Yes, don't call me Shirley. Fuck you. I mean, fuck me. FUCK EVERYBODY!

Sorry, I've lost it and try to regain composure.

"Has anyone seen my phone?"

Terri produces it from the nightstand, but it's dead. Just as she reaches to plug it in, Captain Flynn's goes off—not surprisingly, his ringtone is the Battle Hymn of the Republic. Terri rolls her eyes, and I have no problem imagining her feuding with him as an angry teen.

"Yes, this is Captain Kevin P. Flynn of the U.S. Naval Reserve. I see. Yes. Very well, sir. Thank you, sir. And may God continue to bless America, sir."

"Good news for you, Mr. Carson. Neither the airline or the US Government is pressing charges. After the doctor sees fit to discharge you, you're a free man."

"Thank you Mr…I mean, Captain Flynn."

"As for you," he says to Terri, "I'd like you to come home with me. I've seen enough about you in the news to know something isn't right with you."

The blood drains from Terri's face, and I can see she doesn't have any fight in her.

"Okay. Can I have a moment alone with Cla…Kelly?" She corrects herself by saying my real name—it's the first time she's used my real name since we met on Friday morning.

"You have one hundred and twenty seconds, starting now," he says, pushing a button on his wristwatch. He then turns and marches from the room.

"Did you know?" I ask Terri. The expression on her face gives it away.

"I thought you knew."

My heart sinks—this crazy actress may have just ruined my one shot at getting published.

"Any advice on what to tell the agent?"

"Agent? They diverted a fucking airplane for you. I had to call my fucking asshole of a dad to bail you out. After all that shit, you think your agent is the number one thing on my mind?"

"'All that shit' could have been avoided if you'd just fucking told me there was weed in the gummies. Would that have been so fucking hard?"

"Would it be so fucking hard to offer a thank you? Has that crossed your mind?"

I stare at her in stunned disbelief.

She turns on the TV and navigates to an entertainment channel—clearly, she's aching for a pile-up.

"Of course the big story of the day remains the mystery man in troubled actress Terri Flynn's life," the anchorman says to the camera. "As if yesterday's report from Maui wasn't bad enough, early this morning, the plane Flynn and her male friend were on was diverted to Chicago, and this cell phone footage shows a clearly inebriated Kelly Carson and a disheveled Flynn exiting the aircraft under police escort."

And…here comes another piece of stupid careening into the wreckage—the TV cuts to l' Hole in the Foot Pete Jackson himself. "Kelly worked for me at Omnivore Corporation for almost three years. I always thought there was something odd about him, but I never thought he was a pure wild man." He then turns to the camera and says, "Farmer Kelly, bro, you gotta turn it down a few notches."

"So," the reporter asks, "he no longer works for you?"

"Hell no, brah. We terminated his employment last Friday. We all have different ways of dealing with bad news—I guess Kelly went off the deep end."

"Turn it off," I say, channeling George C. Scott from *Star 80*. That's two George C. Scott references in one twenty-minute period. Who would have thought that was possible? She obliges and tosses the controller into my lap, which, of course, nicks a testicle.

"Well, I guess both our careers are ruined," she says.

I just exhale loudly, and right on cue, Terri's dad comes marching back in.

"Time's up," he barks. "Let's go."

"Thanks for the uplifting experience, Ter," I say as they exit.

"Go fuck yourself, Clark."

"Classy as ever," Captain Major Sergeant Fucking Flynn quips then turns to me as she storms into the hallway. "I don't know you from a hole in the wall, son, but let me give you some advice. Stay away from my daughter; she'll bring you down further than you already are, and that's pretty goddamn low."

He turns on his heel and marches the fuck out of my room. I just shake my head—the picture of resignation— and reach for my phone to see what disasters await there: dozens of messages from my sister, the latest reading "what the fucking fuck?" and a voicemail from the 212 number, Hart Literary.

I'm almost too scared to do it, but I listen to the message and hear the same effeminate voice that greeted me on Friday.

"This is Andre Taylor from Pam Hart's office—please call us back at your earliest convenience."

I call and he picks up before the first ring finishes.

"Hart Literary, this is Andre."

"Hi Andre, this is Kelly Carson…"

Before I can ask to speak with Pam Hart, Andre interrupts.

"Please hold for Ms. Hart."

"This is Pam Hart and this better be good, Carson. No one misses a meeting with me and lives to tell the tale."

Despite the onslaught of shit, I'm still taken aback by her tone. I can't tell if she's joking. I do know the entertainment industry is full of nuts—I just can't get a read on her.

"I am so sorry about this morning…"

"Sorry? Look, I don't know who your PR person is, but your rampage in Hawaii and that stunt on the airplane were fucking brilliant. You wanted to make sure you had my attention—well, you got it."

"I'm just, I don't," I babble—maybe Pam will think it's another clever trick.

"The hardest thing to do is build a platform, but you, Kelly Carson, are trending on Twitter. You're trending everywhere."

I don't even know what it means to trend, but I take it as a good thing.

"Look, I wanna represent you. You're a good writer and your story is interesting, and now that you have an image and are getting noticed, I can really sell you. We just gotta tweak the manuscript a bit."

"What do you mean by tweak?"

"Relax, bubby. It just needs to be punched up."

Bubby? The last time I heard a person use that term, he was shot by Hans Gruber, God rest his soul.

"First things first, I'll send you a contract, which I advise you to look over with your attorney. My fee of 15% is non-negotiable, so don't even try. When the paperwork is done, refresh the manuscript, and if I like it, I'll set you up with my favorite editor. If I don't like it, you can fuck off. I'm just fucking kidding, Carson—I'll just give you more changes. When we get it set, I'll start shopping it around. Be prepared—your life is going to change."

"Pam, I've decided to use a pseudonym."

"Then I can cross one thing off my list because, I hate to say it, but Kelly Carson sounds like a chick and this isn't a chick book."

"What do you think of Hunter Carson?"

"It's strong, but let me chew on it for a bit. You've just become famous under your own name, so we may want to go with K. Carson. Now, there's one more important item."

"What's that?"

"You gotta ditch the girl. Terri Flynn is damaged goods, bubby. She got you some invaluable publicity, but in the long run, she'll be your kryptonite."

Pretty damn ironic metaphor, Pam.

"That shouldn't be a problem," I say. I think Terri and I have had our final alohas and fuck yous, but holy shit, her craziness may be jumpstarting my writing career.

"Good. I'm emailing a contract. Just have your attorney send it back redlined. You're gonna be a star."

"Thank you, Pam."

"Thank you, bubby."

I feel a twinge of guilt about the way things wrapped with Terri but realize she'd advise me not to give a fuck about that. Still, I'm conflicted.

I begin crafting Jo an artful text about this rash of unadulterated insanity when the doctor comes in to say I can go when I feel up to it. I tell him I couldn't feel more up to it, and soon after, a nurse enters with discharge papers, and what do I find in the packet? A brochure for the Stahl Center for Peace and Balance in conveniently located motherfucking Maui. "Humbug!" I exclaim as I crumple it up into a ball and attempt a three-pointer from the doorway, thus completing a George C. Scott trifecta. His portrayal of Scrooge has always been my favorite.

CHAPTER TWENTY

A House Is Not A Home

It's good to be back in Connecticut; now there's something I never thought I'd say. Between the high cost of living, a state legislature that can't control spending, and brutal winters, I often wonder why I stay, but the truth is, it's where my roots are—and my trusty driver, Cesar.

Cesar is a Colombian who's been driving his limo for the past twenty years—that's the same limo for the past twenty years. It's a vintage Lincoln Town Car with well north of 400,000 miles and a borderline crusty interior that's likely hosted the conception of numerous Cesar offspring, a number of whom he likely doesn't know about. But I'm not a prima donna and I like to keep it in the family—his brother Hugo is my preferred waiter at Tequila Mockingbird, my favorite restaurant, and I'd rather a hardworking, albeit horny, guy like Cesar earn my money than some corporate limo company.

Each time he picks me up, our conversation is identical.

"Meester Kelly, did you get any cuca on your treep?" He's been in the country for two decades but sounds like he just learned English yesterday. By the way, cuca is slang for pussy.

"The perseverance in your line of questioning is about to pay off, Cesar, because this time, I did. Flight attendant."

"Really?!" He claps loudly and rubs his palms back and forth as if he awoke to find it's his birthday. "That's wonderful. I so happy for you. Still with the Fish?"

Both my snowplow driver and my limo driver are really creative when it comes to lesbian nicknames.

"We are, but for how long, I couldn't tell you."

"Eef I were you, meester Kelly, I would cut that muff-munching señora out of your life once and for all. I can call some guys who could…"

"That won't be necessary, Cesar, but you are right, I gotta do something about it."

Cesar then takes a call and starts speaking Spanish rapidly into his Bluetooth. I take this as an opportunity to call Jo.

"Well if it isn't my hard-living twin. You still in Chicago?"

"Nope. In the car with Cesar and we just crossed into Greenwich on the Merritt parkway."

"They let you back on a plane, huh?"

"Not without some special attention from the TSA."

"Was it good for you?"

"Well, his name was Mark. He likes long walks on the beach and grazing other men's testicles. I'm going to send him a bottle of Pierre Cardin aftershave for Christmas. Wanted to check in and see if we're still on for tonight."

"Of course. You and me at the Bird—I've been looking forward to it all week."

"Good. Because I have a lot to report."

"Word of warning, dearest brother. Mom's pissed at you."

This is hardly newsworthy—the woman is always pissed at me, even when I don't get a plane diverted to Chicago.

"For once, maybe I earned it."

"Well, she's mostly worried the girls at the club are going to catch wind of your tiny-dicked boss saying you got fired."

My mother is more worried about appearances than reality. She actually doesn't give a shit that I was fired—she's just worried about explaining it to her blue-haired, blue-blood country club bitches.

"My official stance on Mom is 'fuck that shit.'"

"Understood. What time do you want to meet tonight?"

"I need to spend at least a little time with Laura before running out again, so why don't we say eight to be safe?"

"Fine. Give that manipulative sloth my best."

Unlike Angelo and Cesar, Jo doesn't refer to Laura in aquatic terms. She prefers to focus on my wife's talents for manipulation and avoidance of anything that resembles work.

"Also, better call before you show up—you know she could be muff diving." Classic Jo. "Seriously, you gotta do something about that situation…"

"Yeah, yeah. Goodbye, sis."

I hang up and shake my head—I'm doing a lot of that right now.

"Was that your seester?" Cesar pipes. He's met Jo a handful of times and has hit on her an equal number. "Is she steal a lesbian?"

"Yes, believe it or not, she hasn't snapped out of it yet."

"That sucks, man. La Mondada just hasn't found the right polla yet."

My Spanish is poor, but I'm pretty sure "polla" means "cock." Safe bet with Cesar. I'm not sure the fella understands how human sexuality works, but I don't have it in me to argue.

We get off the parkway in Stamford and head to my house, a small, three-bedroom ranch in the center of town. Laura and I moved there after getting married. We intended to upgrade after having kids, but you know how that played out. Cesar parks in the driveway and honks to announce my arrival, a move he's done every time since I told him about walking in on Laura with a mouth full of fur. I'm not kidding, either—her girlfriend Ella had a bush so thick it looked like she had a Wookiee in a scissor hold.

I hand Cesar a forty-dollar tip and he thanks me immensely, not by helping me with my bags, but by stuffing it in his wallet and singing, "I feel like cuca tonight!"

He hugs me, as he always does upon parting, and I head to the garage since there's about a foot of snow on my front walk. I open the garage and enter my house through the door leading to the basement. I drop my bags in the closet-turned-bedroom that I stay in before heading upstairs, where Laura is waiting at our kitchen table.

"Nice of you to come home," she greets me as warmly as ever.

The woman is so cold, eskimos would be like, "Damn, she's cold."

"Nice of you not to be face down in Ella's lap when I arrive."

This catches her off guard—she's not expecting me to

fight back because, well, I never do.

"When were you going to tell me?" she asks, her arms folded across her chest.

"About?" I say with a raised eyebrow.

"Um, your getting fired! I had to hear about it on national TV. And what happened with you on that plane, and why are you hanging with that actress?"

She's only 17 questions away from 20. If I were a betting man, I'd pick the over.

"Peter fired me on Friday while I was in the Delta Sky Club. I was going to tell you when I got home, and here I am," I say through a fake smile.

"Well, what am I supposed to do? How am I going to get insurance? How are you going to pay the mortgage?"

And there's 20. Laura made it abundantly clear early into our marriage that she wanted nothing to do with the finances. She has no idea I paid the house off twenty years ahead of schedule after receiving some very large bonuses in the years before Michele sold the company.

I'm tempted to remind her it's 2017 and women are more than welcome in the workforce, but while I have become more comfortable with conflict, I'm still not an idiot.

"Well?" she says, demanding an answer.

Now the last thing I am going to do is tell her about the possibility of a book deal, because she'll just shit all over it and fuck her. She was never supportive of my writing because she couldn't see how it would directly benefit her, so I've kept it underground, so to speak.

"I'm fine, by the way," I say sarcastically.

"Well that's fantastic," she says, slow-clapping her hands. "How are you going to support us?"

Us. There's still an us when there shouldn't be an us. I'm about to blow up when she catches me off guard.

"I have been thinking about it a lot, Kelly, and I want a divorce."

I hear a record screech in my head for the second time in as many days.

"What?" I say, sounding more confused than surprised.

"You've made a spectacle of yourself and you're unemployed—I just don't think I can be married to you anymore."

I could cry, I'm so happy. I want to do Balki's dance of joy, but I don't think Laura could hold me the way Bronson Pinchot did Mark Linn-Baker on *Perfect Strangers*.

"Have you spoken with a lawyer?"

"What do you think, I'm an idiot? Of course, I did. I called Jim Peters, Ella's friend."

"The guy on TV?"

"Yep," she says, smiling and looking me straight in the eye.

My wife isn't the brightest bulb on the tree. She assumes attorneys who buy a lot of airtime must be the best—in fact, the exact opposite is true. Ambulance chasers and divorce lawyers who advertise all over the place are on the bottom rung of the legal profession.

I suppress a smile—don't wanna tip my hand.

"Don't worry," she says. "All I want is half."

My guess is Ella told her to go after me now to maximize her windfall, presuming my recent employment change means I'll have to spend down our savings.

"What about the house?" I ask.

"Let's just sell it and split the proceeds. Ella and I have been talking and I may just move in with her."

We bought the house at the height of the market, and now, it's probably worth one-third of that. I doubt she knows this.

The truth is, this may be the push I need to extricate myself from Connecticut.

"I guess this means I'll need an attorney, too."

"Jim can recommend one."

I bite my lip to stifle a laugh.

"I'll ask around."

"I'm sorry it's come to this, but Ella and I have come to view you as a liability," Laura offers.

Wow, how sweet.

"Me too," I say somberly, then turn and go back downstairs for a shower—I need to get ready to celebrate.

CHAPTER TWENTY-ONE

Dinner With Jo

I like to think I'm smart with money, so I do things like pay off debt quickly and keep stuff around for as long as its usefulness persists. This is evidenced by my car, a 1989 Volkswagen Golf GTI that pretty much everyone I know has been begging me to ditch since I started making real money. It doesn't have power steering or power windows, but it still runs well and is a beast in snow. I bought it in high school with money I earned as a swim instructor and I just can't seem to part with it—its usefulness persists.

I nicknamed it Eddie after the demonic mascot of my favorite band, Iron Maiden; I know it's customary to give vehicles female names, but come on, I already have a girl's name. Besides, the car looks like an Eddie. I park it behind the restaurant and enter through the back door. I walk through the dining room adorned with Mexican clichés— inflated Corona bottles, pictures of Our Lady of Guadalupe, piñatas hanging from the ceiling. Ironically, the speakers are blasting pop country rather than traditional Mexican folk.

I stop and say hi to Hugo, Cesar's brother, who gives me a big hug; the Garcia family is big on hugs.

"Sounds like someone has been a bery bad boy," he says, and I assume he's talked to his brother. Hugo is shorter than his sibling and a little more stocky—but they have the exact same thick Colombian accent. V's sound like B's.

"I'm not even capable of bad, Hugo. Jo here?"

"I just came from da bar and she no there. You wanna wait at da bar or you wanna jour table?"

Jo and I come here so often we have our own table— the perks of loyalty.

I look to the bar and see Ryan's tending tonight instead of Jason. Both are great, but Ryan's drinks are a little weaker. Given the events of the last 24 hours, that isn't such a bad thing.

"I'll wait at the bar and catch up with Ryan."

Ryan is one of three gringos who work at Tequila Mockingbird, the others being Dallas, the owner, and Jason. Everyone else is from Mexico and Central or South America—there are more Spanish dialects in the place than a linguist could count.

"Well, if it isn't crazy Kelly Carson," Ryan says while dipping the rim of a tumbler onto a wet sponge and then coating it with salt. "You flying solo tonight or will Jo be joining?"

"She'll be here."

Ryan has a degree in economics from UPenn but makes more tending bar than he would at an entry-level corporate job. Plus, he's an entrepreneur at heart and the thought of crunching numbers at a desk all day makes him cringe.

"Have I told you about my new business?" he asks, sliding a margarita in front of me.

"Fire away."

"I'm using drones to take aerial footage of houses for realtors."

This is actually not a half-bad idea, certainly better than his others, which have included a vegetarian bar-b-que catering business and a hip-hop clown enterprise—apparently the one-percenters of New Canaan eschewed the idea of gangsta clowns at their kids' birthday parties. Who would have thunk it?

"What do you charge per house?"

"Fifty bucks, and if they want, I can shoot video inside the house that looks like some HGTV shit."

I raise my glass to him and take a sip; it's just what the doctor ordered. I fill Ryan in on the events of the past few days, including my pending divorce.

"You gonna call her?" he asks, referring to Terri.

"I don't even have her number."

"That fucking sucks." His attention goes towards the door to the bar. "And here she is, Jo Carson in the flesh," Ryan says, grabbing a tumbler to prepare my twin a matching margarita.

I don't turn because I know how Jo likes to greet me, and then there it is, her customary slap on the back of my head; I prefer the Garcias' hugs.

"Look what the cat dragged in. Ryan, don't give this man any gummy bears—he can't handle them."

I neglected to tell Ryan that the edibles I ingested were in the form of gummy bears. Ryan flashes a look of confusion and hands her the drink.

"Don't worry about it," she says and then takes a big

sip.

"You actually look pretty good, Kelly, all things considered."

"That's because it's nonstop good news since the overdose."

"Tell me."

"Laura just asked me for a divorce!"

"No fucking way! It's about time, you pussy."

"My passive aggressiveness finally paid off."

"You got a lawyer? Because there's a guy in Stamford named Stanley Rothstein who'd be a good person to start with. He handled Vanessa's divorce."

Vanessa is Jo's current girlfriend. She's a local TV news anchor and her coming out caused a bit of a scandal due to the fact that she was married to the network's president. They were all set to fire her, but ratings have never been higher.

"Do you think he can look over my contract from the literary agency too?"

"Of course. He can also look at your employment separation agreement, too. He's very good."

I forgot about the separation agreement I got after Peter fucked me, I mean fired me, on Friday. Freudian slip.

"Three birds with one stone."

"Three mockingbirds?" Ryan chimes in.

"Don't quit your night job, Ryan," Jo chastises.

"Have you heard about his new day job?" I ask.

"You are not actually going to sell those prosthetic toe vibrators, are you?"

I forgot all about this. The last time we were here, Ryan pitched the Vibratoe, a fake toe that's actually a vibrator. His hook, aside from the play on the name, was that women could keep it in their purse without worry. Jo tried to explain the many flaws in his thinking, of which she had two major concerns: What the fuck kind of maniac has a prosthetic toe in her purse? And what the fuck kind of maniac masturbates in public?

"No," he says, and then explains the drone business.

"I'm impressed. That's the first good idea you've ever pitched."

Ryan takes the backhanded compliment gracefully and asks whether we'll be eating at the bar or a table.

Ryan is always trying to get us to eat at the bar, but I prefer a table. Plus, it will afford us some privacy.

"Don't take it personally, Ryan, but we're going table tonight."

"I figured. No charge for the drinks."

I slap down a twenty because I like the kid, and Jo and I walk to the dining room and take our table.

Emilio, a short Mexican who's been busing tables since we started coming here, brings a carafe of water, chips and salsa, and guacamole.

"How you doing tonight, guys?" Emilio asks.

"Not bad, Emilio. How's your cousin?" Jo asks.

Emilio's cousin Lino had the flu last week and neither of them have health coverage, so Jo went on a house call to their place.

"He's doing better but had to miss work this week—we may not be able to make rent."

My heart goes out to these two. They bust their asses but can barely make ends meet. It's not as if they are refugees or illegal immigrants either—both were teachers in Mexico, but their credentials meant nothing in the States. Neither could afford teaching certificates here, so they took jobs as busboys. Jo and I slip them a few bucks whenever we can.

"Tell him to keep drinking fluids," Jo replied. "And remember that beer doesn't count."

"Si, señorita!" Emilio replies and walks to another table.

"Those two guys work harder than most of the girls in my office," Jo says. "Even so, they still can't afford health insurance and now they're getting penalized for not having it."

"It's total bullshit, but listen, I talked to the agent today…"

"That's right! You were supposed to be there. She's still interested after all this shit in the news?"

"That's the fucked-up thing—that's practically why she's taking me on. Apparently, all this Terri Flynn airtime has made me more interesting."

"My God, you have a fucking edge now."

"I know. I should feel great, but the way things ended with Terri is putting a serious fucking damper on everything."

"She'll come around. Call her tomorrow and straighten things out."

"I can't! I never got her number. All that time together and we never exchanged digits."

"There's gotta be a way. But you really give a fuck about this girl, don't you?"

"Yes, I suppose I do."

CHAPTER TWENTY-TWO

Attorney Stanley Rothstein

Shortly after nine this morning, I called Rothstein and set up an appointment for early this afternoon. I'm sure the fact that I was bringing a contract, a separation agreement, and a divorce made it a little easier for him to find time on his schedule.

For the remainder of the morning I try to work on my novel but keep coming up empty.

I have what I think is a great premise, but the story still needs that tension. And unfortunately, what I don't have is inspiration. I'd love to pick Terri's brain but don't see that happening any time soon. After staring at the manuscript for two hours without writing a word, I decide to pray to Our Lady of Google and see if there's any way I can track down the red-haired train wreck herself.

Google offers little more than *Temporary Layoffs* gossip and fan pages, one of which completely creeped me out. It was called Master Bates and was a fan fiction site devoted to Terri's character Nikki Bates of *Our Boy Roy* fame, though it took the point of view of Nikki's father.

Odd, right?

After tightening my search, I find a press release clearly crafted by Terri's people that says she's taking time off to deal with personal matters and that the split between actress and studio was amicable. I don't believe that shit for a second.

This might be impossible, but then again, I guess there's good reason famous people are hard to track down. What about the old-fashioned White Pages, though. Seems that might be a good place to find an old-fashioned guy like Sergeant Major Attorney Asshole Flynn, and what do you know, there he is—Kevin Flynn in Deerfield, Illinois.

My computer then warns me that it's fifteen minutes until my meeting with Stanley, so I scramble and leave the house—time flies when you're stalking.

Stanley's office is in a rotund three-story building right off the Merritt Parkway. Eddie and I get there with a couple minutes to spare, and I hurry up the stairs to the third-floor office suite and am more than a little winded when I enter and introduce myself to whom I think is his receptionist, only it's actually Stanley himself.

"Kelly Carson here to see Stanley Rothstein," I huff.

"Kelly? Damn, I expected you to be prettier," he quips and extends his hand, "Stanley Rothstein—nice to meet you. The girl is out for a few days, so I'm pulling double duty. Let's sit in my office."

I follow him through a doorway and into his office, where he decides it's the perfect time to squeeze some drops into his eyes. "Sorry about this—I'm a dry-eye sufferer."

At least it's not restless dick syndrome. Where did that thought come from? I have no idea.

"So, you're going through some shit, huh?" he says, drops running down his cheeks—goddamn if he doesn't look sympathetic.

"I suppose you could say that."

"First things first, your separation agreement sucks. They're terminating you without cause and want you to sign a waiver saying you won't sue them for age discrimination. They're also only offering eight weeks of severance, though you've been with their company for two years and the legacy company for fifteen. That's a shitty offer. How much do you need the severance?"

"Excuse me?"

"Would you have enough to live on if you didn't get anything?"

"Yes, I've been good about saving, but I'm not prepared to turn it down."

"Of course not. But I want to go for the jugular. You should get two weeks for every year of service, which is more than half a year. How old are you?"

"Forty-two."

"Anyone else over 40 in your department?"

I close my eyes to think but can't come up with anyone else over 35, let alone 40.

"Nope."

"Good. We'll tell them we're exploring a suit for age discrimination—that should make them a little nervous."

"And if they don't bite?"

"They'll bite, trust me. The last thing a big public company wants is lawsuits brought by former employees. It makes them look bad and may threaten client relationships. We may not get 34 weeks, but we'll do better than eight."

This guy is aggressive, my total opposite—I like him.

"The other thing—when you were hired 17 years ago they didn't make you sign a non-compete, did they?"

"Correct. Michele Stahl, the founder, didn't believe in such formalities."

"That's good because technically, nothing prohibits you from offering your services to previous clients."

Until this point, I hadn't even give that a thought, not because I'm afraid of the legalities, but because I haven't taken a second to consider how I'm going to support myself.

"Here's how we're going to play this—you need to walk them through these concerns so they don't get their lawyers involved."

Hello darkness, my old friend. While I've become more confrontational since my impromptu trip to Maui, the thought of addressing these issues with Pete and the idiots in HR makes me squirm—I'd almost rather take their shitty deal. Stanley must read my nervousness.

"Look, Omnivore has a lot more money than you do. We do not want to deal with their attorneys. My advice, work on your poker face."

"Okay."

"I'll advise you every step of the way, but you'll do the talking. It will be simple."

I nod.

"Okay, onto the agreement with Pam Hart Literary. This is a pretty standard contract—they're taking fifteen percent of any deal they structure for you."

"Is that a lot?" I ask, showing my ignorance.

"It's on the high side of normal, but I've looked into their client base and they represent a large number of bestselling authors, many of whom have gone from print to the big or small screen. She's the real deal and apparently worth every penny."

"Great."

"Not so fast." He waves a fat finger at me. "This agreement cuts her in on the deal for this novel and its corresponding screenplay—apparently, she thinks you've got something worthy of theatrical release."

"What does that matter?" I ask, showing more ignorance.

"It means you're going to be doing a lot of work, not only fine tuning your novel but rewriting it as a screenplay. She may encourage you to work with another writer, but that's a bad idea."

"Because?"

"Because then you lose creative control and you do not want that. Look, I've had clients walk off movie sets because their work's been butchered by Hollywood screenwriters. Books are always better than the movie— the only way to keep a movie true to the book is to have the author write the script."

"So what do you suggest?"

"That you retain copyright of the novel and subsequent screenplay. We'll include language that protects you on that front, and if they're fine with that, then you sign."

"What's the book about anyway?"

I tell him, and his eyes light up. "That's very original. You should make Blaze's agent colorful but conniving."

"I'll keep that in mind."

"Okay, now the last one, your divorce. How long have you been married?"

"Ten years."

"Kids?"

"Nope."

I then explain how I found my wife in bed with another woman and that we've been in an open marriage since.

"Connecticut is a no-fault divorce state, so the facts of why you're separating don't really matter. You want my advice?"

"That's why I'm here, isn't it?" Of course, I think it but don't say it. Instead, I just nod.

"I'll talk to her lawyer and try and convince him to go to mediation instead of litigation. Maybe you can just split everything fifty-fifty and call it a day."

"That's all she says she wants, but if that's true, why did she hire Jim Peters?"

"Fuckkkkk. That numbskull is going to complicate things."

"I'm assuming she wants to get this settled ASAP, though, because she's worried I'm about to burn through our savings."

"She sounds like a real prize," Stanley jokes. "Okay, litigating a divorce takes more time and more money than settling through mediation. I'll call Jim's office and ask him to talk about it with her. He may be bent out of shape because it'll mean less money for him, but it also means a lot less work, and I know the guy avoids real law work like the plague. I'll let you know what he says."

"Thank you."

"Quick question, does she know anything about the book?"

"Not a thing."

"Good. We'll structure this so she isn't entitled to future earnings. Justice will be served if you earn a few million off the book and movie after your divorce is final."

"Millions?"

"Don't get your hopes up too high," Stanley retorts. "Unless a book goes to auction, a basic deal for a first-time author is a ten-thousand-dollar advance and quarterly or semi-annual royalty payments. Of course, they may subtract printing and distribution costs and money spent on marketing. And don't forget, Pam is going to get her vig. That being said, if the book becomes a best seller, you get a cut of every copy sold. Sell a few million books and do the math."

"What if it goes to auction?"

"Sky's the limit. I've seen seven-figure deals for first-timers, but they are most definitely the exception, not the rule."

I start to smile.

"Of course, real money is well down the road. In the best-case scenario, a publisher releases your book about twelve months after they buy it—their publication calendars are planned years in advance. Then it will take at least six months for the book to get traction and payment won't follow until sales are reconciled. You're looking at eighteen months minimum before you're drawing an income on this thing."

The smile is wiped off my face.

"Also, with her taking half your assets, you're going to need some cash flow coming in, but I don't recommend getting another job because then she can predict future income and go after that."

Now I know why people hate lawyers—they confuse the piss out of you.

"Soooo?"

"So, you've been in your industry for almost two decades and don't have a non-compete clause to worry about. Start your own business and do some hunting."

If I had a spear, I'd chuck it through his heart for invoking Pete Jackson. But I'll be damned if that's not a good idea. I close my eyes, tilt my head to the ceiling, and there it is—Carson and Partners is born.

CHAPTER TWENTY-THREE
Zora's Place

I leave Stanley's office and head to my favorite coffee shop in town. It's not a Starbucks or a national donut chain, but a small place called Zora's run by, you guessed it, a woman named Zora. Hailing from Montenegro, Zora is tall and brunette with some of the loveliest green eyes I've ever seen. I would've pursued her if we weren't double-blocked by marriages.

"Well, look who is here, Mr. Maui. Or should I say, Mr. Chicago?" Zora asks with a devilish glint in her eye. "What the fuck happened on that plane?"

Her facility with swearwords would make Samuel L. Jackson jealous.

"Food poisoning," I reply.

"You looked stoned out of your mind, man."

I couldn't help but laugh. "I didn't know the gummy bears weren't just gummy bears."

"Fuck me! You know they hit you harder than smoking that shit. They hit you slower though, too, because they have to be digested—a lot of times, people don't think they're working so they eat more. Then, bam!" She underscores her bam by slapping the counter. This causes me to jump back.

"You wanna coffee or are you here for a blowjob?"

Jesus, it's impossible to get your bearings around here.

Zora is always unpredictable, but there is a story behind the question. When she was new to the States, she went into a salon and asked, "How much for a blowjob?" but meant to say "blowout." A woman in there called her a whore and told her to get out. A friendlier patron informed Zora of her mistake and she ran out of there red faced. It's my favorite Zora story.

"I think I'll take the blowjob today," I respond.

"Too bad," she laughs. "I just ran out. Plenty of coffee though."

"Then I'll take a coffee."

"Sit anywhere you want, I'll bring it to you."

I take a seat in the corner and thumb through the emails on my phone. I come across one from my former client Natasha, of condom and lube fame.

"Kelly, rumor has it you are no longer with Omnivore. I have a project you might be interested in, call me sometime to chat."

Holy shit, it's as though Natasha somehow learned of Carson and Partners as soon as it slid from the brain-womb. I'm eager to get back to her but see Zora coming with my coffee and a plate of pastries.

"I brought you some sweets because you might still have the munchies." She smiles and slides into the seat across from mine.

"How's the bitch?" she asks, referring to Laura, whose reputation precedes her.

"She wants a divorce," I say.

"Really, man? Oh, that's fucking great!"

Now, upon hearing the news that a friend's spouse wants a divorce, most people would offer condolences. But all my friends want to give me high-fives. It makes me realize just how bad my marriage is.

Before she can continue, the bell above the door chimes and in walk two middle-aged women in yoga pants.

"Fucking Lulus," Zora whispers. "They come in here in their goddamn Lululemon pants and do nothing but bitch; the flashier the pants, the bitchier the woman."

I, for one, believe the inventor of yoga pants should be canonized—then again, I'm likely the target audience.

"Will you stay for a while?"

"Yeah, I'll be here."

"Good. Maybe I'll make your wildest dreams come true after they leave, but probably not." She laughs and heads back to the counter.

I re-read the e-mail from Natasha and can hear her thick Australian accent as I call her cell. It's a running joke we have; she plays up Australian stereotypes and I overdo Irish ones.

"G'day mate!"

"Top o'the morning to ya, Natasher," I say in a brogue. "Ya makin' any money ta-day?"

"Aye. Just selling me shrimp skewers out by the Opera House."

I start laughing and lose the accent. "It's good to hear from you, Natasha. Thanks for reaching out."

"I called your old place this morning looking for you and heard they let you go."

I fill her in on last Friday's unceremonious firing.

"Well this may lift your spirits, I got a fun one for ya."

"I'm listening."

"Our market penetration in condoms, pun intended, has been flat for the past few quarters, so we've done some product development and have come up with a new line of cum stoppers that focus on playfulness."

Natasha is a bit of a wild child if you haven't guessed.

"Our hypothesis is that protection is a given when it comes to the category, so in order to grow, we need something that will get people excited about cumming in a Popeye."

Popeye is the name of the condom brand in question. The company founder thought it was perfect, since the Popeye character is a seaman and condoms are all about semen—maybe they should have market tested that one.

"Sounds like this could be interesting research. Do you have a target in mind?"

"Swingers."

I can't tell if she's serious.

"Like key party, *Ice Storm* swingers?" The *Ice Storm* is one of the top couple-swapping movies of the 90s; I'm sure everyone here agrees on that.

"Yep."

She's serious.

"Interesting."

"The lifestyle is actually pretty common. Our creative agency wants to test these with power users—we need to target people who play a lot. You up for it?"

The little boy inside me is jumping up and down. "Absolutely. Can you give me a few days to get back with a proposal?"

"I kind of need something by tomorrow."

This doesn't give me a lot of time to figure out how to round up a bunch of swingers, but I'm willing to give it a shot.

"Then you will have it tomorrow."

"Wonderful! And it would be great if we could actually test them at a swingers party!"

And I should probably start freaking out about now. I don't know how I'm going to pull this off—it's not like I have access to databases of people in open relationships, but it will be fun trying. Plus, it's not a problem until she agrees to the project.

"I'll keep that in mind."

"Great. I'll be on the lookout for something from you tomorrow. And now, mate, got to get back to me shrimps."

"And I gotta be getting back to me Guinness."

I hang up and sip my coffee. What the hell am I getting myself into? But I have a feeling Zora might be able to offer some insight. I fill her in once she's done with the Lulus, who seem no more than a little displeased.

She laughs, of course, but then she leans in. "It's more common than you think."

"That's what I hear."

"You know how many bored, rich bitches come into my place? Swinging is their cure. If you see a house with a white rock at a certain spot in the lawn, that signifies that they're into the life."

"Really?"

"I'm not shitting you, man. I hear women talking about it all the time. Those Lulus in the corner are probably talking about fucking each other's husbands now. You need people to participate in your study, just ask Zora to help."

"Is there like a president of the local swingers' chapter?"

Zora smiles and goes to the counter to scribble something on a napkin. She comes back and hands it to me.

"Gail Dexter. Tell her you're a friend of Zora's and she'll be happy to talk."

The bell on the door chimes again and Zora leaves to catch flak from another Lulu. My phone rings and I see that it's FuckFace, aka Pete Jackson. I want to send it to voicemail but know I can't ignore him forever. I reluctantly answer.

"Farmer Kelly, it's Pete Jackson. How you doin', wild man?"

I hate this fucking guy the way fire hates water.

"I'm doing great, you fucking cock." I'm sorry, but I don't say it.

"Hey, buddy, have you had a chance to review the severance agreement. I'd love to get that signed, sealed, and delivered ASAP, kemosabe."

"I printed a copy but couldn't make sense of it because it was covered in my shit."

Sorry, again.

Instead, I say this.

"I have looked at it and have some questions, but now is not a good time. How about we discuss it in your office tomorrow morning at 8:30?"

I can tell I've caught Pete off guard—he's not expecting push back from a humble farmer.

"Sure, but can you send me your comments in email?"

"I could, but I won't."

"Can I ask why not?"

"You could, but I won't answer."

I can hear him getting frustrated on the other end of the line.

"What's gotten into you?"

"I'll see you at 8:30. You may want to have an HR representative there to address the allegations I'm going to make."

"What alleg…"

I terminate the call while he's mid "allegation." Acting like an asshole doesn't come naturally, but it feels kinda good.

He calls back, but I silence this one. Instead, I tap a note to a friend in a different division of Omnivore who was pressured into hiring Pete's bumbling son. I'm looking for as much dirt as possible on the guy before meeting with him tomorrow.

Once again, Zora and I are alone, but instead of coming back to chat, she turns on the TV.

"Gotta catch up on the gossip," she says. She's a pop-culture addict. I can't imagine giving a fuck, but my stomach drops when I hear the following.

"Troubled actress Terri Flynn has responded to the announcement that she left *Temporary Layoffs* to seek treatment for substance abuse. The following video was posted to her Instagram account just moments ago."

And then they cut to Terri, who looks better than I expected. Her red hair is pulled back in a ponytail, and it's clear she's not sporting any makeup, making her look more her age. It seems to me, at least, that she's relaxed.

"I am not an addict and am not getting treatment for substance abuse. I left *Temporary Layoffs* because the dirtbag director wanted me to show my tits for no reason other than to see them. We couldn't come to an agreement on this, so I left."

The anchor continues, "And there you have it from the horse's mouth. When *Temporary Layoffs* star Jimmy Walker was asked for a comment, he said, 'That girl was dy-no-mite.'"

"Please turn it off," I say.

"Why? This is the only time I'll have today to catch up on gossip, man."

"I'll tell you whatever you want to know about me and Terri, okay?"

"Deal," Zora says while pointing the clicker at the TV.

I spend the next thirty minutes answering questions about the Terri Flynn I know.

When I'm done, I suddenly feel the need to talk to her, but the only way I can get to her is through Sergeant Major Shit Fuck Flynn, and that man is not my biggest fan.

CHAPTER TWENTY-FOUR

Domino College

I leave Zora's with a powerful caffeine buzz, a stomach full of pastries, and the phone number of the preeminent local swinger; not bad for a day's work. I'm feeling great, but I need to go home and deal with that unpleasantness —Laura and I have too much to figure out.

And as soon as I walk in, there it is.

"I talked to my attorney today," Laura says, not even looking away from the TV. Apparently, this is an especially riveting episode of *Keeping Up with the Kardashians*. "Where were you?"

"Well, I met with my attorney, too, and then I grabbed a coffee at Zora's place."

"Ugh," she says, "I don't know why you insist on going there, I can't understand a word that woman says."

My wife has an issue with immigrants; her family practically came to the United States on the Mayflower and anyone who appears too ethnic is immediately in her crosshairs—I'm shocked she allowed me, the son of Irish and Italian immigrants, into her vagina, on those rare occasions when the stars aligned and permission was granted.

"She's a nice person," I argue. Plus, she's hooking me up with a swinger. Of course, I leave that last part out.

"That's your problem, Kelly, you see the positive in everyone."

If this is a problem, then the world certainly needs more problem children like me.

"That's the strangest thing I've ever heard," I reply.

"You give everyone the benefit of the doubt. That's why people take advantage of you."

I look her directly in the eyes and say, "That's interesting coming from you."

"Care to expand?"

"As a matter of fact, I do." I can tell she's not expecting this. "You've been taking advantage of that same character flaw since I found you face down in Ella's lady parts."

She has no valid argument to my claim, but I know she'll try anyway.

"I can't help the way I was born."

"Of course you can't," I agree. "But you could have been honest with me about it. Instead, you got married just so you could have someone take care of you."

"Oh come on, haven't you gotten over that yet?"

For the life of me, I don't understand how she thinks time can heal this mega-fuck. The woman isn't right in the head.

"Um, no. So I should just not give a fuck that my wife, whom I've supported for ten years, is a lesbian in a lesbian affair but still expects the benefits of marriage?"

"What harm did it do?"

How do you even have a conversation with someone self-centered enough to assume that our marriage vows required me to support her affair? But for the first time, I am ready to have that conversation. "You stole over ten years of my life!"

"Boo fucking hoo. At least you didn't have to pretend to be in love with someone."

That's a simultaneous kick in the balls and knife in the heart, a nearly impossible move. They should base a character on her in the next version of *Mortal Kombat.*

"I don't know what the fuck I did in a past life to deserve a woman like you, but it must have been pretty bad, like torching a village or greenlighting *Grease 2.*"

"What the fuck are you even talking about? Jesus Christ, you think you're ever going to find a woman with your constant movie references?"

Terri would have understood perfectly—God, I miss that crazy redhead.

"This Cool Rider isn't sticking around here any longer." And that's another *Grease 2* reference for her.

"You didn't even hear what I had to say about my lawyer."

I stop, turn around, and lock eyes with her.

"He advised me to consider mediation. It'll be quicker and less expensive. Are you on board with that?"

Fuck yeah I'm on board with that. Remind me to give the wizard Stanley Rothstein a big fat tip.

"I'll talk it over with my lawyer," I say, not admitting it was his recommendation in the first place. "I'll have him call Peters tomorrow."

"Be sure you don't forget." She underscores "forget" by pointing to her head. "I know you have a lot on your mind these days."

This is coming from a woman who loses her car keys multiple times per day only to find them stuck in her ignition.

"Scout's honor," I say and then walk down to my dungeon bedroom.

"You were not a Scout!" I hear her shout but ignore it.

It seems there's no better time than now to call a swinger up, so I dive in.

"This is Gail," a soft voice comes over the line. Dana Plato, whom you may know as Kimberly from *Diff'rent Strokes*, immediately comes to mind—not because their voices sound similar, but because Dana seems like she would have been a swinger.

"Gail, my name is Kelly Carson. I'm a friend of Zora's."

"Well any friend of Zora's is a friend of mine. How can I help you?"

"This is going to sound a bit odd," I say with a trembling voice, "but I'm a marketing consultant and I'm working for a condom company on a study amongst people who live…a certain lifestyle."

I'm trying to be delicate, but apparently that's not necessary with this subset.

"You want to talk to swingers?"

"Yes," I say and breathe a sigh of relief. "Zora said you might be helpful."

"Well, of course. My husband and I have a very open marriage. What do you want to know?"

"Would you be open to speaking with me in person?"

"Well, I'm leaving town to meet him in Rogers, Arkansas tomorrow"—for a swingers convention?—"so if this is urgent, I suggest we chat tonight. My place?"

As enticing as this sounds, I'm a little weary.

"How about Coraline's?"

Coraline's is a trendy bar in downtown Stamford and is run by Zora's sister.

"Perfect. Six?"

It's 4:45, which should give me enough time to think of what in the fuck to ask.

"Ideal," I say. "See you there."

#

I arrive at the bar and find that it's surprisingly busy for a Tuesday evening. I scan the place for a swinging Gail—what does that look like? Leather pants? Leather everything?—but only spy a bunch of older men in the corner playing dominoes.

"Welcome to Domino College, Kelly," Coraline says as I walk up to the counter. "These guys are from Croatia. They come here every Tuesday night to play."

"Damnit!" I hear an Eastern European voice shout.

"You are not your normal self tonight, Ivan. Too much stress at the office?"

"Shut up and shuffle, Aleksander."

"All right, all right, boys, don't get testy," says an older man standing behind the table.

"What do you know from nothing, Karlo?"

After taking a seat at the bar I see a middle-aged woman walk in. Coraline grabs my attention before I can approach.

"Do you want anything to drink, Kelly?"

"Just a light beer please," I reply and then turn my attention to the woman who's joined me at the bar. She's unfortunately—fortunately?—not wearing leather anything. She's dressed...normally. "Are you Gail?"

"Yes. Kelly?"

"Guilty as charged. Do you want anything to drink?"

"White wine," she says towards Coraline.

"Have a seat and I'll bring it over to you."

Gail and I take a seat in the corner, as far as we can get from the domino players.

"So I have to say, I was intrigued by your call."

"I imagine it's not every day someone calls out of the blue to ask about your lifestyle."

"That's putting it mildly."

I explain what I do for a living and the purpose of the study.

"That's actually really smart for them to talk to people like us."

"Why's that?"

"Because we are power users!" She laughs.

Caroline comes with our drinks and Gail lets her get a little distance from the table for powering on.

"Power. Users. Condoms are not optional in our community—they are essential. And we use a lot of them."

"Actually, before we talk about that, can you tell me a bit about how you got into the life? I've led a pretty sheltered one myself."

I decide to leave out the part where I'm married to a lesbian.

"My husband's company sells everything from laundry detergent to body wash. Their biggest customer is in Arkansas..."

"Walmart?" Wally World is the biggest customer for most consumer and package goods companies, and they are based in Northwest Arkansas.

"Yep. He goes down there at least twice a month for meetings. Once while he was there, I'm sure after a number of drinks, one of his colleagues confided that he and his wife were into swinging. Apparently, there's not much else to do down there."

"I've been that way a few times myself, and you're right about there not being much to do."

"Charles, my husband, took me there once because we were considering relocating. We were going to keep his New York salary and live on Arkansas prices. It was very tempting. But anyway, we were invited to a party hosted by one of his colleagues, and when we entered, we had to put our keys in a bowl. I thought it was a drunk driving precaution, but that wasn't exactly the case."

"What do you mean?"

"Well, at the end of the night after we were all liquored up on top-shelf booze, the host called everyone into the great room—the men sat on one side, the women on the other. And that's when the bowl of keys made an appearance."

"Oh my god, I've heard about these things but thought they were myths."

"Well, this is one myth that was definitely confirmed. The bowl went around to the women, who closed their eyes and picked a pair of keys at random. Whoever's keys you got, you went into another room with."

"Wait, they did it in the house? How big was this place?"

"Huge," she says with a laugh. "But many couples wound up in the same room. It's not that uncommon."

"So did you guys participate?"

"I closed my eyes and my heart was racing when my fingers went into the bowl. Luckily, though, I picked our keys. We both breathed a sigh of relief."

"What would you have done if you hadn't?"

"I don't know, but that night we had our most passionate sex in years. Something came over both of us. We were both a little excited by it, a lot excited by it I guess."

A look of serenity comes over face—no doubt, she's reflecting on her swinging career—and she sips her wine. You know, this is a small sample size, but swingers seem pretty content.

"So we talked about the idea of trying it and agreed to a few simple rules: We could only play with another couple while both of us were present, a condom always had to be used, and we had to openly discuss our experiences afterward."

"So how long did you wait?"

"One night! Charles approached the host of the party, and he and his wife coached us on the life. In our uptight culture, we're led to believe that being with another partner will ruin a marriage, but it intensified ours. Over time, we altered the rules a bit so we didn't both have to be there if the urge to play came on, so long as we were honest with the other about what we did and who we did it with."

"Okay, so I understand this going down in Arkansas, where there isn't a lot to do, but what about here?"

"It's all over, right under your nose. New Canaan, Darien, Greenwich, Wilton—major swinging scenes in each of those towns. What do they have in common?"

"Money?"

"Bingo. Money, huge amounts, largely from guys working in finance. There's so much money that regular life becomes boring. Enter swinging."

"So in Arkansas they're bored because there isn't much to do. Here they're bored because they've done it all. Amazing."

"The best swinging scene ever, though, is in Illinois."

"No way."

"Oh yeah. Little town called Deerfield, an upscale suburb of Chicago. My friends there nicknamed it Swingtown."

Holy fucking Deerfield, home of Sergeant Fuck Flynn, where Terri may be sequestered at this very moment. I know my client would be interested in a Mid-America market for this study—Deerfield is definitely making the short list.

"Would you be able to introduce me to some people in Deerfield?"

"Just say the word."

"Thank you."

"Say, what are you doing tonight? My husband is away, but you know, we did change that rule."

She finds my knee and slides her hand up my thigh toward my dominoes.

"Raincheck? My wife just asked me for a divorce—I'm still processing that news."

Gail's hand ceases its march.

"I totally respect that. If you ever want to play, just call."

She looks at her watch and stands up. "Time for me to fly."

I thank her for her time and watch her leave, and fuck

me, her butt does look delicious. I somehow hadn't noticed that before. And I'm apparently not the only one who's second-guessing my decision.

"You crazy," I hear one of the old men call from the corner.

"Excuse me?"

"It pains me to witness what you've done. You like guys or something?"

"Shut up, Karlo," one of them says. "Excuse my friend, he hasn't been with a woman in years. His wife is colder than a nun."

"Like you are one to talk, Aleksander. When was the last time you fucked something aside from your hand?"

It's comforting to know men are the same, regardless of ethnic background.

"I'm in love with someone else," I blurt. This puts a cessation to gameplay. And I'm as shocked as Karlo when I shunned Gail. Am I really in love with Terri? I fucking think I am.

"Love is a powerful thing," Aleksander says. "Not something to be wasted."

"The problem is, I don't know if she feels the same way," I clarify.

"There's only one way to find out," Karlo pipes up. This is Karlo's kinder, gentler side. "Go find her and tell her, boy."

"Gentlemen, I believe I have a trip to plan."

"Na zdravi!" Karlo says, and all the men around him raise their glasses and say the same.

"Na zdravi!"

Who knows what that means, but it feels like encouragement.

I leave Coraline's and go back home to outline my thoughts for Natasha. I fire them off just before midnight and make a note to call her in the morning after my showdown with FuckFace Jackson. Then, lights out.

CHAPTER TWENTY-FIVE
The Trains Of Our Lives

Omnivore's offices are in Midtown, which means (well, meant) a "delightful" ride on the Metro North every day I wasn't in the field conducting research. Luckily, since I was the most productive moderator in the company, I was only in the office a few times a month; the other days, I was out in the world interviewing people about credit cards, body lotion, cell phones, cheeseburgers.

But if you ever want to know what it's like in a third-world country—excuse me, that's not politically correct—I mean, if you want to know what it's like in the developing world, you can get a glimpse on the Metro North. The trains are rarely on time, the cars are always crowded, and everything inside smells like urine because everything is coated in urine, albeit a thin layer.

Since I've been commuting into New York for almost two decades, I've gotten to know a lot of the regulars at my station. There's "How are ya?" Ed, who, as you may have guessed, is very solicitous. Crazy Tom is an older guy who's a former financial analyst turned IT consultant; he couldn't take the finance industry anymore, so he joined one that is shipping jobs overseas faster than Trump tweets responses to negative press. We call him crazy because after a few Foster's oil cans on the commute home he starts asking fellow passengers if they've seen his uncle Phil. The thing is, Tom doesn't have an uncle Phil anymore. He electrocuted himself after pissing on the third rail twenty years ago.

Then, there's a girl I can only refer to as "Hey Mom." She's newer on the platform and I don't know her real name, but I know just about everything else about her because she talks to her mother while waiting for the train. She's about 24, has a pixie cut, and lacks awareness. She assaults the platform (and her mother) with diatribes that primarily feature intimate details of her dating life—which should be made into a film called *Train Girl and the Adventures in the Forbidden Zone*. Absolutely nothing makes this girl happy, and I pity the self-abusive fool who marries her. It pains me to admit it, but I'd take a selfish lesbian any day of the week.

Now, though, the platform is quiet and I take a few moments to scan my email. Silence is broken when I hear Hey Mom coming.

"No Mom, they were doing it all night like a bunch of jack rabbits... Well, maybe it's good for her, but it's not good for me. I can't sleep when they go at it like that... Mom, stop telling me to go back out with Mike! I told you I hate fucking him. All his moves are so fucking predictable... No, I'm not a lesbian!"

This hyper-personal conversation goes on for another five minutes before the train whistle announces the on-time arrival of the 7:17 to NY. I'm a little disappointed—I wanted a little more on this lesbian matter.

Ed and I wish each other a good day when the doors open, and I spend the next hour making notes in the margins of my manuscript. At this point I just need to ratchet up the tension between the main characters, break one out of a nursing home, and stick the landing.

Before I know it, we're pulling into Grand Central Terminal. I leave through the north exit, which drops me off at Madison and 47th, a few blocks from Omnivore's offices in Rockefeller Center.

My office is (was?) in 50 Rock, just across the way from NBC's headquarters. As I stare at the skyscraper where *The Tonight Show* is shot, I imagine swinging by on tour, Jimmy telling the audience how hilarious my book is. I'm brought back to reality by a burly woman in a fur coat who's encouraging me to cross the street by shouting, "Walk, asshole!"

Right. Right. And it's an important reminder—I need to be a primo asshole right now. There's a FuckFace to fuck with.

I enter and am relieved my card key still lets me through security. I make my way to the elevator bank, thankfully, without encountering any of my colleagues, likely because it's 8:25 and those lazy assholes don't show up until well after nine.

I make a left off the elevator and head into the office, stopping to say hi to Sharon—our delightfully bubbly office manager/receptionist who took over the latter role when Pete fired the actual receptionist as a cost-cutting measure. I wonder if he used the line about being a lever on her.

"Kelly, it feels like it's been ages. I miss hearing your

singing in the office."

It's true, I do sometimes sing in the office, largely because I know it annoys Pete and, well, annoying Pete makes me feel good.

"I was in California…"

"And Hawaii apparently."

"You saw that?"

"It was hard to miss. How did you meet Terri Flynn?"

"That's a story for drinks."

"Promise?"

I'm guessing no one knows my news besides Pete and a few people in top management.

"Let's just say, you may be all taking me out for drinks sometime soon."

"Are you finally getting out of this hellhole?"

"I'm sure there will be an announcement later today, but right now, I have to meet with Pete."

"I haven't seen him wobble in yet. Did you hear he shot himself in the foot?"

"In more ways than one."

"What?"

"I'll explain later."

The office layout is full-on open floor; some genius in Silicon Valley decided that taking down walls helps foster collaboration as well as a culture that's less cloistered and hierarchical. Companies in non-tech industries soon caught on and found another benefit—open space is much cheaper than cubicle farms and actual offices. After the acquisition of Stahl and Partners, Omnivore moved us into their open space and now on those rare days when I'm in the office, I feel as if I work in an Indian call center, not a top consulting firm.

I'm grateful the office is basically empty now, but I do see my friend Mara sitting in front of her computer. She works in our field management group, the team responsible for finding all the people that moderators like me interview.

"Hi Mara," I say, but she doesn't look up, so I wave to catch her attention.

She then darts up and gives me a big hug and says, a bit loudly, "Did you bag the redhead?"

I shake my head. "She's just a friend."

"What?"

"She's just a friend," I say louder.

Mara points to her ear and shakes her head. She lost most of her hearing after giving birth to her first child; her doctors can't explain what happened, and her hearing aids only work intermittently. She hands me a yellow Post-it note and a pen—she goes through more Post-its than anyone in the office, a fact that's undoubtedly on Pete's radar.

"She's just a friend," I write, but Mara still shakes her head because I happen to have horseshit handwriting. Finally, I take out my phone and tap, "We are just friends."

She nods and says loudly, "Just friends, huh? I'd hit that if I were you, lesbian wife and all."

Before she can ask me a follow-up question about Laura, I see Pete Jackson from the corner of my eye.

"Hey there, Farmer Kelly, you ready to do this, kemosabe?"

Farmer Kelly and kemosabe. This fucking guy.

I tap a quick note to Mara, telling her I'll catch up with her later. She winks at me and then, trying to whisper, says, "Kick that idiot in the nuts for me," but she says it loud enough so that Pete turns his head and gives us both dirty looks.

"Now or never, Kelly boy."

I leave Mara and follow him to a conference room called Tesla. It's not named after the company or the scientist but the 80s metal band. In fact, all our conference rooms are named after 80s music icons; I'm secretly wishing we were in the Bryan Adams room—a space named for the guy who wrote *Cuts Like a Knife* is the perfect locale for a conversation about severance.

I sit, and Pete remains standing—it's a power move and probably a painful one; never ever forget that Pete FuckFace Jackson literally shot himself in the foot.

"Where's HR?" I ask.

"Destiny is running a few minutes late. I thought we could chat before she got here."

Destiny is a few minutes late. Pete's one of the few people in the world who could say that without realizing it's hilarious.

But to his credit, Destiny is an actual person. She's the new HR Generalist assigned to our business unit. To say she's worthless is an understatement. She has no idea what we do in my group and therefore, every candidate she identifies for a job is missing key qualifications, namely the ability to hold a conversation with another human being. Talking is pretty much the cost of entry for a moderator, but she mainly hires statisticians, assuming that a researcher is a researcher.

"The things I have to address in the severance document need to be heard by HR," I say.

"No doubt, Kelly. No doubt. I wanted to hear about your trip to Hawaii and that babe you were with."

This fucking idiot fired me over the telephone like I worked at a Burger King WHILE I was on a business trip that brought in six figures of revenue—and now he's seriously trying to have guy talk with me.

"Did you tag that shit?"

This is a message to all women, on behalf of all decent men: I'm sorry for the existence of Pete Jacksons everywhere.

"Come on, Pete."

"Fucking farmers never bag the 10s."

I'm about to tear into him, but we're spared the altercation by the arrival of Destiny.

"Hi Kelly. Hi Pete. What are we talking about today?"

I roll my eyes. She doesn't even know what the meeting is about, nor is she bright enough to put the simple equation of terminated employee plus idiot boss together in a conference room with HR.

"Kelly's termination," Pete says.

"Oh yeah. Okay. What about that?"

Pete looks at me, an invitation to begin. I take a minute to collect my thoughts—all morning I was stressing over whether I'd be brave enough to speak up for myself. I remain quiet as I think about Hawaii with Terri and, for some reason, I flash to the cliff jump and how I emerged from the water a seemingly changed man. That shit Saffron at the Stahl Center for Peace and Balance said about the hike I "survived" changing a man was pretty damn true.

"Earth to Kelly," Pete says.

It's now or never. I remove a printed version of my severance agreement and place it on the table. I then pretend to look for a pen.

"You need a pen to sign that, Kelly? I have one right here," Destiny says.

"No, I have one in my pocket."

I reach into my pocket, grab a pen, and then turn on a portable audio recorder I use to record interviews. Ironically, it was a gift from Pete to everyone in my department last year.

With pen in hand I pretend to look through the agreement one last time. I then write NO in big bold letters across the front and push it across the table.

Destiny looks at Pete, and Pete looks at me.

"What's the matter, Kelly?" he asks, a dumbfounded look on his stupid face.

"What's the matter? I've been with this company for over seventeen years and you offer me eight weeks of severance. Industry standard is two weeks for every year, and by my math, that's 34 weeks."

"Whoa whoa whoa, Kelly old boy," Pete speaks up. "Technically you've only been with Omnivore for three years—we feel we're being more than generous with offering eight weeks versus six."

"Thirty-four weeks, or I don't sign."

Destiny gets up from the table. "I guess my work here is done," she says.

What? Fucking baffling.

"I'm not finished," I say. She remains standing and glances at me. "You may want to sit down for this."

She drops her bag and sits.

"Do you have anyone left in my department over the age of 40?" I ask.

"What are you getting at, Kelly," she says with a stern look.

"It seems like maybe you want old guys like me out. I mean, Petey Pop over here told me I'm too expensive to keep around, even though I bring in most of the revenue."

He gives me a nasty look.

"Your point being?"

"Age discrimination is a real thing in the corporate world. You should really consider such things before terminating anyone over 40 without cause."

"You don't seriously think..." Pete pipes up, but I cut him off because I'm fucking feeling it.

"That age had anything to do with it? You tell me, Petey Pop." I fully realize that Pete is older than me and I'm the one claiming age discrimination. I'm using irony, and the nickname Petey Pop, hoping to unnerve him and get his anger up so he slips and says something he shouldn't.

"Stop calling me Petey Pop," he protests.

My plan may be working.

"I also heard something really interesting."

"What's that?" Pete and Destiny ask in tandem.

"Pete, you have a son who's about to graduate business school this December, right?"

The blood drains from his face.

"Point please, Kelly," Destiny chimes in.

"I heard you were pressuring analytics to hire your son and lost your cool when they decided there were better candidates in the pipeline." I then turn to Destiny and add, "But isn't it true, Destiny, that an offer went out to Peter Junior yesterday?"

"I'm not at liberty to discuss..."

"Save it," I cut her off. "Age discrimination and nepotism...tisk tisk tisk," I say while waving my finger. "A recipe for disaster if word got out."

Pete looks at me like he'd shoot me in the foot if he had a gun.

"Are you blackmailing me?"

"Well, Petey Pop, let's just say I took your advice and did some hunting of my own."

"You are a real asshole."

"No, if I were an asshole, you wouldn't have fired me. Assholes climb the ranks here—the good guys get fired."

"What's the big picture here, Kelly? You are a dinosaur in this business. No one will hire an old guy like you—this is a young man's game," says the guy approaching sixty, though you'd never know it given the money he's spent on plastic surgery, Botox, and highlights. He looks more like an out-of-work reality TV star than a general manager.

"You know what killed the dinosaurs, Kelly?"

Is this motherfucker going to say hunters? I stare blankly, afraid I'll choke him if he says it.

"The inability to adapt to new circumstances," he says, offering a refreshing factual error. "Farmers like you can't adapt to new ways of doing research because you are of the old school. Let me tell you this: You are a dying breed and we are investing in younger people who are more willing to take an innovative approach to our business. I am getting five of them for one of you."

I see Destiny turn that stern look on Pete.

"Well now that he's supported my hypothesis about age discrimination, I can turn this off." I remove the audio recorder from my pocket.

"Fuck," he says.

"That won't hold up in court," Destiny argues. "We didn't know we were being recorded."

"Maybe not in a court of law, but absolutely in the

court of public opinion."

"What do you want?"

"Fifty-two weeks' severance and full healthcare for a year."

"But you said 34 before," Pete protests.

"I gave you an opportunity to accept that, but you didn't. My price went up, call it Dino-inflation."

"We can't decide that now," Destiny says. "We have to run this by Omnivore."

"I've got an open calendar today. I'll just sit right here and wait for your answer."

"It could take days before Omnivore responds," Destiny counters.

"Bullshit," I reply. "You have some big contracts coming up for review in January. You think our clients will want to keep doing business with a firm accused of age discrimination and nepotism? I assume no, but if you want to test my assumption, take all the time you need."

"Kelly, can you…"

"I'm done talking to you both. The next time I see either one of you it better be with a revised severance agreement in hand. You can go now."

They look at each other stunned and get up to leave.

"Oh, Petey Pop," I say, knowing the nickname has gotten so deep under his skin.

"What?"

"Would you mind closing the door on your way out?"

He slams the sliding door and storms off. My heart is beating a mile a minute, but holy fuck if I didn't just beat the shit out of that. I am fucking Superman.

CHAPTER TWENTY-SIX

Pitching Swingers

Assuming I have a fair amount of downtime before Pete and Destiny return with the revised agreement, I take out my phone and call Natasha to walk through the proposal I sent last night.

"G'day mate," she answers.

"Top o'the morning to ya," I reply, but my heart's not in the accent—I want to get straight to business.

"How the hell did you pull this together this quickly?" she asks. "It's fucking brilliant."

"Like you said, the swinging lifestyle is more common than I realized. I just asked around and learned a lot."

"So Deerfield, Illinois huh? I figured you'd come back with something in LA or New York. I like it—if our proposition can play in the Midwest, it can play anywhere."

"Agreed," I reply, not letting on that I have ulterior motives for choosing Deerfield.

"Why is it so cheap? I would have expected this to cost twice as much?"

I quoted $75,000 to run a series of interviews with couples and to host a swingers party at a home we'll rent in Deerfield.

"I don't have to pay a recruiter to find these people," I reply. "I'm doing it myself and that cuts cost significantly."

"Well, this will certainly make me loyal to you."

Omnivore wouldn't have thought twice about quoting double. I'm going to run my business with more integrity —it's the key to long-term client relationships.

"I wouldn't have it any other way."

"Do you think we can do this in two weeks? We go into a planning session with our agency the first week in January and I want this to feed into that."

"Well, Christmas is coming so not in two weeks, but if we offer a high enough incentive, we can do it the week between Christmas and New Year's. People won't turn down money that will help offset Christmas expenses."

Given the timing, I'm seriously considering going to Deerfield early and seeing if I can spend Christmas with Terri, assuming she's still there. I think to look up her Instagram post from earlier in the week and see that it is geotagged with Deerfield, IL, so there's some hope she remains in Swingtown.

"Sounds good. I'll sign this today and get a PO over to you after we file some paperwork to get you set up in our system. I'll have my assistant send that to you later today."

"Always a pleasure doing business with you, Natasha."

"G'day, you fucking MICK."

"May the road rise to meet you," I say with a fierce return of my brogue and end the call.

#

After hanging up with Natasha, I remove my tablet, but

before I even get it fired up, my phone starts to buzz. It's Pam Hart—I'm pretty busy for a guy who just got fired.

"This is Kelly."

I hear Andre's soft voice come on the line.

"Please hold for Pam Hart."

"Is this my new client?" says a cheerful Pamela.

"I take it you heard from my attorney," I say with a little laugh.

"Very shrewd, Mr. Carson. Most first-time authors are happy to sign whatever we put in front of them. Not you."

"I'm smarter than your average bear."

"I have no problem with you maintaining creative control over the eventual screenplay, bubby, but we are getting ahead of ourselves a bit—we need a best-selling novel first, and we aren't quite there yet."

"I have a few thoughts on that," I say. "I'm working on some changes, specifically in the relationship between Allison and Blaze."

Allison is Blaze's love interest and the brainchild behind the reality show he's considering—while he hates the genre, he'll do anything to get closer to her.

"I've thought of a clever way to increase the tension and add a major twist. I'm also rethinking how I break Victor out of the nursing home."

Victor is a key cast member in the show *Casa Grande* and he has to participate in the reunion Allison is orchestrating. I wrote a scene where he breaks out with the help of another character, but it isn't funny enough, so I need to punch it up. The truth is, I want to break him out like members of The A-Team would free Murdoch from the psychiatric hospital, but I can't figure out how to execute it.

"All good things, bubby. When do you think you'll have another draft for us? I want to start pitching this immediately after the holidays, and your new editor is going to need time to read it."

"Soon, I hope. I know what to change—I just don't know how to change it yet."

"A word of advice, Hemingway," Pam says. "Get out of Dodge and have an experience, not like getting stoned out of your mind on an airplane, but something out of the ordinary. Meet some weirdos—that'll do the trick."

Meeting weirdos shouldn't be an issue—I'm about to embed myself with the Deerfield Swingers Association.

"How about I send you guys what I have by New Year's Eve?"

"I'll spend all New Year's Day reading it in Chatham with a bowl of clam chowder as my reading companion."

"That's pretty specific."

"It's my routine the first of every year. I meet my favorite client, Mick George, for a bowl of chowder at his favorite restaurant, The Bleeding Seal. If you want, I can share it with him—it's right up his alley."

"You have my permission," I say and then see Destiny and Pete standing at the door.

"Pam, I have to go. Is there anything more we need to chat about?"

"I'm going to send a revised agreement over to your lawyer. Just print it, sign it, and get it back to me so we can make this legit."

"You got it."

"I'm looking forward to working with you, Kelly Carson. You are going places, but don't forget to enjoy the journey—it's the best part."

She hangs up and I motion for Pete and Destiny to join me in the Tesla room.

"We have a revised agreement with the 52 weeks you're asking for," Destiny says. "Though we've included a clause that prohibits you from disparaging Omnivore and its employees."

They hand me the agreement and it takes me a good ten minutes to read through the legalese.

"Everything satisfactory?" Destiny asks.

"On the surface, it looks good, but I need to have my attorney review it. If he's comfortable, I'll sign it and get it back to you tomorrow."

"Really?" Pete asks. "We can't square this away now?"

My guess is some higher-up in Omnivore has taken a very special interest in this matter and won't leave Pete alone until I sign on the line, but I'm not letting him off that easily.

"No, we cannot, Pete. I don't want to shoot myself in the foot by not letting my attorney check this."

I'm surprised by Destiny's reaction—a chuckle. Pete gives her a dirty look. I can almost hear him make a mental note to fire her.

"You're way more of an asshole than I ever thought you could be, Kelly. I underestimated you."

"I'm a modern-day cowboy," I reply—that's a Tesla, the band, reference.

Pete shakes his head and gets up to leave. Destiny, still giggling over my badass line, follows suit.

"I just have one more condition," I say.

"What's that?" they ask in tandem, again.

"I want Pete to send an Omnivore-wide email explaining it was his decision to eliminate my position as a cost-saving measure."

"I was planning on doing that anyway," he states. "It's part of my Fuck the Farmers Campaign."

"Great," I say and pack my bag. Admitting he cut the most productive member of the team will be akin to shooting himself in the other foot.

CHAPTER TWENTY-SEVEN

I Won't Be Home For Christmas

I leave Omnivore's office, presumably for the last time, and take a late morning train back to Stamford. I swing by Rothstein's office to hammer out the final details of my severance agreement as well as my contract with Hart Literary.

After looking over the agreement from Omnivore, Rothstein observes, "If all my clients were like you, I'd have a lot less stress in my life. How the hell did you get 52 weeks out of them?"

"Let's just say the age discrimination threat made them nervous, but the nepotism accusation was the real kicker."

I explain what I knew about Pete forcing someone in another department to hire his son.

"You are a machine," Stanley says. "And that guy is a fucking idiot."

"When God handed out brains…"

Stanley hands me the revised agreement. "Sign away."

I hand it back to him happy to be done with it.

"The agreement with Hart Literary is also ready for

your John Hancock."

I sign that with a Hancockian flourish.

"Lastly, we lucked out with Jim Peters. He didn't put up a stink about mediation, said he actually preferred it since he could still bill hours but do a shit-ton less work. That guy is a real prize."

"So what are next steps there?"

"The first step is for you and Laura to have an initial consult with the mediator —that can happen as early as next week. Then, depending on how much stuff you want to split and how long it takes to come to an agreement, you're looking at a process of anywhere from two to four months. Since you don't have kids, though, it should be on the quicker side."

The other day, Laura told me she simply wants half of everything, though I'm sure that ambulance chaser attorney of hers wants to go for more. "For argument's sake, let's say on day one, we agree to split everything fifty-fifty. How long would it take, then?"

"I've never seen that happen, but presumably, it would only be one or two meetings, which could happen within weeks. Then it's a matter of finalizing it legally, which can also be expedited."

"Any chance we can get this marriage dissolved by the end of the year?"

"Whoa! That's pushing it."

"I just want this behind me."

"In that case, you may not need a mediator at all. If you already have something in mind, let me present it to the other side."

"My best offer is she gets the house, half of our investments, including my retirement, and I pay her legal fees. She can't touch future income."

"That's extremely generous, but might I offer a suggestion? You're leaving no room for negotiation. She may have told you she only wants half, but they may surprise us and push for more. I would advise you to say split everything fifty-fifty, including the house. And if it comes to it, then we'll throw in the entire house as sweetener."

"Okay, and we're firm on no future income."

"Absolutely, just don't go mentioning anything about the book or your new separation agreement. Along those lines, I would advise you to take a lump sum payout in January so you don't get nailed with taxes."

"Good thinking."

"I'll shoot you a note later when I hear from your wife's attorney."

"Sounds good," I say and get up to go.

Maybe I'm making a mistake by not fighting harder to keep more of what I worked so hard for, but the truth is, I don't give a fuck about any of it—I just want to be free.

#

On my way out, I realize I haven't lived up to a promise I made to Jo the other night—I haven't seen our fucking mom. Reluctantly, I drive to our parents' home, where I find my mom glued to the TV in her kitchen. She's watching very conservative cable news; she often complains about not being able to sleep at night but simply can't link her insomnia to the fearmongering she absorbs all day every day.

"You've been home since Monday and it takes you until Wednesday afternoon to come see your mother?"

This guilt coming from the woman who didn't come to

my college graduation because she was playing in her country club's member-guest tournament. Nothing comes between my mother and golf.

"I've had a bit of a hectic schedule since coming back," I say defensively.

"And what made you too busy for your own mother?" she says, pouring on the guilt.

"Let's see, I was fired on Friday, so I've been dealing with that, and Laura asked me for a divorce on Monday, so I spent yesterday meeting with a lawyer. Today, I met with my former boss and then went back to my lawyer to finalize my severance agreement." I omit the part about getting an agent for my book—if I told her, the whole town would know, and then Laura would find out and try to negotiate for a piece.

"So it's clear—your mother comes in last place."

I'm about to respond, but my mother's attention is diverted to a story on the news about a Muslim man who throws September 11th parties.

"Deport them all," she mutters.

Now I know what my mother saw in Laura.

"When was the last time we had a meal together, just you and me?"

I'd love to be able to point to my senior year mother-son banquet, but in addition to missing my college graduation, she had her sister, my aunt Mia, step in for her at that event because she was playing mahjong.

"Do you remember what song we danced to at my wedding?" I ask.

She looks down. "Trick question, we did not do a mother-son dance at your wedding."

"Do you know why?"

"I can't for the life of me remember."

"Because you were busy arguing with Dad over whether or not the valet was a Muslim and totally missed the announcement of the dance."

"Well, I never liked "Catch a Falling Star" anyway. Perry Como was a sap."

"Enough, Mother. Jo says you're angry at me, what gives?"

"Well, you got fired. And you embarrassed this entire family with your antics in Hawaii with that second-rate actress. What were you doing with someone like that? She's not exactly an upgrade from that lesbian you married…"

Before she finishes, I instinctively come to Terri's defense. "She's a nice girl, Mom—a little impulsive maybe, but she showed me things about myself I didn't even know were there."

"Like how to get kicked off an airplane?"

"That was an accident!" I protest. "Besides, all charges were dropped and it was declared a case of food poisoning."

"That is immaterial, my dear boy. The minute my friends saw it, my phone rang off the hook."

Her first instinct wasn't to see if I was okay—it was to conduct damage control with her blue bloods. I immediately think about asking Terri for advice on handling my agent after waking up in the hospital and not thanking her for taking care of me and arranging legal support—apparently, insensitivity runs in the family.

"You're going need a better story than food poisoning when all the ladies at the club ask you about it on Christmas Eve."

My mother retired from cooking when Jo and I graduated from college. As a result, every year we have Christmas Eve dinner at the club.

"I won't be joining you for Christmas Eve." I see the blood rush from her face.

"Uh, no, Christmas Eve dinner at the club is a family tradition."

"I have other plans."

"With who? The ginger from the airplane?"

I sure hope so, I think as I turn and leave without another word.

CHAPTER TWENTY-EIGHT

Getting my Shit Together

In the week that's passed since returning from Maui, I've managed to take my manuscript as far as I can. But I'm still struggling with a few elements, including the ending—I want that big soap opera bang, my own Who Shot JR?

One thing I am proud of, though, is new elements I've given Blaze; since he's an actor looking to make a comeback, I have him participating in focus groups in disguise, taking on new personas each week to build his chops. It's a nice nod to my industry, though I know some of the more uptight research practitioners won't appreciate the humor, that they'll claim I'm denigrating the process by insinuating people lie to participate in focus groups. This is all entirely accurate by the way; participants lie all the time to get selected—it's an occupational hazard for us moderators.

I've also given him a taste for older women and a love of Zima, which he imports from Japan, the only country still celebrating the drink's 90s moment. Little elements like this add dimension to characters and make them more memorable.

I'm flying to Chicago tomorrow, Christmas Eve, and plan on showing up at Captain Major Shit's house unannounced to try to make amends with his daughter. A lifetime's worth of things had happened in the days I spent with her, and yet she was the only thing that I really gave a fuck about. Perhaps I'm obsessed, perhaps I'm crazy, but fuck if I don't give a huge fuck about her.

These days when I'm not fantasizing about Terri or working on my novel, I'm swinging, or rather, I'm immersing myself in the culture and I'm starting to think maybe there's something to the lifestyle. After all, divorce befalls about half of all marriages—I'm right in the thick of divorce myself. But, then again, our marriage was (is?) open, sort of. I guess there's no solution if the couple kind of despises each other.

I've arranged to interview eight bonafide swinging couples in the Deerfield orgy-house I've rented for the week. I will be staying in the house, though not orgy'ing, unless something truly unforeseen occurs.

I plan to host the interviews in a small den just off the foyer. I'll set up a video camera and stream the footage to a larger family room in the house, where my clients will watch in real time. It's a unique setup, but I think it'll work for a project of this nature.

After interviewing the couples over two days, I'll host the party—a true swinging fuckfest—on the third night, which happens to be New Year's Eve. Thank goodness for Gail. I never would have been able to arrange this without her. She wanted to come along, but she and her husband are double-booked; apparently, they're also ringing in the new year with a bang!

Yesterday, attorney extraordinaire Rothstein received the fully executed severance agreement from Omnivore. They agreed to hold off until the second of January to disburse my payout. He also set up a meeting for today between the two of us, my wife, and her attorney. The objective is to get this shit done—I don't want it on my mind when I'm in Deerfield. Stanley insisted the meeting be held on neutral territory so, in ten minutes, I'm heading for the Courtyard Marriott in downtown Stamford.

The hotel only has valet parking, and I pull up behind a man in a horrible toupee who's raging at the valet.

"There's absolutely no reason it should cost that much to park for a fucking hour or two."

"Look, I'm just the valet, I don't set the prices."

"And why valet parking anyway? I never like handing my keys to someone I don't know."

"I assure you I'm trustworthy, sir, but again, I don't make the rules. If you prefer, you can park at a garage. There's one a block away."

"And walk? It's 20 degrees outside! This is absolute piss."

But the poorly toupee'ed man finally capitulates. I make a mental note to give Blaze's agent a bad toupee and a raging disdain for valet parking. And then the guy turns around, and I see it's Jim Peters, my soon-to-be-ex-wife's lawyer.

After the lawyer's car is taken into the garage, Eddie and I pull up. We shift into neutral and raise the parking brake as a valet comes over.

"How long will you be here for, sir?"

"I'm not sure, but at least two hours. Do you know how to drive stick?"

The valet's eyes light up. "Is that a five-speed?"

He's a little too excited and I recall the iconic scene from *Ferris Bueller's Day Off* when the parking attendants take Cameron's father's Ferrari for a joy ride—but I have a feeling I'm the only one capable of joyriding Eddie.

"Yep," I say.

"Fucking A!" He hands me the ticket and takes Eddie downstairs. I don't hear any tires screeching, so I'm feeling okay.

I walk into the hotel lobby and find Stanley waiting for me.

"They're here," he says. "Peters walked in red-faced. I assume he was arguing with the valet." Rothstein is the fucking man. And his hair is real. "Ready to get this done?"

"Now or never."

We walk to the conference room where Laura and Peters appear ready for battle. He still looks furious, and Laura looks as if she's going on a job interview, not that she's been on one in over ten years. We shake hands and Peters tries to take immediate control of the session.

"Let's get right down to business," he says. "Here's what my client wants. Half of all liquid assets; half of the home, which is to be put up for sale immediately; health insurance; her car; half the couple's investments, including the vested balance of Mr. Carson's 401K."

This is exactly what I'm prepared to offer, except for health insurance. Legally, I couldn't put her on a policy if we're divorced. Jimmy the Rug should know this.

Rothstein begins to ask a question, but Peters dives back in with a whammy.

"That's not all. We also want alimony of one hundred

thousand a year for ten years, the length of the Carsons' marriage."

"I wouldn't consider the last nine years a marriage," I argue. "Given that she's been fucking women the entire time."

Laura rolls her eyes.

"Control your client," Peters warns Stanley.

Stanley touches my arm, and I'm instantly relaxed. Seriously, he's something else, something magical.

"Where do you think this alimony will come from?" he says. "My client was just let go from his job. He may be unemployed for a while."

"Not my client's problem."

"I beg to differ," Stanley says.

"Explain."

"You see, my client has enough evidence to prove that this marriage is actually not valid. Mrs. Carson admitted early in their marriage that she's a lesbian and the two have not been a traditional couple since. Further, she suffers no ailments that prevent her from working. Given that, should this go to litigation, you will lose."

A four-way staring match ensues—Stanley versus Peters and me versus Laura. Both Stanley and I emerge victorious. Things are looking good.

"I am requesting a break to confer with my client," Peters says.

Stanley and I respond with controlled, confident nods and leave the room to confer in private.

"I really want to reach an agreement today," I say.

"I understand, Kelly, but if you concede too quickly, they may get suspicious. So far, they haven't brought up a claim on future income, aside from the alimony."

"Trust me, I'm not ready to wave the white flag. That alimony would be a million dollars over 10 years."

"Yeah, but based on what your new business could do and your earnings potential from the novel, a percentage of future earnings could be a lot more."

I know Laura and I know she thinks if this gets wrapped quicker, she'll get a bigger haul. We can get this done today.

"Go back and offer the entire house," I say. "She can keep everything left over from the sale. Let's see if that appeases her."

"House time, huh?"

"House time."

"Okay," Stanley says, and we head back in.

"I've talked it over with my client and…"

But I cut Peters off and launch, looking directly at Laura.

"You went through with our wedding, knowing you weren't in love with me, never had been, and never would be. You used me for over ten years and you expect me to fund the next ten years of your life…"

"Control your client, Rothstein."

I ignore the opposing counsel's warning and keep going.

"I stayed in this marriage against the advice of everyone I know. For some reason, I still had feelings for you. I did my best for you, by you. And this is how you treat me."

"Rothstein!" Peters slams his hands on the table.

Laura takes the bait. "You should have known I wasn't into you when I stopped fucking you before we were married."

"You told me that was because you needed a commitment from me."

"And what did I do after you put that engagement ring on my finger? Did I suddenly open my legs and let you in? I didn't even fuck you on our wedding night. I waited until two days later to consummate our marriage and thought about a woman I'd met at the pool the entire time."

Peters spikes his pen, clearly upset by his client's admission.

"And that is why I want to end this once and for all. You can have everything you asked for, minus alimony. After I give you half of everything I've earned, you won't get anything else from me. Ever. As a point of concession, I am willing to leave you with 100% of the house. Sell it and keep everything."

"I'd like a moment with my client," Peters says.

"I'll take it!" Laura interrupts.

Peters exhales loudly. "Laura, I advise you to not…"

"Shut up, James—you get paid either way."

"I'll draw up the papers this afternoon," Stanley pipes up, "and send them to James for review. If they look good to you, James, have your client sign, and I'll have Mr. Carson do the same."

"Fine," Peters says.

I get up to leave, as does Laura, although she surprises me by walking to my side of the table and offering a hug. As we embrace she whispers in my ear, "Guys like you will always finish last because you're too nice."

A wide smile spreads across my face, but she can't see it —my head is buried in her shoulder. "It will all work out in the end," I say.

Rothstein and I leave the room, and as soon as the door shuts, we hear hooting and high-fiving. We exchange a glance and a smirk.

"Shall we high-five, Stanley?"
"No," he says, "let's wait till we get outside."

CHAPTER TWENTY-NINE

El Capitan

Cesar and I pull up to the curb at LaGuardia, and I know we're in for a tender moment—after all, it's the holiday season.

"Good cuca in Chicago, mi amigo," he says.

See, there it is.

"Merry Christmas to you, too, Cesar."

He gets out to hug me as I leave. I sort of hug him back.

The terminal is packed with families looking to get to Chicago early so they can spend the entire afternoon with family. As I look around, I experience a twinge of sadness that, at 42, I have no family of my own. I'm beginning to think I'll never know what it's like to raise kids and live vicariously through them, to burden them with one's own disappointments. As I ponder, I see a toddler walk onto the luggage carousel and fall down as it starts moving; if it weren't for the quick reflexes of the child's father, junior would have taken the trip of a lifetime into the inner workings of airport baggage.

This being a small terminal, there's no special treatment line for those of us with status, but the security line is moving quickly and thanks to my recent Chicago detour, I'm once again selected for extra screening and enjoy a particularly rigorous pat down, which some may regard as special treatment, by an agent named Fred, who, judging by the way his hand goes over my ass, once dreamt of becoming a proctologist.

Amazingly for LaGuardia, my flight leaves as advertised and I land around 10 a.m. Central. I navigate my way to the rental car shuttle and take some time to thumb through emails. There's one from Stanley letting me know he received the fully executed agreement from Peters and that he'd be filing it later that day. There's also an email from Pam asking where I am with the revisions—I write her back, assuring her she'll have something in the next seven days. I'm pretty confident I can keep that promise.

A few minutes later, I'm Hertz'ed up and on my way to Deerfield, Swinging Capital of Middle America and hopefully, current/ temporary residence of troubled actress/Kelly Carson soulmate Terri Flynn. I contemplate plugging in the address I tracked down for Sergeant Major Terri's Father into my GPS but decide to stop to eat first. As I pull into the parking lot of a Toby Keith's I Love This Bar and Grille, my phone starts ringing. It's Gail Dexter.

"Gail, you calling to tell me you changed your mind about Chicago?"

"No, baby, still can't make it to your New Year's Eve swingfest, but I got some great news for you."

"I'm intrigued. What's up?"

"The biggest player in the suburban Chicago swinging scene heard about your party and wants to come, in more ways than one."

"Are you shitting me?"

"I shit you not. This guy has been living the lifestyle ever since he got divorced, which was a long time ago. There's just one catch, though."

"He wants a higher incentive?"

We're paying each of the couples a cash incentive of $200, though I get the sense that most would do it for free.

"No, he's a very private person and only goes to such things in a disguise. A real pillar of the community type. Rumor has it he works for the government. Anyway, no one knows his real name, but everyone calls him El Capitan."

She says the name in a very thick Spanish accent and I immediately picture George Hamilton from *Zorro the Gay Blade*. I can't help but quote from the movie: "Have you ever heard of the ships in the field, the little bah bah bahs?"

"What are you talking about?"

My sister and I watched that movie at least a hundred times when we were younger—she would have caught that reference in a heartbeat, same for Terri, but I can't hold it against Gail for having no clue what I'm talking about.

"Never mind, I just had a momentary lapse of reason."

"You are an interesting man, Kelly Carson. Can we hope for any other lapses given your new relationship status?"

The truth is, I have no idea how I am going to behave once the party's in full swing (pun intended). I'm guessing it depends on where things stand with Terri; I haven't even fantasized about another woman since we parted ways, the last time I was in Chicago. This also begs the question of what my client intends to do, as she'll be playing the part of co-host.

"Gail, I kinda doubt it."

"I know you might feel nervous, but remember, you'll be with the most nonjudgmental people you'll ever find. My advice: Be safe, be open-minded, and have some fun."

"I appreciate your calling. But tell me this, how will I know El Capitan when I see him?"

"Don't worry, I guarantee he'll be hard to miss."

CHAPTER THIRTY

Nose Job

After finishing a red Solo Cup full of *Beer for My Horses* IPA, I leave the restaurant and decide to do a Sergeant Fucker Flynn flyby. I remember Terri telling me he still works part time, so my fingers are crossed that this is part of that time. If she's home alone, we'll have the opportunity to chat one on one without his running interference. But my hopes are dashed when I see a vintage Oldsmobile Cutlass Ciera parked in his driveway —based on what she's told me and my brief encounter with him, the car suits him well—old and conservative.

I park across the street. His house is a center-hall colonial with white shingles, dark blue shutters, and a red door. Nothing screams proud American like a house that's literally painted red, white, and blue. To boot, there's a flagpole in the lawn flying Old Glory and the blue and yellow flag of the US Navy. Pretty sure I've found the right place.

From my vantage, I have a clear view of the upstairs windows and see a figure open the shades to the set just above the front door; based on my limited knowledge of architecture, I know it's rare for a master bedroom to be located in the center of the second level, and I estimate it's a child's room or a guest room. As the shades rise, I'm praying it's not Sergeant Major Shit Ass, and then there she is, a beautiful woman with beautiful red hair—Terri Flynn.

I want to shout. I almost honk the horn, but that's a pretty unrefined way of announcing one's presence. No, the right thing to do is to go up to the front door and knock on it like a man, a man who doesn't give a fuck—well, about anything other than Terri Flynn—well, Terri Flynn and his novel.

As I walk up the driveway, my heart begins to pound as if I'm running a marathon, but I don't let the imminent blackout deter me. At the bright red door, I extend my right hand to knock, but before my knuckles hit wood, the door opens. I'm expecting to see Terri, but instead, I'm greeted by the barrel of a hunting rifle. If Pete Jackson had this at his disposal, he'd have blown his entire foot off.

"You have approximately sixty seconds to leave my property, son, and if you have not hightailed it out of here by then, you are leaving here in a bag."

"Terri!" I shout.

"Fifty-nine, fifty-eight, fifty-seven..." Sergeant Asshole Piece of Fuck starts counting backwards.

"Clark?" I hear a voice call from upstairs.

"Just a college kid looking to sell magazines," he yells upstairs then continues his countdown. "Forty-two, forty-one, forty..."

"Terri, I love you!" I cry out and then become intimately familiar with the butt of his rifle.

"What the fuck?" I shout, clutching my nose. I feel blood gushing down my palm. He continues the countdown to my death.

"Twenty-five, twenty-four, twenty-three…"

I decide two things in that instant: one, he is not joking whatsoever about shooting me and two, I am not nearly man enough to take him. So I do the only thing I can: I turn and scurry to my car. I look back to see Sergeant Cock standing on the porch, his rifle at ease (or something), pointing straight up but directly toward Terri's bedroom. My eyes shoot up and I see her standing in front of the window with her arms folded. I shout out, "I'm staying on Mt. Pleasant Street," before heading into my car and leaving the neighborhood.

Apparently, I've underestimated the lengths Terri's father will go to prevent his daughter from chatting with me.

#

I plug the address to the house I'm renting into my car's GPS and stop at a convenience store just short of my destination to pick up some necessities for my (likely broken) nose. I'm met by an overly talkative employee named Piper who greets me with the following, "Do you know your nose is bleeding?"

I flash Piper my best no-shit-Sherlock expression.

"There's an urgent care center just one block away if you want to get that looked at. What happened?"

"An A-list actor's father just clocked me in the face with the butt of his rifle."

"What?" Poor Piper looks so puzzled—I just want her to feel okay.

"Sorry, bad joke. I walked into a door earlier. Thought

it was one of those automatic *Star Trek* jobs."

"Oh, my dad loved that show. First-aid stuff is down aisle five."

I return with gauze and some Band-Aids.

"You from out of town?"

"Why do you ask?"

"You have an accent."

I've never thought of people from Connecticut as having an accent, but I bet people from Chicago don't think they have one either.

"Yep."

"Visiting family for the holidays?"

Actually, I have no family to speak of and will be spending most of my time here interviewing people into partner swapping and group sex. I decide it's against my better judgment to admit this—I've already put Piper through a lot—so I just say, "Something like that."

"Oh, it looks like it will be a white Christmas after all," Piper says, looking like a gleeful child who's just spotted a mound of presents under the tree.

I gather my things, thank Piper for her service, and head to my car and home for the next week where I want nothing more than to clean my nose, rest my feet, and spend some time digesting the *Made in America* Cheeseburger I had for lunch back at Toby Keith's.

CHAPTER THIRTY-ONE

It Came Upon a Midnight Clear

After settling into the house and cleaning myself up, I decide to lie down and take a nap. I'm astonished when I wake up at 9:30 p.m. having slept most of the day away. I'm hungry and have to venture out for food since I didn't think ahead to stock the fridge. It's Christmas Eve, almost everything in town is closed, but according to Google there's a nearby mall catering to last-minute shoppers, and there, I'll find a perfectly open American Steakhouse.

The restaurant bar is actually busier than I imagined. I quickly learn why, and it's not simply because it's the only open restaurant in town.

"Are you with the orphans?" the hostess asks.

"The who?"

"The orphans. It's a group of family-less people who come here to party every Christmas Eve."

"Well I fit the criteria, but I'm not with them."

"Would you like to sit at the bar?"

I glance at the crowded bar and decide to take a seat at a two-top in the dining room. I order a vodka and soda with a splash of cranberry and immediately start thinking of Terri—I was with her the last time I had one of those.

I look through the menu and decide on filet mignon. It's a steakhouse after all—when in a Roman steakhouse… I slam the drink quickly and order a second one, and then a third. By the time my steak arrives, my face is numbish and my enunciation loses some crispness.

Patrick, my waiter, comes by to check on me and asks if I parked my car in the lot.

"Why, is it being towed?"

"No, just a clever way for me to confirm that you drove here."

After ordering crème brûlée for dessert and paying my bill, the waiter comes back to ask if he can order me a cab. What a prince. And he's right. I know better than to drive with this much liquor flowing in my system. I tell him I'll Uber but hold off on making the request.

There are almost three inches of snow on the ground now and the world looks as pure as it ever has—immaculate, even outside the American Steakhouse.

I hear church bells in the distance—houses of worship preparing for midnight services. My phone tells me it's 11:30, and since I'm intoxicated and have no place to go except a big empty house, I let my curiosity guide me toward the bells.

When I get to the steps of the church, I realize the walk from the restaurant has not done much for my level of inebriation. If anything, I feel a little more buzzed. I'm trying to read the name of the church, but the letters are all blurry. I can make out a priest in colorful robes atop the stairs greeting Christian swingers as they pass, and likely because I can't walk a straight line, he calls down to me.

"You there, are you okay?"

"Physically or spiritually, Father?"

"Either!" he says with a laugh. "You should get out of the cold and come inside. You've got ten minutes before Mass begins."

"I'm not sure you want me in your church, Father. Do you have insurance against lightning strikes?"

"Ha! This is a hospital for sinners, not a museum for saints."

I've never met a jovial priest before and am into it. I follow my curiosity up the stairs, hopefully not struggling too discernibly.

"Let me guess, you are all alone on Christmas Eve and found yourself having dinner and a few drinks down the street."

"How did you know that?"

"Because twenty people referring to themselves as 'orphans' just walked in. I figured you were one of them."

"I'm just a guy who came to Deerfield to express his love for a woman whose phone number he doesn't have."

Again, because I'm a good person, I omit the part about the fuckfest I'm hosting in a week.

"Well, I hope you find her," the priest says. "What's your name, son?"

"Kelly. Kelly Carson."

"A nice Irish name."

And he's such a nice guy, he doesn't make a crack about my name.

"What's yours, Father?"

"Daniel Joseph, but everyone calls me Fr. Danny."

"Well Fr. Danny, I'm about to step into a church

voluntarily for the first time in over twenty years, but first I need to relieve myself of the vodka I borrowed over the past hour."

"Enter the church and go down the stairs. The men's room's on the right."

I head into the church cautiously—when I see no signs of abnormal electrical activity overhead or rumbling below, I breathe easier and head downstairs. After a prolonged bladder evacuation, I head back upstairs and find a seat in the back, near a confessional. I notice a red light above its door and assume someone is in there spilling their beans, probably regrets about this or that fuckfest. I'm caught off guard when the door opens and Terri emerges—oh man, I hope she wasn't talking about swinging.

Our eyes meet, but the moment is interrupted by the booming voice that commands, "All rise." As the congregation stands, I lose sight of Terri and the organ's loud opening riff (is that what you call it in church?) to "Oh Come All Ye Faithful" knocks me off balance. Damn vodka.

After the opening prayer, the congregation sits yet I remain standing for a few beats, hunting for Terri. No dice, Chicago.

After the first reading, the psalm, and the second reading, it's time for the Gospel and Fr. Danny tells us how Christ came into the world, not as king or conqueror, but as a humble child. He then preaches one of the most touching homilies I've ever paid attention to.

"Merry Christmas, everybody. Today is the day we have been waiting for since the beginning of Advent, but your children have been waiting for since, well, last Christmas."

The congregation laughs, and Fr. Danny continues.

"Why is this day so important?"

He lets the question hang in the air so long I'm tempted to shout out an answer just so he might get on with it.

"Because it's the day we remember that our Father in Heaven loves us so much that he sent us his only Son to teach us and carry the cross of our sins."

Fr. Danny leaves the ambo and moves down the center aisle of the church.

"Did you think I was done? You are not going to get off that easy on Christmas Eve. Ohh, by the smells I'm smelling, I'm guessing we have a few Eye-tal-yans with us. How many of you enjoyed the feast of the seven fishes tonight?"

I see a number of hands in front of me go up, and this underscores my decision to sit in the back.

"That's a wonderful tradition. My German family could never pull it off. We stuck with the classics like red cabbage and potato dumplings, apple and sausage stuffing, and a roast. My great-grandparents were fond of rabbit, but chose to serve that on Easter instead."

This guy has a sick sense of humor. I like it.

"So Christ is born, yea!" He says "yea" like Jim Gaffigan's inner voice.

"And in a few months, we will mourn his death on the cross, boo."

This time, Fr. Danny channels Dana Carvey imitating President Bush—the first president Bush, not the second. His humor has the congregation's attention. They are totally with him.

"But why do we care about all of this? Why do we care about events that happened not hundreds, but thousands of years ago? What difference will it do in today's modern world?"

Again, he lets the question hang out there.

"Because He asked us to. The night of the last supper, Jesus asked his followers to repeat His actions of breaking bread and drinking wine in order to remember not only the events leading up to his death, but to remember His teachings of love, compassion, and forgiveness. Our culture is so self-centered that we don't give a care about much beyond what impacts us directly."

The word processor in my head is doing a find and replace with the word "care"—I'm changing it to "fuck."

"But we are here tonight, celebrating the birth of a man whose teachings of love, compassion, and forgiveness were considered revolutionary by His contemporaries—so revolutionary that he was put to death. But we are here, and we remember. Now the question is, what do we do about it?"

Fr. Danny pulls up his robe sleeve and looks at his watch.

"It is now thirty minutes into December 25th and I am guessing Santa has delivered all his presents and put them under the tree. But there are a few gifts I want you to give to yourself and to others on this Christmas Day. I want you to offer the gift of compassion to those who need it, forgiveness to those who ask for it, and love to those who seek it."

Fr. Danny then mimics the voice of the movie trailer voiceover guy.

"In a world where people are taught not to give a care about anything other than themselves, one congregation breaks convention and starts…to…care!"

Fr. Danny smiles and reverts to his normal voice.

"Merry Christmas everybody."

I'm either so touched by his words, or maybe it's the vodka, but I start to cry there in that pew in the back of whatever church this is in Deerfield, Illinois. It starts as a whimper but builds to a full-blown bawl once the congregation stands to recite the profession of faith, which I try to recite from memory, only to find they changed the words on me!

As the congregation sits back down, I catch a glimpse of Terri—she's staring at me, no doubt filled with questions about my puffy eyes and the tears running down my cheeks.

Something certainly happened in Hawaii that impacted my life, perhaps changed its course—my father would claim I finally grew a pair. Now, sitting in this church, I feel as if I'm changing once again.

Then I don't know what in the (I'm not cussing because I'm in a church) is happening. I'm taken out of this meditation of sorts as everyone stands again and then kneels and then stands once again and then kneels. Am I in a church or an exercise class? Ecclesiastical calisthenics? How would Richard Simmons look in clerical robes?

Next thing I know, I'm in line for Communion and saying "amen" when offered the Body of Christ. As I walk up the side aisle back to my pew, I catch Terri's eye as she kneels. I do the same and take a few deep breaths as I feel the tears start to bubble up again.

Next thing I know, I'm standing and Fr. Danny proclaims, "The Mass is ended—go in peace to love and serve the Lord and one another."

"Thanks be to God," the congregation says in unison.

The cantor then announces the closing hymn is "Joy to the World" and the organ booms to life once again. I watch as the altar servers, Eucharistic Ministers, lector, and Fr. Danny recess up the aisle and out through the back of the church. There is a long line of congregants following them, but I decide to swim against the tide and hunt for Terri. As I pass a group of Italian women I experience first-hand what Fr. Danny referred to in his homily as the scent of fried fish hits my nose.

I get a bunch of dirty looks from parishioners trying to get out and am about to duck into a pew for cover when I catch Terri out of the corner of my eye. She sees me, and I yell, "Meet me in the confessional." She gives me the thumbs up sign to let me know she heard me. I can't imagine what the other worshipers think as they flock towards the exit.

Terri enters one door and I enter another and remove the divider that separates priest and penitent.

"Your nose looks like shit," she says in place of "Bless me father for I have sinned."

"You can thank your handler for that."

"He's just looking out for me. We've come to an understanding of sorts."

"Where is he?"

"Dad? Ha! My mom was the Catholic, Captain Flynn thinks Catholics are too liberal. He's spending the evening with Baptists."

"Hardcore?"

"He's core to the core," Terri says while giving me a salute.

"I thought he was in the Navy."

"All the same to me. Where's your car?"

I'm embarrassed to say it, but I tell her I had too much to drink earlier and had to leave it at the restaurant.

"Vodka?"

"Bingo. You remembered my love-hate relationship with the spirit."

"Want a lift to wherever you are staying?"

"Yes, but before that I just want to tell you how sorry I am for the way I acted in the hospital. I was insensitive and not thankful for all that you did for me. So, I'm sorry."

It's her turn now to apologize.

"I was overwhelmed that day. We'd been up for a while and the flight from LA became a bit stressful. I should have warned you about the gummies."

"You are forgiven," I say and make the sign of the cross over her the way Fr. Danny did over the congregation as he closed Mass.

"Still friends?" she asks.

"Still friends," I confirm.

"Did you shout that you loved me back at my dad's place?"

"Before he took out my schnoz? Maybe."

"You are in a confessional, Kelly Carson, tell the truth."

"Then yes."

"Let's get out of here."

We exit the church and see that the snow has started falling harder and both our heads are immediately covered in white.

"About that ride?"

"Of course, Kelly."

She doesn't call me Clark. Perhaps she's changed as well.

We walk to her car, which I'm guessing is a rental,

seeing as it's a Japanese import and there's no way Sergeant American Soldier owns one of those. My house isn't that far away, but it's enough time to start catching up.

"So give me the scoop, what's happened over the past few weeks?" she asks.

"Well, let's see, I negotiated a 52-week severance package from my idiot boss, my wife asked for a divorce and we've already filed papers, and I officially have an agent."

"Wow, that's a lot of incredible developments. So you're a free man?"

"On the market and open for business." But she's the only person I want to be with.

A few minutes later, we're parked outside my house.

"Got any booze?" she asks.

"No booze, but I've got a Keurig. Care for a cup?"

"That actually sounds lovely."

I brew a cup of coffee for her, then one for me. We sit down on the couch in the den and catch up.

"Your turn," I say, sipping from my cup. "Tell me everything."

"Let's see, my career is pretty much over, my agent dropped me, and the studio wants to sue me. I'll probably never work on big screen features again."

Instead of looking sad, she actually laughs.

"What's so funny?"

"What's funny is that I really, really, really hated Hollywood. It pushed me to become someone I wasn't. I started not giving a fuck about anything, and while I thought that was liberating, it was actually quite isolating."

"So does that mean you're done with acting?"

"Oh God, no. I have no other marketable skills. I'm just not going to act in films that ask me to play by bullshit rules. I'm going to take a drastic pay cut and only do independents. I've heard the more independent studios run by streaming services are much more humane to work for. I've been hustling for scripts to read; that'll be easier when I land another agent."

"I'm surprised you can get any scripts without an agent."

"Today's entertainment business is like the Wild West, and there's gold in them thar hills."

She hasn't lost her sense of humor.

"So did you come to Deerfield just to stalk me?"

"Actually, you're only part of the reason I'm here." I then go on to explain what I'll be doing here the week between Christmas and New Year's.

"Swingers, huh…in Deerfield? You are barking up the wrong tree."

"I don't think so. From what I've heard, this place is the Swingtown of the Midwest. Wanna see for yourself? Come watch the ball drop on New Year's Eve, if you know what I mean."

"Well, I don't have anything going on that night—surprisingly, I know—so put me down as a maybe."

"Give me your number and I'll text you the specifics."

I tap her number into my phone and send her a text message to make sure I got the number right. A buzzing from her purse confirms I'm good.

"Not hanging out with Sergeant Major Corporal Flynn on New Year's? I figured he's a big partier."

"Actually, he's going to some party with his girlfriend. They didn't invite me, though. But…are you going to play,

I guess is the term, at your swingers gala?"

I leaned in closer to her. "There's only one woman in Deerfield I want to play with."

She embraces me and we kiss like teen lovers who have a house to themselves for the first time, and what happens next is maybe the most beautiful thing I've ever experienced.

Terri slows the pace of our kissing and looks at me in the eyes. And there, that instant, her wet lips parted slightly, her eyes meeting mine, reaching in to gently stroke my soul—that's maybe the most beautiful moment I've known.

"Let's take this slow," she says.

I remember Terri Flynn's Sex Advice from Maui. I feel my heart rate instantly slow. I feel so wonderfully calm. We lie down on the couch and keep our clothes on, her red hair spilling over her white blouse. As irresistible as she looks, I don't want to ruin anything bubbling between us by taking things too fast, too soon so we just spoon. Apparently, caffeine doesn't impact her the way it does me, as she's sleeping shortly after her head hits a pillow. I'm up for a while, soaking up the moment, but finally succumb to sleep around three.

I wake up around eight the following morning, only to find that Terri's gone. Thankfully, though, I now have her number and can at least get in touch without going through Major Dad and his arsenal.

CHAPTER THIRTY-TWO

Merry Christmas To Me

I go for a run in the cold Deerfield air to sweat out the alcohol remaining in my system. While I didn't go to bed drunk, vodka always makes me dizzy the following morning. The only cure is sweating out the remnants, and who knows, maybe a new Christmas tradition is born: sweating out vodka on the swinging streets of Deerfield.

As I run, I have an epiphany and almost run into a mailbox. I know exactly how my novel has to end, and I've just devised a major twist between Blaze and Allison.

I run back to my room before the inspiration passes and fire up my laptop. I then rewrite the ending of *Return to Casa Grande* and continue working until the Christmas sun goes down, rereading the manuscript multiple times and making small tweaks.

I also work in a confessional scene that came to me last night at Mass and add quirky character traits to flesh out my children, which is how I've come to regard these characters.

By five, I've gone through it twice and think it's set. I

email it to Pam Hart with a "Merry Christmas" subject line and leave the body blank—the attachment speaks for itself, I hope.

A minute later, I get her reply: "I'm Jewish. Hart is short for Hartman and you have officially ruined my Christmas. I know this will do nothing to help Jewish stereotypes, but I was supposed to go out for Chinese food and see a movie with the other nonbelievers. Now I'm going to be stuck at home reading a manuscript. If you hear back from me tonight, it's good news. If not, you have some work to do."

I just realize I haven't eaten since the American Steakhouse. I'm starving, but if Pam can't have Chinese, maybe I can. I tap a quick text to Terri, seeing if she wants to grab a bite.

"Options are limited," she responds with Pam Hart quickness.

"Chinese?"

"Chinese! I'll pick you up in 20 mins."

A Chinese dinner on Christmas with troubled actress Terri Flynn—sounds perfect. I dance my way into the shower to rinse the festering vodka sweat.

#

Terri picks me up and drives us to an upscale Chinese restaurant in nearby Northbrook. It's relatively empty, aside from a few Jewish swingers; it seems safe to assume the Deerfield swinging scene spills into Northbrook. Instead of ordering an alcoholic beverage, I ask for seltzer with lime, and Terri gets the same.

"Did you get in trouble for coming home this morning?" I ask.

"Turns out, I beat my dad and Joan home."

"Joan?"

"His lady friend."

"How long have your parents been divorced?"

"Almost twenty years. Mom and I stayed in Southern California and he moved here. I used to pester my mom for details about the final straw. She'd always avoid it and just say we were better off without him. I couldn't help but agree with that fact, considering how much of a dick he was."

"And now?"

"Now I see an old man who only wants the best for his daughter, to protect her from the cruel, cruel world."

"What changed?"

"I don't know, maybe I matured. He's still not the loving father every little girl wants, but he's tried hard these last two weeks to get me back on my feet. He's changed, too, though, in some pretty unexpected ways."

"Don't tell me he's mellowed," I say, rubbing the bruise on the bridge of my nose.

"Well, he's still a prick, but it seems like he's living a little more. Back in California, he would be in bed religiously by 10, but since I've been here, he and Joan go out all the time and most nights, they don't even come home until early morning. Maybe he's having his midlife crisis in old age."

I laugh and she does the same, but for longer.

"What's so funny?"

"There's more. This is going to sound nuts, but I think he and Joan are into playing dress up."

"Run that by me again?"

"One morning I got up early for a run, and he and Joan were just getting home. I swear to God on the holy Bible it looked as if he was wearing makeup. He darted to their bedroom before I could question him about it and I went for an extra-long run in the cold December air to rip the image from my mind."

"People are getting freaky in Deerfield. But you know what, good for him if he found something he's into," I say. "My parents have been married forty-five years and barely look at each other anymore. Maybe I should have bought my dad some Mary Kay for Christmas."

Terri laughs. I'd be more than happy spending the rest of the night talking about Sergeant Major's makeup fetish, but I know Terri doesn't like to spend a lot of time on personal stuff, and I don't want to push her.

"So what's next, Kelly Carson?" she says.

See what I mean?

"Well, after I wrap up work next week, I don't plan on going back to Connecticut to stay. I've been thinking about going to Scottsdale for a while."

"What's in Scottsdale?"

"I've always liked the desert, and I could use a little break from the ordinary. I'll have a year of severance coming my way and money from this current gig, so I'm thinking about moving out there. I can run my business from anywhere, so why not someplace warm?"

"Want company?"

"Seriously?"

"I can't stay here forever, but I don't wanna go back to LA either."

"Do you mind a detour to Stamford so we can pick up Eddie?"

"Dog?"

"GTI."

"Five-speed?"

"Yep."

"Sweet."

The waiter comes with our appetizers and we dig in. I'm ravenous and pushing to eat as much as I can before Food Thief Flynn's latest heist, but I'm interrupted when my phone starts buzzing. Please be Pam Hart. And it is.

"Do you mind if I get this? It's my agent."

"How Hollywood, go ahead."

"Hi Pam…"

"Kelly, bubby, I'm halfway through and this is ten times better than it was before. I'm laughing on every page—it's a satire on both Hollywood and the business world. People are going to love it. Listen, my little goy, I'm going to send this to your new editor tonight—she's also eating Chinese, if you know what I mean. You may hear from her in the next few days. All good things. Mazel."

And then she just hangs up, as though she was leaving a voicemail. I'd be offended if she hadn't just given me the finest ego stroke of my life.

"Annnnd?"

"She loves the latest version of *Return to Casa Grande*."

I'm not happy—I'm stunned.

I share the big changes I made and the huge twist I devised at the end.

"That's fucking brilliant."

"I thought so too."

"Watch out, Kelly Carson—you're going to become a big star one day and I'll be able to say I knew you when."

It's just one good thing after another—until Terri's mouth falls open, dropping a lump of dumpling and an "oh shit."

I look around to see what's the matter and find a red-faced patriot charging toward us.

"Merry Christmas, Captain…"

"Shut the hell up, son," he says, aiming a finger at me, then redirecting it toward Terri.

"You, come with me now."

He's practically rumbling with anger and causing a scene—all the diners in the place are staring squarely at our table.

"She's 42 years old," I say. "Can't she make up her mind about who she wants to have dinner with?"

The other fingers on his right hand extend to meet his pointer, and then he slaps me in the face; I actually would have preferred a punch, as it would seem a more manly thing to experience in front of the woman I love.

"Dad!" Terri shouts.

"Five, four, three…" He starts counting down, letting her know how much time she has before he presumably picks her up and carries her from the restaurant. By now, I know his countdowns are no joke. She complies before detonation.

"And don't try calling her," Captain Foundation says. "I'm confiscating her phone and her car keys."

I've just witnessed something out of a John Hughes movie, except it happened to a 42-year-old woman, not a 16-year-old Molly Ringwald.

CHAPTER THIRTY-THREE
Pasta LaVista Baby

Two days go by and I don't hear a thing from Terri. I've texted her a couple times, but no response—I guess her dad held true to that promise. Of course, I could swing by the house, but I'm wary of more gunplay. Pam's editor has been feeding me developmental suggestions bit by bit, and since I have nothing else to do, I've been addressing them as they come in. After the developmental phase, she's going to line edit, or so she tells me.

A knock at the door takes me out of my revisions, and I open it to see a diminutive older woman wearing nothing but curlers and a bathrobe standing on my doorstep—she's got to be freezing her saggy tits off.

"Are you on the lease for the Willette house?"

"Yes, I'm hosting the fuckfest. You're early."

No, I don't say that. I introduce myself and tell her I've been here for a few days now and ask her name.

"I'm Jeanette Wainwright and just got back from spending Christmas with my kids in Indiana. I've lived in this neighborhood for over sixty years, and sir, I'm the president of our neighborhood watch. You aren't one of those meth heads, are you?"

A little laugh leaps from me.

"No meth here."

"Okay, because Bobby Williamson was one of those meth heads and he blew up his mother's house not but two streets over from this one, don't ya know?"

She peeks into the house and eyes the mound of video equipment I've yet to find a home for.

"What's all that you got here?"

I can't just come out and tell Jeanette I'll be using the Willette house to interview swingers and host a group sex party, so I think on my feet.

"My cousin is getting married and my aunt asked if I could film the wedding. We're having the reception here on New Year's Eve."

"Well, I'm sure you cleared having a party with the Willettes, but don't be surprised if Harold and I stop by to make sure you don't get out of hand."

I can only imagine the look on this woman's face when she walks into a full-on swingers party. I'm guessing she might have a heart attack and good old Harold might suffer from an erection lasting longer than four hours the whole time he tends to her.

"Strict invite only," I say. "Believe me, I won't do anything that threatens my security deposit."

"Okay," she says, turning to go, "just keep the noise level to a minimum."

I'm pretty sure I just successfully navigated my first orgy-house obstacle. I figure there's no time like the present to start setting up the video camera in the den off the foyer where I intend to film my interviews. The only downside is a bay window—anyone looking in will see a camera pointed at the couch. As such, I make a mental note to close the fucking shutters, all the shutters—Jeanette will be watching.

Camera ready, I run a cable to the upstairs sitting room where my clients will observe each interview in real time. I tape down the wire and hook it up to the flatscreen hanging on the wall. I turn on the TV, select the appropriate input, and there we are, a beautiful live-feed of the empty couch.

I take a quick shower and then check my phone again—still nothing from Terri. My overactive imagination has her locked in the basement alongside Dr. Dre and a gimp chained to a trunk.

Eminem and *Pulp Fiction* references aside, I realize there's not much I can do for Terri at this point; she has to put her foot down and get out from under his watch.

With no emails from my agent, editor, or client, I decide to take the rest of the evening off and grab a beer with a friend from college who moved to Chicago a few years back. I grab an Uber, but on the way out, I notice I've forgotten to close the shutters, but what's the worst that can happen? The sun's down and this doesn't seem like the kind of neighborhood with a lot of breaking and entering, especially with Jeanette on the lookout. But that could be the problem—Jeanette's on the lookout.

#

Andy Wind and I were in the same fraternity, and to this day, I consider him one of my closest friends. After twenty years as an auditor, Andy decided he was through crunching numbers all day and opened a restaurant in Chicago's trendy West Loop neighborhood. He had a vision, a calling—a fusion of Mexican and Italian cuisines called Pasta LaVista, a name inspired by his favorite movie, *The Terminator*.

I walk in shortly after eight—the dining room's abuzz and packed, but I find him beside a saved seat at the bar.

"Well, well, well, if it isn't Carson himself."

"In the flesh," I reply.

"Beer?" Andy asks.

"Yes please. I need to carbo load, big day tomorrow."

"What are you researching now? Toothpaste? Credit cards? Mobile phones?"

"Swingers," I say after a pull on my Corona.

"I really want that to be true."

He narrows his eyes at me. I narrow mine back.

"It is. Swingers."

"Well, fuck me in the ass and call me Charlie."

I'm pretty sure Terri used that same line back in the Delta Sky Club when I met her. I have no idea where it's from, but it's not easy for me to admit when I don't get a reference; I realize this is a character flaw.

I move on and explain why I'm on the swinger hunt and why it brought me here.

"Up in Deerfield?"

"Apparently, it's ground zero for the swing scene. There's a guy up there who goes by the name El Capitan who's apparently the kingpin of all swingers. And he's coming to my party."

"You gotta let me come, brother."

"No can do, unless you bring a date—that's the give and take of the scene."

"My girl wouldn't be into that," he says with a sigh. "But I bet I could find one on Backpage!"

"Sorry, no professionals either."

Andy looks at me and frowns.

"Hey, I don't make the rules."

He accepts that he can't come to my orgy and goes on to fill me in on his life and the freedom he now feels being outside of corporate America. I reward his storytelling by sharing the doozy I've been living since my airport axing.

"That shit is movie worthy," he says. "And holy fuck if Flynn's father isn't a sociopath."

"He makes Reagan look like Pelosi."

"Here's the thing," Andy says, leaning closer. "Guys that far to the right have secrets. Big secrets. I bet Papa Flynn is into some dark shit."

Hmm, maybe he is a clowner. Is that what people into clowning are called?

"Trust me, brother, you ever watch the news when a Democrat gets busted for something? Take Clinton, for example—he got head from a woman who could stand to lose a few and then checked her oil with a cigar. No big deal."

Well, in my mind the president shouldn't cigar an intern —or anyone, for that matter—but I don't want to argue the point.

"When some far-right douche gets caught, though, there's usually a male hooker and a bag of designer drugs involved. Remember that guy trying to solicit sex in an airport bathroom?"

"Oh yeah," I say. "Ol' Wide Stance. Freaky."

"That's what I'm saying." Andy takes a big swig of beer and laughs. "What else you got going on?"

I tell him about the book but don't give too much away about the plot, assuming he'll want to read it when it comes out.

"Well, here's to my buddy the author. Next round is on me!"

"All these rounds are on you."

We both laugh and Andy raises his glass.

"To El Capitan!"

"Salud to El Capitan," I say and take a big pull.

For dinner, I order a combo plate of rigatoni con carne and he gets tacos al carbonara. Neither sounds particularly appetizing, but the food was fucking great.

"You've clearly struck a nerve with this place," I say. "It probably wouldn't have tested well in one of my focus groups, but here you are, printing pesos and lire."

"You know, I spent the first half of my career in a risk averse industry—my job was to minimize financial risk! I can't tell you the number of people who told me not to pursue this thing, but here I am."

"I've got a stack of rejection letters from agents who told me my manuscript wasn't good enough to shop around until one actually took a chance on me. Maybe that's the problem with the world today."

"What's that?"

"People are playing it safe all the time. The age of risk takers has passed. Every new product I test is just a variation on a theme, and all Hollywood does is remake the same five movies over and over. Do we really need another reboot of *Spider-Man*?'

"Preach it, brother—preach it."

"Originality is dead and safety is in. You know what safety breeds?"

"What's that, brother?"

"Contempt! I lived the first 42 years of my life playing it

safe with work, with relationships and look where it got me?"

"Well, you do have a book coming out…"

"Yes, but it got me unemployed. It got me in a dead marriage and it got me…bored. I don't want to be bored anymore."

"You've got the world at your fingertips now. You're going to have some jingle in the bank, even after giving your soon-to-be-ex half. How is she, by the way?

"She's…not my problem anymore. I really don't care how she is."

"So back to what you want to do now that you're free from the bonds of marriage to a lesbo and the bindings of the corporate world. What's the plan?"

"Run away into the sunset with Terri."

"How you gonna get past the father?"

"I'll think of something."

"So for the short term?"

"All I've got so far is fly back to New York, pick up Eddie at my sister's house, pack him with the few material possessions I have, and start driving out west. As Terri says, 'there's gold in them thar hills.'"

"Eddie still lives, huh?"

Andy is a fellow fan of Iron Maiden; Eddie Lives was a popular message on Maiden tee-shirts and posters back in the day.

"He's got more than nine lives."

"To Eddie," Andy offers with a raised glass.

"To Eddie," I reply.

CHAPTER THIRTY-FOUR

Meet The Swingers

I return to the orgy-house shortly after midnight and do a quick walk through—my clients are expected to arrive around 11, and our first couple will arrive around noon. Then we have another at two, four, and six. We'll follow the same schedule the following day, and of course, this all builds up to the grand finale on New Year's Eve. With the house in order, I call it a night.

I wake up early, shower and get dressed just as the caterer arrives. I put the food away and my attention is called to the front door where I assume Natasha and her team are waiting. I open it and am surprised to find Neighborhood Watch.

"Mrs. Wainwright, what a surprise."

Instead of a bathrobe, she's wearing a house dress beneath a winter coat. The curlers are still in full force.

"Expecting company today?" she asks. "I just saw a catering van leave. I thought you said the reception was the day after tomorrow."

"We will be having friends and family coming in

throughout the day today, Jeanette—nothing to get worried about."

"I walked my dog Tucker by last night and saw what looks a camera pointing at the couch. You're not one of those porno makers, are you?"

"No porno, Jeanette. We'll be using the room for couples to record their well wishes to the bride and groom. Nope, no porno whatsoever."

"But…I'm getting an idea. Do you have any porn acting experience, Mrs. W?"

No, I didn't say that because I'm not a fucking monster.

"I'm going to keep my eye on you—the first sign of trouble and I am calling Deerfield's finest."

A car pulls up and I'm relieved to have this interruption interrupted by Natasha and her team.

"Kelly," she says. "So good to see you."

Natasha is dressed, as usual, to the nines—designer coat, tight black pants, high heels. She's with two men, creative directors from her ad agency who are dressed provocatively, like creative directors are apt to do. One is wearing a fur coat and fedora while the other is dressed in all black; he's so skinny he makes David Bowie look like John Belushi. Mister Fur Coat, AKA Steven, is an art director and Skinny Man is a copywriter named Oliver. They are tasked with taking this research and coming up with advertising ideas for the new line.

"Hey, Kelly," Steven says, sounding very gay. "Ready to par-tay?"

Oliver is much more subdued: "Hey Questions, how's it going?"

Since I met him a few years back, Oliver has called me Questions because…it's my job to ask questions.

Their appearances and these exchanges only raise Jeanette's suspicions. She seems utterly scandalized.

"G'day, Kelly, is this one of our swing-as?" Natasha says in an overdone Australian accent.

"What's this about swingers?" Jeanette says.

"You are so funny, Natasha. No, this is Jeanette—he lives directly across the street and just wanted to make sure the people renting her neighbor's house are fine, upstanding citizens."

"I'm going to keep a close eye on all of you. I don't like this one bit."

She walks back to her house, looking over her shoulder multiple times on her way.

"I'm sorry she isn't sticking around," Stephen says. "Crazy bitches love to fuck."

I show the team around inside and take them to the room where they'll be observing the interviews.

Oliver, who typically doesn't say much, which is odd, considering he's a copywriter, says, "It's kind of like *Candid Camera*, but with swingers." His dry tone, style of dress, and odd hairline are reminiscent of Steven Wright. Come to think of it, they may be related.

"Kelly, that means you're Allen Funt," Steven quips. "I hope you have some good one-liners. I need some ha-has after that flight."

"Kelly, what happens if we want to ask you a question?" Natasha asks. Unlike her compatriots, she's all business.

"I thought of that. I'll have an iPad in the room. Just send me a message if you want me to expand on anything."

Everyone follows me downstairs to the kitchen and I take the sandwiches from the fridge and fill a bucket with ice.

"This is ground zero for calories. I've got everything you'd find in a focus group facility and more. M&M's, chips, pretzels, sandwiches, beer, wine—you name it."

"Looks like you've thought of everything," Natasha says.

"It's about 45 minutes to showtime, so I'm going to go through my question guide a few times. Feel free to make yourselves at home upstairs. I'll let you know when the first couple arrives."

"*Candid Camera* was an underrated show," Oliver adds out of nowhere.

The three of them go upstairs and I take a seat next to my camera and reread my guide a few times while making notes in the margins. Next thing I know, the doorbell rings —I'm praying it's not Jeanette again.

Happily, I see a middle-aged woman with a much younger guy. She has gigantic manmade boobs, and he looks like an extra from *The Outsiders*—a greaser, not a prep.

"My name is Adam and this is Eve. We are here to be interviewed."

Swinging 101: Swingers use fake names.

I show them in and look across the street to see Jeanette on her porch, looking our direction through a pair of binoculars. This is going to be an interesting day.

I send a quick text to Natasha and the team upstairs, letting them know we're about to begin. I turn the camera on and explain that I'm recording this so I don't have to take notes while I interview them because I'd rather spend my time listening than writing. They are totally cool with it—are swingers cool with everything?—so we begin.

My questions will be about how they got involved in the

lifestyle and their practices. Eventually, I'll build to a discussion on condoms, including my client's brand and their perceptions of it. I'll also give each couple samples of the new product line and instructions on how to provide feedback after they have a chance to use them.

It turns out Adam and Eve got into the scene on a whim. Eve was married to a man closer in age and invited their new neighbors over. As you may have guessed, the new neighbors were Adam and his now ex-wife. After a few too many cocktails, the topic of wife-swapping came up and they agreed to give it a try. Afterward, Eve's husband and Adam's wife were deeply regretful, but the floodgates were opened for Adam and Eve—they wanted that all the time. Their respective marriages quickly dissolved while they paired up to explore the lifestyle together.

I hear a variation on this story with the next pair—Jack and Diane were invited into the swing club by another couple. They are older, in their late sixties, and started swinging in the 1970s. Unlike Adam and Eve, whose marriages dissolved, Jack and Diane stayed together and credit the openness of their marriage as a reason their union has remained strong for over forty years.

The next couple, Ross and Rachel, almost broke up when Ross had an indiscretion with a co-worker, but his honesty about the dalliance intrigued Rachel. She became even more intrigued when Ross shared a picture of the girl he'd slept with—instead of kicking him out, Rachel asked Ross to invite her over for a threesome. They've been hooked on the life ever since.

Billy and Allison, on the other hand, were in a traditional relationship when they happened to move into a trendy condominium complex where swinging was the norm. Every night was a swap-party; eventually, their complex earned the nickname Melrose Place.

While I show Billy and Allison out, I see a cop car parked in the Wainwrights' driveway. She's pointing at our orgy-house and giving the officers an earful. Eventually, and seemingly with some reluctance, the cops start walking in our direction with Mrs. Wainwright in tow. She's in the same house dress from this morning and the curlers are still in. I'm now convinced it's some kind of hair replacement system, and the curlers are a way of reducing suspicion—but I'm not fooled. She's not only president of the Nosey Neighbor Association, she's also a client.

"I have to take care of something outside for a minute," I yell upstairs and then walk outside.

"Good evening, officers, would you like some coffee?"

"Pay no attention to his bribes, officers," Jeanette shouts. "Do what you came here to do."

"I am sorry to have to ask you to do this, sir, but can we take a look inside?" His name tag reads Officer Wilcox. "Mrs. Wainwright over here is convinced you're up to some illegal activity."

Thankfully, Natasha didn't come in with the gigantic box of Popeye rubbers—that would be a dead giveaway that some unorthodox shit is going down.

"Come right in, but can I ask you to remove your shoes? I don't want to track any dirt inside."

The officers and Jeanette follow me in.

"Can we start in the kitchen?" Baker, the other cop, asks.

"No problem." I walk them to the kitchen and offer the

cops a sandwich and drink.

"Are these Jimmy Johns?" asks Wilcox.

"Only the best!" I reply. They both accept the sandwiches.

"Officers, I am going to make a note that you accepted a potential bribe."

"Follow me to the den where I've been interviewing people all day."

"This is what I was talking about. This is where he's filming porno!" Jeanette accuses.

"If you like, I can show you what I was filming. I can't share the sound, as we're experiencing some technical difficulties, but the video will show it's clearly not porno."

While I switch the camera to play mode, I tap the mute button—I do not need the officers hearing a second of this.

"Doesn't look pornographic at all," Baker accurately observes.

"I can even scrub through the footage so you can see the clothes stay on for the duration."

I speed through the footage and the officers nod with satisfaction.

"I am so sorry to have had to bother you, Mr. Carson," Wilcox says.

"No worries at all. Would you all like a few more sandwiches for the road?" I'm careful to make sure Jeanette is sure that she's included in the offer.

"Whether it's porno or methamphetamine, there's something going on here, and I'm not consuming any turkey submarines that have been associated with it," Jeanette says, but Wilcox and Baker take me up on the offer before I walk the three of them out.

Before I close the door, Jeanette extends her foot to prop it open and issues a final warning. "I'm keeping my eyes on you."

"Have a nice night, Jeanette."

"Sorry again, sir," Wilcox offers and follows his partner across the street.

I close the door and regroup with the team to chat about today's sessions and then take them out to dinner in downtown Chicago, as options for swanky eateries are limited in Deerfield. It's not that I'm feeling generous, it's that I'm just going to bill it back to them anyway, so why not live it up?

#

Swing Day 2: Natasha and her team return to the house around 11 and we briefly discuss today's agenda before meeting Luke and Leia, fortysomethings who are deep—so deep—into cosplay; Ricky and Lucy, baby boomers into S&M; Joanie and Chachi, college students at Northwestern; and Mulder and Scully, goths who seem to be into group vampire fucking.

Thankfully, there's no interference from good old Jeanette Wainwright, but I know it's coming—Neighborhood Watch doesn't simply lie down when a potential meth/porn factory pops up across the street.

CHAPTER THIRTY-FIVE
Party Planning

Orgy day has finally arrived. Natasha shows up around 11 and tells me Steven and Oliver are on the way back to New York. She's wearing extra-tight jeans and a hoodie and looks more relaxed than I've ever seen her. She goes from Type-A marketer to laid-back party co-host pretty seamlessly. She's also toting a pink overnight bag.

"What's in there?" I ask.

"Just some necessities a girl might need," she says with a wink and a smile. "What time does the planner get here?"

Since I've never thrown a swingers party before, I hired someone who has to consult with us on how to throw a successful bash. She's come highly recommended from Gail who said that this woman has hosted some of the best parties she's ever been to.

I look at my watch. "Any minute now. I've spoken with her a few times over the phone and she sounds normal."

"You sound surprised. Most of the people we spoke to yesterday seemed beyond normal given their kinky hobby."

"Right. Who am I to judge?"

As the words leave my mouth, there's a knock at the door. We both walk over and find a professional-looking woman with shoulder-length brown hair standing on the porch. She's dressed in a very conservative black suit and, if I didn't know any better, I'd have assumed she was a high-powered lawyer. Which, she may very well be—I've learned in the past couple of days that swingers work in all sorts of industries, including the legal profession.

"I'm Pepper Gardner, are you Kelly?"

Her tone is strictly business and I'm wondering if she knows my former boss who now goes by the name Vanilla.

"Yes, come on in."

I let Pepper through the door and look across the street. Wainwright is back, binoculars in hand. I smile, wave, and close the door behind me to attend to my guest.

"First things first," Pepper says. "Don't look me in the eyes. If you look at me in the eyes, I walk."

Natasha and I exchange confused glances.

"May I take your coat?" I ask, averting my eyes from hers. She hands it to me, but I'm nervous and don't grab it in time. I pick it up and hang it on the rack by the door.

"First things first," she says very businesslike, "you are going to have about 40 people here tonight and this coatrack won't handle the demand. Where's the coatroom?"

"Ummm," I say.

"Okay, at most straight parties you would use a guest bedroom as the coatroom, but you don't want to do that tonight. Do you know why?" Her tone has become militant as if she's related to Terri's father. She answers before either Natasha or I can chime in.

"Because there's going to be some serious fucking and sucking going on in the bedrooms. Must I teach you everything?"

"There's a mudroom just off the garage," I point out and walk her there, careful not to make eye contact lest I turn to stone.

"Halt!" she screams as we enter. "Aussie chick, put a sign above this doorway saying coatroom. Clear signage is just as important at swingers parties as it is anywhere else. Do you understand?"

"You fucking imbeciles" is implied by her tone. I mentioned before that swingers are pretty normal people, but Pepper proves there are outliers in any population.

"Keep up with me now because the following is important. We need to divide the rest of rooms into mingling rooms, playrooms, and utility rooms."

"Can you explain the difference between the three?" Natasha asks sheepishly.

"Fucking newbies!" Pepper shouts, but not at us due to her no eye contact rule. "Mingling rooms are common rooms where people can get to know each other and hold a casual conversation. I recommend the kitchen as a mingling room because everyone always winds up there anyway. You also have a great room with a nice stereo system just off the kitchen, which would also be a good mingling room."

"There's also a den upstairs…" I'm cut off by Pepper, who is holding a finger up to me.

"You will only speak when spoken to!"

I wonder if she knows the dominatrix who got my clothes in Hawaii.

"Generally speaking, upstairs rooms are play rooms.

More on that in a minute, I'm not done talking about mingling rooms. Rule of thumb, no dingaling in the mingling. Got it?"

She doesn't wait for our reply.

"One more thing, in the mingling rooms you want to avoid a few things including loud music and bright lighting. I would recommend putting some trivia game cards at different spots in the room to encourage interaction, and maybe as hosts you two can introduce an icebreaker game to get people talking. Is that so hard to understand?"

"I was going to ask you what we should do as hosts," Natasha says, her Australian accent is muted by fear.

"You have a very calming voice, I like it," Pepper says in a more subdued tone while smiling at Natasha. "What's your name again?"

"Natasha," my client says while trembling.

"I'm going call you Barbie from now on. You'll find that most people go by nicknames in the swinging scene and I've just given you one."

I've never seen Natasha, I'm sorry—Barbie—blush before, but there's a first time for everything.

"But your number one job now is to listen and to stop asking fucking questions. Got it, Barbie?"

Sergeant Gardner is back.

"As hosts your primary job is to make everyone feel comfortable. The key to hosting a swingers party that no one will forget is to make everyone feel relaxed with each other so that connections are made. To do that, you will be friendly and greet everyone as they come in and then make introductions to people who don't know each other."

Got it, we just have to do the exact opposite of Pepper

and we'll be all set.

"If you make sure everyone is having a good time, you are doing your jobs correctly. Okay, I think that's enough on mingling rooms. On to utility rooms. Can you two geniuses guess what they are?"

"Wash rooms?" Natasha says inquisitively.

"You are a smart little shrimp eater, aren't you? Exactly. Bathrooms are utility rooms and, generally speaking, are not play rooms because nobody wants to be using a toilet while two people are playing in the shower, or someone is bent over a sink."

I walk Natasha and Pepper over to one of the two half baths that are located downstairs.

"You'll want to put clear signs over each utility room so that the flow of a conversation doesn't have to be interrupted by someone trying to find out where they can tinkle."

"Makes sense," I say.

"I'm glad you're taking it all in, lover-boy. In each utility room you will want to have some core toiletries including washcloths, hand towels, hand soap, lotion, mouthwash, tooth brushes, and toothpaste. Also, I highly advise that you put a sign up telling people that nothing but toilet paper should be flushed. More on that when we get to the playrooms."

We leave the bathroom we are standing in and Pepper's voice rises a few octaves. "Now to the fun part, the playrooms. Playrooms are just what they sound like, places where your guests will go off to get off. These should be clearly marked as group playrooms and individual playrooms as, for whatever fucking reason, some people don't like to play in groups."

I show her the room we have been conducting interviews in for the past two days.

"This would make a good small group playroom, but you've got to lose the camera. As kinky as these people are, no one wants to be filmed at one of these parties. You'll have some pretty high-powered people here who go to great lengths to protect their anonymity."

"The camera will be gone shortly," I confirm.

"God damn right it will, Scorcese. Now, in each playroom you are going to want a few essentials. Condoms, lots of them. If possible, a nice variety of playful styles, some lubed and some not lubed. Individual lube packets are preferred to bottles, and maybe have some female condoms too. To that end, as I mentioned before, toilets do not always handle condoms well, so be sure to have clearly marked receptacles in each playroom where people know to put their used items. Also, put on your shopping list Kleenex, spare towels, and maybe even some moist towelettes as some people prefer to clean up with those. Most people don't want to be reminded of their children when they are playing, so I don't recommend baby wipes. There's a new product on the market called Swipes, short for sex wipes, that are more appropriate. You can find them at CVS."

For the life of me I had no idea that hosting a swingers party could be this much work.

"Okay, final logistics what are you serving to drink?"

"I told everyone we would be providing red and white wine, but any other alcohol is BYOB."

BYO? I know she'll correct me if I'm wrong.

"Smart," she says—I guess I'm in the clear. "This isn't a party where you want people getting blitzed, just nicely buzzed. What are you doing for food?"

Gail told me that it's best not to serve heavy food as people tend to not want to play hard when they have full stomachs, so I planned accordingly.

"I have some light appetizers that I will put in some chafing dishes that I have rented, as well as a fruit and mild cheese tray."

"Well, someone gave you some good advice, lover boy."

This is the first time she's said anything remotely complimentary to me and I allow myself to feel a hint of pride. It's ruined a moment later.

"Just promise me you will wear something a little more sophisticated. No one wants to go to a swingers party hosted by Mr. Rogers."

Natasha looks at me and lets out a laugh.

"Well, you both have your shopping lists, so I better let you get to it. Coat please. Now!"

I walk to the door and hand Pepper her coat as well as an envelope that I've had in my pocket that includes a token of our appreciation for her time.

"I just have one question, Pepper, it's been on my mind since Gail told me."

I'm afraid to ask her due to her unpredictable outbursts, but the question has been gnawing at me for a few days.

"What's that?"

"What do you know about El Capitan?"

She breaks her own rule and looks at me square in the eyes.

"He's a legend in the scene but super secretive."

"I've heard that."

"Believe me, whatever your mind has conjured won't prepare you for what you are about to see tonight. There isn't one woman in the greater Deerfield scene who hasn't been with him."

Pepper's body shakes as she says this. Either he gave her the best toe-curling orgasm of her life, or he's a complete creeper.

"I'm intrigued," Natasha says.

"Just know he will be the absolute last to arrive and likely the very last to leave as he likes to make a grand entrance and have as much fun as he possibly can. The truth is, I believe he leads a very sheltered life in the real world and therefore takes full advantage of parties like these to let his true colors shine through."

Pepper leaves, and Natasha and I follow her out the door to shop for all the items we'll need later tonight. It's only after I go into the cool December air that I've realized I've sweat through my undershirt.

CHAPTER THIRTY-SIX

Scarilyn Monroe

It's Orgy Day, an hour before party time, and I find myself wondering if Terri will actually show, but for all I know, Captain Cockblock has her chained up, a chastity belt affixed as an added precaution.

I shower and change into my outfit for the evening, a trendy black suit and crisp white shirt with no tie—an open collar seems fitting orgy host attire. Once I give myself the okay in the mirror, I head out and find Natasha lighting candles in one of the playrooms. She's wearing a long and very sheer dress. She has her backside pointed toward me during the lighting ceremony, and I see she's got nothing on underneath but a black thong. My heart starts racing, and I imagine that won't stop for the rest of the evening.

"Enjoying the view, Kelly?" she asks mischievously. As she turns around, I see the front of her dress is as sheer as the back. "When in Rome," she says with a wink.

"I guess this is a pretty Roman event, but now I feel overdressed."

"Nonsense." She strides to me and grabs my lapels—I manage not to orgasm. "You look sexy, nothing like a boring moderator."

"Hey, I'm not a boring moderator!"

"Just fucking with you, baby. It's New Year's Eve, so let's have some fun."

I follow her out and almost roll down the stairs because I can't take my eyes off her perfectly shaped backside—it's going to be a night of nonstop adversity.

"I guess we're all set," she says.

"Now we just need our swingers."

And just like that, the doorbell rings and the party's underway.

People arrive in groups, and Natasha and I are playing the part of co-hosts quite well. We take turns greeting newcomers and passing out drinks—Swinging 101: The first drink of the fuckfest is the most important.

Once just about everybody has arrived, we transition to full-on mingling. I have a few trivia cards stuffed in my pocket, and when I go up to a couple I didn't greet, I pull out a card and ask a question; I stick with the entertainment category, as it's the most amenable to conversation. It's such a great icebreaker, but warning: If you try this at your own party, people may start fucking.

Little by little, we notice people are leaving the mingling rooms and heading off to play—there's lots of hand-holding and giggling. I feel like a proud father, a proud swinger party host father.

I find that, on average, couples are playing for twenty minutes and then rejoin the party looking refreshed and relaxed. I use their refractory periods as an opportunity to ask for feedback on the setup in the playrooms and find nothing but glowing reports; without even having to ask, the swingers are raving about the condoms. Natasha is holding similar conversations and is all smiles.

"I think we have a hit on our hands with this new line," she says. "I'm going to consider this research a success and start having some fun. You in?"

The truth is, I'm painfully horny—literally, it hurts—but two things are holding me back: my feelings for Terri and my anticipation for the arrival of legendary swingman El Capitan.

"Go have fun," I tell her. "I'm holding out until the big guy gets here."

I watch Natasha approach a couple who, to my knowledge, has yet to visit one of the playrooms. A moment later, the three of them head to the staircase—man, Natasha doesn't fuck around, and by that, I mean that she does.

But the elusive three-way is not so elusive here—the offers start coming my way, but I pass; as horny as I am, and with zero career three-ways under my belt, I'm still not interested in going guy-guy-girl, which is the three-way combo du jour of the party.

I grab a drink and the doorbell rings. It can be one of three people, and I only want to fuck one of them.

We aren't making too much noise, but I can't shake the feeling that old Mrs. Wainwright is here to fuck me, fuck all of us, really—but not literally, probably. I peek out and see another cop car in her driveway—damnit. The doorbell rings again and I answer it, good host that I am.

I open the door and find something completely unexpected—a silver-haired woman dressed like Charlie Chaplin, Hitler mustache and all, and an older man dressed as Marilyn Monroe. His face is powder white and his lipstick is the color of blood. There's no question, I'm standing face-to-face with the legend, El Capitan, though Scarilyn Monroe would be a more fitting nickname.

"Please come inside," I say enthusiastically. "Let me get you a drink."

My enthusiasm is not matched—I see pure fury as if El Capitan is staring face to face with a guy who wants to fuck his only daughter. Scarilyn's face turns bright red, actually a nice shade of pink given the white makeup, and he screams, "You son of a bitch!" while charging at me.

I'm caught completely off guard, and he knocks me to the ground and straddles me—is this a sex move? I don't know if I'd prefer that or a punch to the face. Realizing it's going to be a pummeling, I bump my hips upward and wrap my legs around his waist and cross them, holding him firm so he can barely wiggle. I lock my right foot behind his left and roll him onto his back. Right before I drop an elbow on his chest, Officer Wilcox barrels in and tackles me off.

"What's going on here?" Officer Baker says, Mrs. Wainwright trailing behind.

"I opened the door and this man attacked me."

Scarilyn is now back on his feet and looking nervous as hell—El Capitan is about to be unmasked (demake-up'ed?). I look into his eyes and immediately know I've seen them before. They belong to Capitan Kevin Fucker Flynn. He's El Capitan? My God, this is incredible.

"I told you this is some kind of drug-fueled party," Jeanette says triumphantly. "Who else would come to such a thing dressed like this?"

Officers Baker and Wilcox look around and see that

everyone else is dressed quite normally. Fortunately, they don't insist on going upstairs where they'd see baskets of condoms and piles of fucking.

"No loud music, no one appears to be drunk—everything looks okay to me," Baker says.

"Agree," says Wilcox.

"Mr. Carson, do you want to press any charges against Mr…Monroe here?"

"That depends," I say, looking Scarilyn in the eyes.

"On what?" Baker says.

"On what happens next. I'd like a minute alone here with Mister Monroe if that's okay with you fellas."

"Have at it."

I walk Capitan Marilyn Flynn to the den—I wish this moment could last forever.

"Sit down," I say.

"Who do you think you…"

"I think we got off on the wrong foot, El Capitan. Sure would be a shame for everyone in this lovely, quiet community to know you're a swinging cross-dressing fucker."

"You don't have the balls."

"Really, well how about this. You relinquish your control over Terri and I don't expose El Capitan."

"You have no proof," he says, at which point I take my phone from my pocket and snap a series of pictures.

"I'll break that phone in half."

"Go ahead, and I'll press charges. The pictures are already on the cloud anyway."

"You little piece of…"

I hear a car pull up and peek through a crack between the shutters—ah, if it's not beautiful redheaded troubled actress Terri Flynn!

"Looks like your daughter's come to say hi. Wanna see her? I know how close you two are."

"I have to get out of here."

"Do we have a deal?"

"Fuck you!"

"Have it your way. Terri…" I shout, but he cuts me off.

"Fine. Deal. It's her life—she's free to ruin it as she pleases."

"Good," I reply and poke my head out the door. And see Charletta Chaplin cowering behind the staircase to avoid being spotted by Terri.

"Hey, Clark!"

She's taken to calling me Clark again. I'm not sure if that's a good or bad thing, but I really don't give a fuck about that at the moment.

"Glad you could join. Officers, I do not wish to press charges."

"Sorry to have disturbed you again, Mr. Carson," Baker offers.

"You can't just leave now!" Mrs. Wainwright protests.

"Lady, it's New Year's Eve and you need to get laid," Natasha offers, strolling down the stairs, cigarette in hand. "Why don't you come up here and let me show you something."

I am dumbfounded, but good old Mrs. Wainwright heads upstairs and doesn't come down screaming when she finds out what's going on.

"Is everything okay, Clark?"

"Just finishing something up," I say. "Why don't you go to the kitchen and get a drink?"

"Okay," she says slowly, clearly convinced I'm up to no

good. I turn my attention back to Scarilyn.

"By my estimation, you have twenty seconds before she comes back into the foyer and sees you." I then start counting down, "Nineteen, eighteen, seventeen…"

Sergeant Defeated Fucked then bolts from the room like a bat out of hell and takes Charlie Chaplin with him. Terri returns to the foyer to the sound of a car peeling out in the background.

"What was that all about?" she asks.

"Uninvited guests," I say.

With all the excitement, the couples begin to slink out. Jeanette Wainwright is the last to leave and avoids all eye contact on the way out. We've finally heard the last from her. She'll definitely have a sore pussy tomorrow, and an uncomfortable conversation with dear old Harold.

"Well, I'm heading back to my hotel," Natasha says. "Unless you two want to play."

I look at Terri, and we both shake our heads.

"That's a very kind offer, though, Natasha," I say.

"Your loss."

She leaves, and Terri and I are alone for the first time since we were so rudely interrupted on Christmas Day.

I look at my watch. "Shit, it's two minutes to midnight."

We dart into the great room and turn on the TV with thirty seconds to spare before the ball completes its descent in Times Square. Once the clock reaches zero, we kiss, softly at first and then passionately. She leads me upstairs and we do a little playing of our own.

Epilogue

The past three years have been a roller-coaster unlike any other. Terri's father lived up to his word and backed off his daughter, allowing her to fly back to New York with me. She helped me pack up Eddie and we drove out to Arizona.

For six months, I worked with Elizabeth, the editor Pam hooked me up with, to fine tune *Return to Casa Grande*. Getting Terri's freedom wasn't the only gift her father gave me—his dressing like Marilyn Monroe inspired me to use drag as a way of breaking one of my characters, Victor, out of a nursing home! I love it when a plan comes together.

Pam underestimated the level of interest in the book and we wound up putting the manuscript up for auction. It sold for a $100,000 advance and a high-dollar marketing plan paid for by the publisher, unheard of for an unknown author. The catch is, they want two follow-up books within the next eighteen months—a prequel and a sequel.

I quickly learned that writing is the easiest part of the process—marketing is the real bitch. I started with book signings at the major chains and was disheartened when almost nobody came to the first few. As sales grew and as word of mouth spread, though, attendance got bigger and bigger. In fact, we ran out of copies in New York with the last one being sold to none other than Pete Jackson himself. I wonder how he liked the way I signed it, "To Pete, you are still a fucking idiot. Hunter Carson." Maybe I'm being too hard on him—without Pete, I may never have gotten divorced.

Which leads me to the book signing I did in Stamford. My sister was by my side the entire time and pointed out that Laura had come with Ella, my former and her current handywoman, in tow.

"A $100,000 advance, huh?"

"And a piece of every copy sold thereafter."

"Well played," she said.

I sure hope they are doing well.

As the book's popularity skyrocketed, so did interest in the author. My dream of being a guest on *The Tonight Show* came true! While I was the second guest, I had a good time getting to know the main guest, podcaster Farrah Graham. I've been listening to her Uncorking a Murder podcast for years and decided it would be a good place to advertise my book. After that deal was inked, sales of my book doubled.

With all the press my book was getting, the movie studios took notice and a bidding war went on for who would option the screenplay. My agent encouraged me to sell to one of the major studios, but I went with a streaming service that offered the most creative control. Also, they were open to having Terri play a key part in the movie. In addition to her, Ted McGinley, Andrew Shue,

Jennifer Grey, and Jack Wagner all have starring roles in the film.

We moved from Arizona to California as *Return to Casa Grande* was shot on location in LA. We bought a modest home in the upscale suburb of Westlake Village, just a fifteen-minute drive to Malibu but with none of the pretension. Terri was happy to be working again—and on her terms—and I was happy to be beside her during her fourth comeback.

After a rigorous sixty day shooting schedule, Terri and I took a vacation back to Maui, where I started writing the prequel to *Return to Casa Grande*, which focuses on the lives of the main characters before and during production of the soap opera that made them household names. I've also finished a fictitious Casa Grande episode guide that will be put in the back of the second edition of *Return to Casa Grande*. There are rumors that Netflix actually wants to produce the series itself.

I look back on the past three years of my life and see how far I've come. I'm no longer averse to confrontation and conflict—that's the cost of entry in my new industry, the entertainment business. And while I've learned to give a fuck about the important things in life, I'm all out of fucks for the rest.

Acknowledgements

This book is my return to comedy—having written two mystery/thrillers (*Uncorking a Murder* and *The Last Homily*) as well as one deeply personal book (*Winning Streak*), I wanted to get back to making people laugh like I did with *Return to Casa Grande*, my very first full length novel. What prompted me to start writing though, was no laughing matter. Art imitates life a bit in this book and my position at a large consulting firm was eliminated in early 2017 and for those paying attention to the conversation between Kelly and his boss, my manager at the time did characterize me as a lever he had to pull. This was, however, the best thing that could have ever happened to me as it prompted me to start writing again and this book is the result. My private consulting practice as has also blossomed confirming what the late great Randy Cappiello believed is true, **success is the best revenge.**

I am indebted to my editors at Word Mule—Joe Gartrell and Ben Gibson—whose tag-team approach turned my manuscript into a novel. Their copy editing is superb and to say that their developmental suggestions made this a better book is an understatement. Thank you

Joe and Ben.

My proof reader Eagle, from Aquila Editing, certainly has an eagle's eye for typos, missing words, and shifting tenses. I am forever in her debt for helping me to make this book as good as it is.

I also need to thank my beta readers Rebecca, Sue, and Tracy for their keen eyes in helping me spot the typos that I could never find as well as providing their valuable feedback along the way. You guys rock!

I'd like to apologize to my parents for the overuse of profanity in this novel as well as the adult nature of key scenes. I can hear my father saying to my mother, "What have we raised?" Please chalk it up to Michael being Michael and don't forget that I love you.

At the end of the day, I wanted readers to root for a guy whose non-confrontative nature makes him a bit of an underdog. I wanted people to see Kelly Transform from Clark Kent to Superman and then eventually land somewhere in between. I hope you enjoyed following his journey and sincerely thank you for buying this book.

—Michael Carlon, May, 2017

Sneak Peek - Return to Casa Grande

Sneak Peek:

Return to Casa Grande

Thanks for the Memories

Blaze Hazelwood lifted his hands up to his eyes and rubbed them hoping that doing so would reduce the sting of the hangover that was setting in. It was sometime after three a.m. and the snoring coming from the other side of the bed reminded Blaze that he wasn't alone. He lifted up the sheets to get a glance of the woman he picked up earlier in the evening and shook his head knowing that, in his heyday, he could have done much better.

Knowing that sleep was not going to come back to him anytime soon, he got out of bed and walked over to his television and ejected a tape from his VCR. You read that right, a VCR; Blaze was an actor past his prime and stuck in the 1980s. He looked at the tape to confirm what was written on it and saw that the label read May 8, 1989. Satisfied, he popped the tape back into his VCR, rewound it, and hit play. He sat at the end of his bed to re-watch the last news story done about *Casa Grande*, the 1980s primetime soap opera that made him famous.

The picture was fuzzy, so Blaze had to adjust the tracking on the machine. Once the level of clarity was passable, he saw the image of Kitty Carson, then a fiftysomething reporter for a magazine devoted to soap operas, standing in front of the nightclub where the wrap party for *Casa Grande* was held twenty-five years prior.

"Greetings soap opera fans, Kitty Carson from The Soapdish reporting. It's truly the end of an era—after 10 years on prime time, Casa Grande has closed its doors forever, leaving a hole in the hearts of the show's millions of devoted fans who will now have to turn elsewhere for their weekly dose of drama.

"*Casa Grande* was the very definition of the '80s soap opera. The show chronicled the lives of California winemakers the Thornridge family and featured every element synonymous with this golden age of prime-time soap—desire, power, jealousy, greed, murder, infighting and scandal. But network executives say viewer tastes are changing, so they're creating a drama geared toward younger adults for the coveted Monday at 10 p.m. time slot.

"Sources tell The Soapdish that the new show, *LaMaze Academy*, will center on the lives of five teen girls attending a boarding school, who make a pact to all get pregnant during their junior year. Up-and-coming starlet Naomi Stevens is rumored to have a lead role.

"'*Casa Grande* has been a very successful show for the network and it was a difficult decision not to renew the show for another season,' said network executive Geoffrey Crestwood. 'We wish the cast nothing but the best.'

"That's not what this reporter heard. Rumor has it that Crestwood's had it in for the show ever since the writers killed off the character Missy Thornridge, who was played by Crestwood's daughter Vanessa.

"But the *Casa Grande* body is not yet cold! How could I

resist mentioning the revelations made last night? Spoiler alert for any of you who are going to watch it on your VHS players this evening: Madeline Thornridge, matriarch of the family, turned out to be having an affair with JR Solstice, 30 years her junior and the son of her nemesis, Sam Solstice of competing winemaker Global Wine Inc. We all knew she was seeing a mystery man for years, but even this imaginative entertainment reporter with a penchant for younger men didn't see that one coming.

"As if that weren't enough, we learned that Michael Thornridge arranged for the death of his sister Missy. His motive? He admitted to being in love with Kyle Dixon, the dashing young farmhand-turned-wine executive his late sister couldn't keep her hands off of.

"But perhaps the biggest bombshell of last night's series finale was learning that Missy Thornridge wasn't really dead after all—just as the handcuffs were about to be slapped on her brother Michael, Missy walked through the front door, and she was not alone. With her was a four-year-old boy, who we learned is the son of Barton Dixon, Kyle's father and the head caretaker of *Casa Grande*. Emotions changed on a dime for Kyle Dixon, who was visibly elated at the return of his lover yet instantaneously became furious to hear of her affair with his father. Then, in classic soap style, the lights flickered and a scream rang out! When the power came back on, we saw Kyle Dixon lying in a pool of blood, suffering from a stab wound but with no weapon to be found. The curtain closed on Casa Grande, leaving viewers wondering: Who stabbed Kyle Dixon?

"On their way into the after party, held at the ultra-trendy hot spot Vertigo in Hollywood, I spoke with fans on the street about their reactions to the series finale.

"Maria Vacodo had to be consoled by her sister Carol.

"'It's like losing a friend," Maria said. "And I am just dying to know who stabbed Kyle!'

"'I just can't believe it,'" said 22-year-old fan Catherine Rosdale. 'I've been watching *Casa Grande* since its premiere in 1980 and have been hooked ever since. I want to have Blaze's baby!'

"She is referring, of course, to cast member Blaze Hazelwood, who played show hunk Kyle Dixon. Many women wore T-shirts that said 'Marry Me, Blaze.' This reporter, old enough to be his mother, isn't too ashamed to admit she'd like a roll in the vineyard with the 20-year-old actor.

"You may recall the stir in West Germany earlier this year when Blaze was found to be having a secret affair with the mother of one-hit wonder Nena, of the song "99 Luftballons." The Germans love Blaze, with his blond hair and blue eyes, and have caught a bad case of what they call Blaze Fieber, or Blaze Fever (auf Englisch). Apparently Blaze has a thing for older women; maybe there's a chance for me after all.

"I caught up with the cast members during the after-party to find out their plans for the future. Elizabeth Pierce, who played matriarch Madeline Thornridge, says she intends to take some time off."

"'Charles and I are going on an extended honeymoon,'" Elizabeth said. "'He's always wanted to sail around the Greek islands, so that's what my current plan is, darling.'

"That's right—none other than Charles Pinkertoni, the Santa Barbara financier rumored to be connected with an

Italian crime family. You didn't hear it here, lovelies, but the 30-year age difference between the two has left many wondering if Pinkertoni was looking for a beard to counter the rumors that he is a homosexual. If I go missing and my body is found at the bottom of the Pacific wearing cement shoes, you'll know I was right!

"Victor Tillmans, the actor who played head caretaker Barton Dixon, said he intends to buy a ranch in Simi Valley—a case of life imitating art.

"Danny Boy, who played Michael Thornridge, was living up to his Hollywood wild child image and had enjoyed one too many cocktails by the time I got to speak to him. Danny was slurring his words so badly I didn't even get a quote. I was able to make out that he'll be touring with his rock band Sinner's Swing this summer and may entertain offers for TV or movies after that. Oh Danny Boy, good luck with that.

"Vanessa Crestwood, who made her return to the show last night for its finale, says she is eager to show the world what she has to offer on the big screen—and that may mean revealing a bit of what her mama gave her.

"'I've signed on to do a film with director Erick Shon,' she admitted, dropping the name of the Hollywood director whose films border on soft-core pornography. 'So I guess you will be seeing a lot more of me in the future.'

"And when it comes to series star Blaze Hazelwood, there will be no rest for the weary.

"'I want to show the world that there is more than one dimension to Blaze Hazelwood,' he said, 'so I am going to try my hand on the stage this summer.'

"This confirmed the rumors I'd heard earlier this week about Hazelwood getting the lead role of Marty McFly in

Back to the Future: The Musical.

"All good things must come to an end, and such is the case with *Casa Grande*. One thing is for certain: prime time will never be the same, without the colorful cast and equally colorful storylines of *Casa Grande* to keep us entertained. As far as this reporter is concerned, there will never again be a show quite like it."

When the segment was over, Blaze pushed the stop button on his VCR and went back into his bed. He debated whether or not to wake up the girl, whose name he couldn't remember, but decided against it. Instead, he put his head on a pillow and his back toward the girl. He was asleep minutes later.

Blaze's Nightmare

Tension was running high at the Dolby Theatre in LA where the second annual Reality TV Awards were coming to a close and the final presenter of the evening was about to be announced by host Bret Michaels, the lead singer of '80s 'hair band' Poison and former reality TV superstar. The most anticipated award of the night was about to be announced: the award for best new reality star.

"Ladies and gentlemen," Bret said, "to present the award for best new reality star, please welcome Ted McGinley."

The crowd applauded as Ted McGinley appeared onstage. McGinley was contractually obligated to appear on the awards show despite the fact that his own reality show, *Ted McGinley: Sitcom Killer*, had been cancelled earlier that year. It made one question whether or not there would be a third annual Reality TV Awards, or if the McGinley curse would strike again.

"I am honored to present the final award of the evening. The nominees for best new reality star are..." The theater went dark as large screens played clips of each show.

"Willie Aames for *Jesus in Charge*." The audience saw a clip of Willie Aames throwing Bibles at homeless people on LA's Skid Row while shouting, "Repent, repent, repent."

"William Katt for *Greatest American Heroes*." The audience saw a clip of the actor interviewing "everyday Americans" about the good things they were doing in their local communities while sporting curly blond hair and the iconic red costume that made him a household name in the '80s.

"Emmanuel Lewis for *Forgetting Webster*." The former child star was seen in a clip lying on a therapist's couch talking about how all he wanted to do was forget the sitcom character he played in the '80s.

"And Blaze Hazelwood for *Blaze of Glory*." The audience saw 1980s heartthrob Blaze Hazelwood preparing for an audition by speaking lines to his reflection in a mirror. His blond hair was shorter than it was in the '80s, but his eyes were as blue as ever.

The house lights came back up, the monitor showing a four-way split screen with a feed of each nominee's face. McGinley opened the envelope and read: "And the award for best new reality star goes to…Blaze Hazelwood for *Blaze of Glory*."

The crowd erupted in applause, and as Blaze walked onstage the orchestra played a classical rendition of David Hasselhoff's *Looking for Freedom*. Blaze accepted the award from McGinley and then turned his attention to the crowd.

"First, I would like to thank the members of the Reality Show Academy for nominating me for this award. My competition was formidable, and I have a great deal of respect for my fellow nominees. Honestly, I have not felt this excited since a cool November evening 25 years ago when I found myself in West Berlin. When the crowds on the east side of the Berlin Wall pushed their way through to the west, I remember thinking to myself it was the most intense one-sided game of Red Rover I had ever seen."

Blaze paused to allow the crowd a moment to laugh, but no one did. A little shaken, he cleared his throat and continued: "In the 25 years since that cool November night I've learned one thing…" Blaze paused and looked at the crowd, then said, "Who the fuck am I trying to kid?" The crowd gasped at his use of profanity—surely Blaze must have known this was being broadcast live. "I am better than this. What I said about my competition being formidable, that was bullshit. I'm the only star in this room! You can take this meaningless piece of crap award and shove it up your bums."

Blaze then extended his right arm and dropped his award, which broke in three pieces, and walked offstage shouting "Reality TV is bullshit" as the orchestra began to play.

"Blaze, Blaze!" a beautiful brunette said while shaking the sleeping man beside her violently. "Wake up, you're talking in your sleep."

Blaze turned over and looked at the woman who was shaking him. "What is your name again, luv?" Blaze said the word luv with an British accent. While Blaze's hometown of Little Falls in upstate New York was far away from England, he had developed an affectation of speaking with an British accent from time to time. Even though they only met once over two decades ago, Blaze considered Madonna a close friend and saw how her developing a similar affectation helped keep her relevant after almost four decades in show business. Blaze thought that if it worked for Madge, it could also work for him.

The "luv" in bed next to Blaze was a twenty-two-year-old waitress named Betty who had waited on Blaze earlier that evening. Even though he wasn't a household name anymore, his boyish good looks coupled with his blond hair and piercing blue eyes along with his charm kept him a player in the seduction game.

"Betty, you asshole! You were talking in your sleep."

"What was I saying, Betty, luv?"

Betty looked at Blaze softly and her demeanor changed; she softened her tone. "You kept mumbling that reality TV is bullshit."

"Of course it is, luv," Blaze replied. "I was dreaming that I won the award for best new reality TV star. I got angry and stormed offstage."

"Wow, does that mean I just had sex with an award-winning actor?"

"Only in my dreams, luv."

"Well, Mr. Hotshot," Betty said, sliding her hand down his chest, "why don't we celebrate your big award?"

"I won't argue with that, luv."

Meet T-Bang

"I can't believe I have to meet with a guy named T-Bang,"
Allison Hart said to Lucy Nichols, one of her production
assistants. At 30, Allison was the quintessential up-and-
comer at Universal Products Company, or UPC for short.
The multinational conglomerate, which made everything
from bath soap to TVs and was even rumored to dabble in
the defense sector, had been struggling in recent years to
identify a new advertising model that worked. The
fragmentation of the media universe, and viewers
"zapping" their way through commercials, left
corporations struggling to find ways to reach buyers. That
was why UPC had hired Allison.

Allison had seen the popularity of reality television
skyrocket just as network advertising revenue started to
fall. In her final year at Harvard Business School, she'd
made the case that consumer product companies should
abandon traditional TV advertising altogether and focus
instead on product placement in reality TV shows. Then
Allison went a step further, arguing that in order to control
the conversation, consumer goods companies should
create their own programming, since owning the show

means owning placement—an advertising method modeled on the early days of radio and television, when companies such as Procter and Gamble created the shows they sponsored. It was this model that had created the soap opera.

But Allison isn't all brains; in fact, she always felt as if her classic good looks were a detriment to her. At five feet eleven inches, she was taller than most of the girls she went to school with. Her long blond hair and athletic physique also caused the heads of both men and women to turn whenever she walked by. Because of this, Allison felt as if she had to work three times as hard as anyone else in order to be taken seriously.

Through her connections at Harvard, she was able to present her ideas on marketing to Brandon Master, the chief executive officer of UPC. Master hired her on the spot and immediately made an offer to buy Pocket Box, the fledgling online network dedicated to creating custom programming for the 18-to-24-year-old market. Pocket Box would be their distribution vehicle for the programming ideas Allison had, and this is where T-Bang came in.

"He can be an ass, but he's kind of charming in a low-rent kind of way," Lucy said to her boss. "He's actually kind of cute."

It's true; behind the multiple gold chains and the beard that looked as if it could have been drawn with a fine tipped pencil, T-Bang was not what most women would consider ugly. His brown hair was cut very close to his scalp, allowing admirers to see his perfectly shaped head— his mother chose to give birth by C-section for fear of her narrow birth canal causing what was considered an above average-sized head to take on a cone shape immediately after birth. But the pièce de résistance was the cleft on his chin—a cleft so pronounced that he would invite women to sip whatever it is they were drinking right from his 'chimple.'

"Cute or not, I never dreamed I would actually have to interact with talent, and I use that term very loosely," Allison replied. "I have an MBA from Harvard and now I have to spend my afternoon buttering up to someone named T-Bang? I guess if we have learned anything from the Kardashians it is that you no longer have to have talent in order to be famous."

Lucy disagreed with her boss on that point; she was secretly a reality TV junkie and knew the comings and goings of the Kardashians, Tori Spelling, and even the Duggars. Additionally, she was annoyed that her boss dropped the Harvard line again; why do people who went to Harvard always have to mention that they went to Harvard?

Thaddeus Stevens, a.k.a. T-Bang, was the 24-year-old son of '90s TV star Naomi Stevens and her life partner, Eric Peters, a high-profile entertainment attorney. When Thaddeus was conceived during the filming of *LaMaze Academy*, the breakout hit that made Naomi a household name in the '90s, the show's producers decided to let Naomi raise him on set. Since the program focused on a group of girls who had made a pact to get pregnant, the writers had little difficulty writing Thaddeus into the show. Over the years, audiences fell in love with his character, Michael Allen.

Deciding at age 18 to break out of his "goody-goody" image, Thaddeus adopted the name T-Bang. He now can be found running wild in Hollywood with his crew of former prep-school kids turned wannabe thugs. His erratic behavior at Hollywood's nightspots, coupled with the long list of young female celebrities he was rumored to have bedded, earned the attention of a UPC brand manager, who thought T-Bang would be a great vehicle to promote the company's Lust brand of products—a cross-category line targeting the personal care needs of teenage boys, including shaving cream, body spray, and body wash. Now Allison had to pitch a "celebreality" show she had crafted around T-Bang and his "crew"—and do whatever was needed to get him to sign.

Allison's attention was momentarily diverted from Lucy when her instant messaging application started to blink. It was Marios, her personal assistant, letting her know that T-Bang had arrived, along with two members of his entourage. Allison replied to keep them entertained for 15 minutes before showing them to her office. She wanted to be the one in control of this meeting and didn't want to look too eager.

#

T-Bang and his merry band of misfits took their seats in the waiting room outside Allison's office. While waiting for his boss to come out of her office, Marios was privy to one of the most inane conversations he'd ever heard.

"That bitch gonna be like all over the T-Bang, man, know mean?" one of them said.

"Yo yo yo, check it out, T-Bang gonna filet that like the Gorton's mothafuckin' fisherman," replied another. This conversation was accentuated with grunts of "aw snap" and fist bumps.

It took all his strength for Marios not to burst out into

laughter at this exchange. Sitting before him were three of the whitest boys he had ever seen. Beneath the flat-brimmed ball caps, the gold chains, the fake gold teeth, the rings, the vintage Run DMC T-shirts, and the baggy pants worn below the waist, Marios saw three young men of privilege desperately trying to live in a world they clearly knew nothing about.

T-Bang was too busy composing a tweet to respond to his friends. T-Bang saw it as his responsibility to keep his over one million Twitter followers in the know about the comings and goings of his life. His followers knew what he ate for breakfast, lunch, and dinner every day. They knew when he was drunk and when he was horny. They always knew when he was bored, since that was when he tended to tweet the most. The best he could offer to them at that moment was "At UPC/Pocket Box to hear a pitch. Pocket Box—like a sex toy." Within seconds of sending that tweet, T-Bang had multiple offers from women offering their box for his pleasure.

His attention was diverted from his mobile phone when one of his friends asked about the party they were planning for his 25th birthday. "Yo, T, you think your parents will let us host your 25 throwdown at their place in Malibu next month? I got Big Kenny and Road Dawg waiting in the wings." Big Kenny and Road Dawg were the two hottest DJs in LA. "Your parents' place is off the hizzie."

"My moms hasn't given me a straight answer yet, yo. I think she's still bent that we tag-teamed that ho." Earlier that week, Naomi had caught her best friend and former *LaMaze Academy* co-star Jenna Talia in bed with her son and his friend Freddy. Jenna had tried to explain that the boys were just helping her through a hard time, but Naomi was outraged.

"Don't worry, T," his friend replied. "It'll all blow over, just like it always does."

Marios realized he was paying too close attention to this conversation when his phone started to ring. His angry boss asked, "Didn't you see my instant message? I'm ready to see him now, please show him in." Marios apologized to her and then announced to T-Bang that Allison was ready for him.

"Want us to go in there with you, T?" his friend Freddie asked.

"I gots this one, boyz," T-Bang proclaimed. "If the meeting takes more than 10 minutes, you know I be knockin' some boots, ohh." At that, fist bumps were followed by chest bumps, and T-Bang walked into Allison's office.

#

Allison waited a moment after T-Bang sat down before sitting down herself. "Thank you for coming in, Thaddeus."

The use of his first name annoyed him. "The name is T-Bang, the only one who calls me Thaddeus is my moms."

"Do you have more than one mother?" Allison asked.

"Nah, it's like, I say moms when I really mean mom. It's just the way I speak. Dat okay wif you?"

"Of course," Allison said disdainfully. "You have quite the reputation, Mr. T-Bang. You've been involved in multiple altercations in Hollywood clubs, yet you never wind up in the police blotter."

T-Bang smiled, "It pays to have a lawyer in the family."

He was referring to his father.

"You're constantly hired by club promoters to attend events. When you do, there are lines out the door of people wanting to meet you."

"Being bad pays off, I guess."

"It would certainly appear that way. Tell me, T-Bang, how would you like to make some real green?" Allison knew to build rapport by adjusting her speech; she even started to subtly mirror T-Bang's movements. When he blinked, she blinked. When he crossed his arms, she crossed her arms, and when he leaned in, she leaned in. She would know that she had him when he started to mimic her body language.

"Yo—T-Bang is all about the Benjamins," he replied, referencing the founding father whose image is on the one-hundred-dollar bill. "How you gonna make it rain for me is what I wants to know."

"We here at UPC think your life is fascinating. As such, we have crafted a show around it. All aspects of your life will be captured and streamed to Pocket Box subscribers."

"Yo, stop right there. T-Bang don't wants a camera crew following him around. It just ain't natural, you feel me?"

"That's the beauty of modern technology. We will actually plant small pinhole cameras on you and the members of your crew. No one will see them. They will communicate by Bluetooth to a smartphone that we will give you. The video will then be beamed back to our servers, then streamed to the Pocket Box community."

"Wait, so everything we do will be shared? That's not gonna fly—what abouts when I wants to get with a shorty?"

Allison found T-Bang's derogatory attitude toward

women—and everything else about him—extremely offensive. But she bit her tongue; the deal was more important than her opinion on what constitutes acceptable standards of behavior.

"We thought of that," Allison explained. "If there's ever a situation that you don't want to record, whether it be an intimate situation or a situation where legality may be in question, all you have to do is click a kill switch on the smartphone. That will immediately stop the broadcast until you turn it back on."

"Sounds dope. But you still haven't told me how you gonna make it rain money for T-Bang." This was the second time T-Bang had spoken of himself in the third person.

She uncrossed her arms and noticed he did the same. She knew it was time to reel him in.

"All network television is sponsored by advertisers and this will be no different."

T-Bang interrupted her, "Wait, you tellin' me there's gonna be commercials on my show?"

"No, not exactly. We can't have commercials, because the idea of the show is that it is your life unfolding in real time. Real life doesn't have commercial breaks. What we intend to do is have advertisers give you products to use. We simply ask that you use them at some point each day."

T-Bang got up abruptly and exclaimed, "T-Bang ain't no sellout."

Allison had expected this reaction from her guest. "You'll be paid $20,000 a week and be given a contract for 52 weeks, which we will honor even if your show gets canceled."

T-Bang couldn't hide his Cheshire Cat grin as he sat

back down.

"What do you say to that, Mr. T-Bang?"

"There's only one thing to say," T-Bang said. "Bling it on, baby."

And that's how *Bling It On Featuring T-Bang* became the first ever celebreality show produced by Allison Hart of UPC and streamed from Pocket Box.

Blaze Gets Therapy

Blaze was lying on the leather couch in his agent's office as if he were in a therapy session. He was wearing a pastel shirt, white pants and loafers without socks as if it were the mid 1980s and he was about to go on an audition for *Miami Vice*. Stanley, Blaze's agent, put down the current issue of *Variety* he was thumbing through and let out a large sigh. "Can you please stop doing that?"

"Doing what?" Blaze was oblivious to the fact that he was throwing a blue racquetball up in the air and catching it while waiting for his agent to finish the article he was reading.

"Throwing that damn ball up in the air! Why are you here anyway?"

Blaze did not have an appointment to meet with his agent; he popped in unannounced that afternoon.

"You need to get me back on TV, Stanley! Blaze Hazelwood was meant to be seen, not lend his voice to fucking cartoons and video games." One of Blaze's bad habits, aside from his British affectation, was referring to himself in the third person.

In the years since *Casa Grande* went off the air, Blaze

regularly found work doing voiceovers, and he longed for the days of being on screen again.

"Speaking of which," Stanley said while not bothering to look up from the pages of the magazine he was reading, "how did that voiceover work go last week?"

Blaze replied in an agitated manner, "When you told me I would be voicing a character named Winged Foot in a video game called *Flight of Fancy*, I assumed it would be something teenage boys would play. It turns out, I was voicing a fucking pink pony in a game designed for grade-school girls! Do you know what my character's catchphrase was? Do you?"

"Enlighten me," Stanley replied.

"We have pony power!" Blaze said animatedly while making a throat slashing gesture with his finger. "And don't get me started on that fucking voice director, the worst!"

"Did the check clear?" Stanley asked wryly.

"You should know; your percentage was deducted!"

"Hey, I gotta eat too."

Blaze sat up on the couch. "Well you don't seem to be missing too many meals there, Stanley old boy."

"Hey, all I am saying is that unlike your former co-stars, you are making a very good living."

"I am not low on money, Stanley, I am low on relevance. It used to be I could walk into a bar and have any woman I wanted. Do you want to see what I went home with last night?"

"Not particularly, but I have a feeling you are going to show me anyway."

Blaze got up from the couch, removed his phone from his pocket, and found a picture that he took of his overnight guest from the night before.

Stanley picked up the phone and said, "Are you sure that's a woman?"

"Yes, but there were times when I had my doubts."

"Look, my heart goes out to you, Blazey boy, but from where I am sitting, you have it really good. Do you remember Elizabeth Pierce?"

"Remember? I would kill to forget her! That drunken witch made my life miserable on the set of *Casa Grande*. I always imagined her throwing wire hangers at homeless people just for the fun of it."

"Well, the only work I could get for her in the past year was a job on an infomercial pitching reverse mortgages. She can barely pay her bills."

"Karma is a bitch!"

"How about Vanessa Crestwood, do you remember her?"

"I think I was the only one on the show that she didn't screw. How could I forget her?"

"Tune in to the TV Shopping Network later today and you will see her pitching some new kind of toy. She also hasn't worked in years."

"Hey, whatever happened to Danny Boy? He and I used to party hearty together back in the day."

"Danny, now there's a sad case!"

"Don't tell me he died!" Blaze said.

"Worse, he found God and became a priest. He was assigned to a parish up in Agoura Hills and completely turned his life around. Clean and sober for about 10 years now. It's a damn shame. Do you remember Victor?"

"Good old Victor! That man taught me everything I know about picking up women. Please don't tell me he's a priest too."

"He's loopier than a noose in a spaghetti western. Strangest thing, a few years back he started this habit of riding his horse naked through the streets of Simi Valley, kind of like a male version of Lady Godiva. He's now living in some retirement home up in Westlake Village."

"I guess when you put it like that, I'm not doing so bad, am I?"

"Look, I'll do what I can to get you in front of the camera, but the only thing coming across my desk for you these days is rea…"

Blaze cut Stanley off before he could finish his sentence.

"So help me God, if the words reality TV come out of your mouth I will stick a fork into your heart."

"Look, I know how you feel about it, but that's where the opportunities are these days."

Blaze looked at his watch and then looked concerned. "Shit!"

"What's the matter?"

"I just remembered, I have to be in Westwood in two hours."

"That's ten miles away, you'll never make it. What's in Westwood anyway?"

There were few places where you could not traverse ten miles in two hours; LA at rush hour was one of them.

"Do you mind if I change in your bathroom?"

"Go right ahead, but you didn't answer my question. What is in Westwood?"

Blaze walked to the bathroom in Stanley's office and closed the door. "I got a call this morning about participating in a focus group at six p.m. I am supposed to play a teacher"

Stanley rolled his eyes; play was the wrong word.

"You still do those things?"

Blaze came out of the bathroom wearing a button-down shirt, khaki pants, and a tie. Capping off his transformation into a teacher were a wig and glasses.

"How many times do I have to tell you, they are a great way to adapt different personas and build my acting chops."

"You know, you could be just like any other actor and take acting lessons or workshops?"

"But that's the thing, luv," Blaze said with his British affectation. "I am not just any other actor. I am Blaze fucking Hazelwood!"